PRAISE FOR SHARI RANDALL'S
CURSES, BOILED AGAIN!

"A mystery as richly layered as a genuine Connecticut lobster roll!"
—Liz Mugavero, Agatha Award-nominated author of Pawsitively Organic Mysteries

"Curses, it's over already! Shari Randall introduces a lively cast of characters who had me dancing through this book. Allie Larkin charmed me with her sense of humor when faced with a heartbreaking injury. The climactic scene is like nothing I've ever read or seen and I loved it!"
—Sherry Harris, author of the Agatha Award-nominated Sarah Winston Garage Sale Mysteries

"Randall's first in her brand-new Lobster Shack Mystery series is a delicious cozy with deadly outcomes and plenty of probable culprits. The quaint, fictional Connecticut village and snappy title set the perfect scene, while the good flow and tight, *Murder She Wrote*-type storyline keep the pages turning . . . the red herrings Randall adds do a perfect job of misleading the audience until the bombshell ending."
—Debbie Haupt, *RT Book Reviews*

"Randall has achieved a trifecta of triumph here: engaging characters, a welcoming backdrop, and a compelling plot—all of which coexist harmoniously (beyond the requisite homicide) . . . *Curses, Boiled Again!* is an accomplished debut that, like one of Aunt Gully's famous lobster rolls, is fresh-tasting yet familiar—and entirely guaranteed to satisfy. Just know that you'll be back for seconds . . ."
—John Valeri, *Criminal Element*

"It's always a treat to discover a new mystery series, and this one delivers both a strong plot and artfully developed new characters. This debut series introduces a fully developed community that serves as a stellar launching point for more visits to Mystic Bay and the Lazy Mermaid Lobster Shack."
—Cynthia Chow, *Kings River Life*

St. Martin's Paperbacks titles by Shari Randall

Curses, Boiled Again!
Against the Claw

AGAINST THE CLAW

Shari Randall

St. Martin's Paperbacks

AGAINST THE CLAW

Copyright © 2018 by Shari Randall.

All rights reserved.

For information address St. Martin's Press, 175 Fifth Avenue, New York, NY 10010.

ISBN: 978-1-250-11672-7

Our books may be purchased in bulk for promotional, educational, or business use. Please contact your local bookseller or the Macmillan Corporate and Premium Sales Department at 1-800-221-7945, ext. 5442, or by e-mail at MacmillanSpecialMarkets@macmillan.com.

Printed in the United States of America

St. Martin's Paperbacks edition / August 2018

St. Martin's Paperbacks are published by St. Martin's Press, 175 Fifth Avenue, New York, NY 10010.

10 9 8 7 6 5 4 3 2 1

For Jessy and Charlotte

Acknowledgments

I must acknowledge the delicious inspiration of two fabulous lobster shacks right in my own backyard—Ford's and Abbott's in Noank, Connecticut. Many thanks for all the great meals and a special shout-out to Loretta at Ford's for all the laughs.

Many thanks to my wonderful team at St. Martin's—Hannah, Nettie, Amanda, Sarah, Martin, Lesley, Mary Ann, John, and Ragnhild the copyeditor—and to my agent John Talbot. So nice to have you all in my corner.

Chapter 1

For all her MBA, fancy Boston job, and perfect French manicure, my sister Lorel was still at the mercy of her passion for the bad boy of Mystic Bay, Connecticut, Patrick Yardley.

In the frame of the Lazy Mermaid's front window, Patrick and Lorel kissed, Patrick astride his Harley, totally ignoring the "get a room" looks from customers heading into my aunt Gully's lobster shack.

"What's a guy got to do to get some chowder around here?" a customer at the counter said.

"Sorry." I served him a bowl. He added crackers and dropped his spoon in with a splash.

Lorel hurried in, the roar of Patrick's Harley following her as he gunned out of the parking lot.

Aunt Gully shot me a warning glance and grabbed a plate from the kitchen pass-through.

"What?" Lorel smoothed her gold-blond hair.

"I didn't say anything." I wiped drips of chowder spattered by the sloppy customer. He threw me a look. "No need to rub a hole in the counter, honey."

Lorel joined me behind the counter. "Patrick and I were talking about a new social media campaign for New Salt."

"Since last night when he picked you up for dinner?" I muttered.

She brushed past me into the kitchen.

Two men in Harbor Patrol polo shirts bellied up to the counter and scanned the chalkboard menu on the wall behind me.

"What can I get you, gentlemen?" I said, trying to swallow my irritation with Lorel.

Bertha Betancourt, Mystic Bay's Lobster Lady, shifted aside to let the two men get closer to the counter. Bertha's family had been lobstering in Mystic Bay since the town was founded and her Learn to Lobster cruises were a popular tourist attraction. She leaned toward Aunt Gully.

"Gully, when I pulled up those lobster pots, I had a feeling, you know how you get a feeling?" Bertha's round, sun-reddened face crinkled into a grin. "Well, I reached over and what do I see? Some joker's stuffed a wolffish in one of my pots. Ugly monster nearly took my hand off!"

"God bless America!" Aunt Gully chuckled.

"That woke me up, let me tell you!" Bertha swigged her mug of coffee as if it were a tankard of rum. "Shoulda been there, Gully. Ugliest thing you ever did see."

No. The ugliest thing ever was the thought of my

sister rekindling her relationship with the guy who'd been breaking her heart since middle school.

The two men ordered lobster rolls with extra coleslaw. I clipped the order to a metal wheel and turned it into the kitchen.

Lorel frowned at me through the pass-through window. "Don't look at me like that. I know what I'm doing."

I started after Lorel, but Aunt Gully pulled me back. "I don't like it either, Allie, but she's a grown woman. And love is never a mistake." She picked up two plates with overflowing lobster rolls. "Though sometimes it's a learning experience." She brought the plates to a couple seated by the front door.

I sighed. "Everyone loves the bad boys."

Some people would say that Lorel was out of Patrick's league. Others would say Patrick was out of hers. The problem was that they were in different leagues. Patrick's bar/restaurant, New Salt, catered to Mystic Bay's yacht-club set. Rumors, about drugs mostly, drifted around the club like tendrils of fog on the bay. Sure, Patrick looked like the cover of a romance novel come to life, but he'd had numerous brushes with the law. Was I the only woman in Mystic Bay who was immune to his charms?

The wall phone shrilled. I picked it up. "Lazy Mermaid Lobster Shack."

"This is Zoe Parker, personal assistant to Stellene Lupo. I'd like to speak to Gina Fontana about catering." The clipped voice made me feel like I was wasting her time.

"Gina Fontana?" For a second the name didn't

register. My aunt Gully was Gully to everyone from Mystic Bay. No one here called her by her given name, Gina.

Lorel came out of the kitchen's swinging door, tying an apron behind her back.

I caught Lorel's eye and enunciated clearly. "Sorry, we don't do catering."

"Who is it?" Lorel said.

I pressed the phone to my chest. "Somebody somebody, personal assistant to Stellene Lupo." As soon as I said the name it registered. Stellene Lupo.

Lorel yanked the phone from my hands.

"The Stellene Lupo?" Aunt Gully hurried back to the counter. "She owns that big modeling agency in New York."

Bertha turned. "And the Harmony Harbor estate!"

Lorel covered one ear and murmured on the phone, using her money voice, all modulated and clearly enunciated. "Catering? Of course."

Of course? "What?"

Lorel waved me off and turned her back.

Catering? We'd never done catering. My aunt's Lazy Mermaid Lobster Shack had just opened this past spring. Business wasn't just good. It was overwhelming. There was a line waiting to get in as soon as we opened the doors at eleven. We'd talked about what my MBA sister called other "income streams" including catering, but we'd decided to just get through the busy summer tourist season first. Now she was talking about catering?

A group wearing neon-green NEW ENGLAND LOB-STER TRAIL T-shirts surged through the screen door into the shack. Aunt Gully turned to greet them. "Welcome, lobster lovers!"

"I'll have Mrs. Fontana get back to you," Lorel said. "She's in a meeting right now." Aunt Gully posed for a selfie with a stocky guy wearing a baseball hat decorated with red foam lobster claws.

"Thank you so much. Good-bye." Lorel hung up and jotted notes on an order pad.

I put my hands on my hips. "I thought we didn't do catering."

Lorel's green eyes sparkled. "We do now."

Aunt Gully leaned over the counter. "You look like the cat that got the cream, Lorel."

"Our ship has just come in, Aunt Gully," Lorel said.

Chapter 2

After the lunch rush, a couple of Aunt Gully's friends came in to help. Lorel, Aunt Gully, Aunt Gully's assistant manager, Hilda, and I gathered at our conference room: a wobbly picnic table on a patch of gravel behind the shed where we stored live lobsters.

Lorel sat at the very end of the table, as if she were leading a meeting at the big Boston social media company where she worked. She'd taken a week off to help with the Fourth of July rush, then she'd go back to managing accounts for Fortune 500 companies.

I adjusted the high-tech, waterproof wrap on my left ankle. All I wanted was to get my almost healed broken ankle completely healed so I could return to my soloist spot with New England Ballet Theater. In the meantime, I'd accepted a role with minimal dancing in a show at Mystic Bay's Jacob's Ladder Theater. I'd work with Aunt Gully until I got the all clear to dance again from our company doctor.

"Listen to this." Lorel's green eyes glittered. "Stellene Lupo's throwing her annual Fourth of July party. She wants us to serve our lobster rolls, chowder, and coleslaw to her guests. One hundred people. From seven to nine P.M. We've been talking about additional income streams . . ."

Aunt Gully's eyes took on a dreamy, faraway look. *Uh-oh.*

Aunt Gully squeezed Lorel's hand. "I have to admit, I'd love to see the inside of Harmony Harbor. Too bad you didn't see Stellene when she was here a couple of months ago."

"You never mentioned it!" Lorel exclaimed.

"I must have missed her, too," I said.

"Well, Hilda follows the society news and she said it was her."

Hilda Viera and her husband, Hector, were the shack's only other full-time employees—Hector cooking lobsters and Hilda managing the shack with Aunt Gully. Hilda and Hector had both worked in the restaurant industry before retiring and sailing around the world. When their sailboat *Happy Place* docked in Mystic Bay, they'd decided to stay and take jobs at the Lazy Mermaid.

"She was with her teenage daughter, Tinsley," Hilda said. Her big brown eyes radiated concern. "Tinsley has a reputation for being wild. In and out of rehab, poor thing."

"That's not important." Lorel took Aunt Gully's shoulders and turned her toward her van parked by the side of the shack. "This is important. With what Stellene will pay us, you could buy a new van."

I straightened. If Aunt Gully's van had been a cat,

it would be on its seventh or eighth life. The rust-flecked Dodge had more than two hundred thousand miles on her, plus several scrapes from where I side-swiped our mailbox when I was learning to drive.

"One problem." One of us had to be sensible. "How will we be in two places at the same time? How do we keep the shack open and do Stellene's bash? The prep work alone for the party will take hours—"

Lorel cleared her throat. "We could just close the Mermaid early and do Stellene's party." She looked out over the river that flowed behind our shack, avoiding Aunt Gully's eyes.

Aunt Gully, too, looked out over the Lazy Mermaid parking lot to the river. A sailboat with all the time in the world slid past our dock. Aunt Gully straightened her pink Lazy Mermaid apron. "Well, the money is—"

"Crazy good." I sighed.

"Tempting," Aunt Gully said. "But I have to open the Mermaid on the Fourth. We're part of Mystic Bay. We'll have so many summer people here, and people coming after the parade. I want to be part of that."

"Stellene's party's at night." Lorel leaned forward. "We could call in reinforcements. Hector and Hilda can manage."

I was torn. On one hand, we said no catering! On the other hand, great money! Aunt Gully's face was even pinker than usual, matching the pink barrette holding back her silver hair. She was excited, sure, but was I the only one who cared about the woman's health? Aunt Gully's not old but does qualify for the senior center where she takes a Zumba class one day a week. She already worked long days, seven days a week at the shack.

"Did you say yes already, Lorel?" I asked.

Lorel shook her head.

"Good. Because if Stellene's willing to spend that much money, that means she really wants us." It was an insane amount of extra work, steaming the lobsters, picking the meat, toasting the rolls, making Aunt Gully's Lobster Love sauce, coleslaw, and chowder.

"Tell Stellene we can do it if her staff can do all the prep work." I held Lorel's eyes. "It's the only way it'll happen."

"Yes, yes. I can show them how to do it right." Aunt Gully tapped her lips with her forefinger, her thinking pose. Her cheeks pinked and her dangling lobster earrings caught the sunlight. She was getting into it.

What Stellene wants, Stellene gets. The words, unbidden, slid into my mind.

Lorel jotted notes. "I'm sure Stellene can afford plenty of kitchen staff at Harmony Harbor."

"Hilda, would you and Hector handle things here?" Aunt Gully squeezed Hilda's hand.

Hilda nodded. "Of course we can handle things here. Though I'd much rather be there."

Aunt Gully hugged Hilda. "Me, too."

"You'll have to tell me every detail. And I mean every detail," Hilda said.

"Do you really think it can work?" Aunt Gully's brown eyes shone. We were all giddy with the thought of all the money Stellene would pay, giddy at the thought of getting behind the walls of Harmony

Harbor, serving our lobster rolls to the rich and famous movie stars and models who would be there.

"If they give us the staff," I repeated.

"Okay. I'll call Stellene's assistant." Lorel jogged back into the shack. Aunt Gully and Hilda, chatting excitedly, followed.

I stretched my arms over my head and turned my face to the sun. My red hair is the type that comes with sunburns and freckles, but I love the feel of the sun on my skin. Maybe if business slowed, I'd get away for a quick swim before rehearsal.

The blare of a car horn yanked me back into the real world. Voices rose. I hurried to the front of the shack. As usual for the summer, tourist traffic on Mystic Bay's narrow streets flowed like winter sap, slow and sticky. "Honk all you want, won't do you any good," I muttered.

Our parking lot was full. Customers streamed from the sidewalk to the door of the Mermaid. No time for a swim.

A lobster boat pulled up to our pier. The captain waved and I returned the greeting as I went to meet him.

Ten-year-old Bit Markey ran up behind me on the pier. He brushed his floppy black hair out of his eyes and together we hauled buckets of live lobsters into the storage shed.

Bit lived with his mom and dad in a prerenovation 1840 house across Pearl Street from the Mermaid. A sagging front porch and a marijuana flag in the parlor window made it stand out from the other, more carefully restored buildings on the street. Bit spent several hours a day working at the Mermaid, ferrying live lob-sters from the pier to the lobster storage shed, sweep-ing, and what he called "policing the grounds."

A car horn blared as a blue van marked with BEST OF NEW ENGLAND TOURS squeezed into the lot. Ever since the New England's Best Lobster Roll competi-tion in May, the Mermaid had been visited by several tour groups a day.

"Here we go," I said.

Bit and I hurried into the kitchen. I slung a pink Lazy Mermaid apron over my head. Lorel emerged from Aunt Gully's tiny office. She pursed her lips, scribbling on the order pad.

"Well?" I asked.

Lorel hugged Aunt Gully. "It's a go! Stellene's as-sistant says they'll have her staff provide you with everything you need, Aunt Gully. Her daughter wants Lazy Mermaid lobster rolls and Stellene'll do whatever it takes to get them."

"Lorel, that's just grand. Grand!" Aunt Gully twirled me around and then strode out of the kitchen into the dining room. Lorel and I exchanged looks.

"Oh, God, here it comes." I peeked through the pass-through window.

Aunt Gully started singing her victory song, "Get Happy" from *Summer Stock,* a song made famous by Judy Garland.

Aunt Gully's no Judy Garland.

Bit ran out the kitchen door, his hands over his ears.

As Aunt Gully squawked, conversation in the shack ceased. Customers caught each other's eyes and tried not to laugh. Then Aunt Gully hit a high note.

A man in a Red Sox T-shirt, broad and tall as a foot-ball linebacker, set down his lobster roll. Next thing I knew, he was dancing with Aunt Gully and singing along. The diners crowded into our tiny shack all started applauding and talking at once. The tour group stood at the screen door, holding cell phones high.

Next to me, Lorel was quiet. She scribbled on the order pad, avoiding my eyes. I took the pen from her hands. "Okay, Lorel, spill. There's a catch, isn't there?"

Lorel tucked the pad in her pocket. "Nothing to worry about, Allie. Details, details. But Stellene asked for us, you and me, to help serve."

"You and me? Why?"

Lorel waved it away. "Who cares? Come on, Allie, the people at Stellene's party are the type to throw huge parties. Rich movers and shakers. This is a golden opportunity. Stellene chose us because her daughter loved the lobster rolls and Stellene likes Aunt Gully's"—Lorel lowered her voice—"primitive, naïve aesthetic."

"Primitive aesthetic?" I folded my arms.

"Primitive. And naïve," Lorel said. "In the art world it means childlike."

"I know what it means." How could I argue? Most seaside restaurants have that typical old-fashioned nautical look: fishing nets, antique wooden lobster traps, ships' wheels, little statues of lighthouses and pipe-smoking sea captains in yellow slickers and sou'westers.

Aunt Gully had that on steroids and sprinkled with glitter. Shelves that ran along the top of the wall of the shack were crowded with her mermaid collection, what she called her mermaidabilia. It was the kitschiest, tackiest, tchotchke-est mermaid stuff ever—mermaids on dolphins, mermaids with hula skirts. Cowboy mermaids, mermaids with maracas. Customers had started bringing Aunt Gully mermaid tokens from their homes. We even had a life-sized wooden mermaid figurehead standing outside the door of the shack.

Just when I was sure I was getting a migraine, someone dropped a coin in Aunt Gully's jukebox and Tom Jones was singing. I pulled my eyes away from the mermaidabilia. There wasn't an inch to spare in our tiny lobster shack, but now some teenage girls were dancing with Aunt Gully and the man in the Red Sox shirt. A little boy stood on a chair, marching in place, conducting the music with a plastic fork.

It was absolutely nuts. The lobster shack had only been open a few months. We'd never gotten through a Fourth of July holiday. Now we had to get through Fourth of July and cater a party for one hundred one-percenters at Harmony Harbor.

Still, excitement kindled in me. I couldn't wait to get behind the walls of Harmony Harbor.

That evening at Aunt Gully's cottage, which we affectionately called the Gull's Nest, Lorel, Aunt Gully, and I relaxed on the patio, taking advantage of the cool evening air. A storm two days earlier had left behind calm clear weather and a reprieve from the humidity that was typical of summer in Mystic Bay.

The old-fashioned wall phone in the kitchen shrilled. Aunt Gully went inside to answer it.

Music thumped as a car rolled down the street. The scent of charcoal, lighter fluid, and grilled hamburgers and hotdogs was in the air. Summer people were moving in for the holiday weekend. Down on the beach at the end of the street, fireworks crackled in a trial run for the Fourth. The sulfurous smell drifted on the breeze.

Strings of fairy lights strung over the patio mimicked the fireflies over Aunt Gully's garden. Lorel bent over her smartphone. Usually her texting was work related, but tonight I wondered if she was texting with Patrick.

I tried to swallow my words but I couldn't help it. "Lorel, listen, I know your affairs are none of my business—"

Lorel didn't look up. "That's right, Allie, my affairs are none of your business."

I drank the last of my lemonade. Sweet and bitter. Just like my relationship with Lorel.

"I—"

"Allie. I'm not discussing it. If Aunt Gully can stop nagging me about Patrick, so can you."

"I—"

Lorel raised her head, her look hard even under Aunt Gully's string of fairy lights. It's the same hard look she'd give when I wanted to tag along in middle school. The lights highlighted her sculpted cheekbones, her strong jaw. She looked like the cool blond heroine of a Hitchcock movie.

I changed tack. "Well, I took your morning shift today. You owe me."

Lorel scrolled on her phone. "I already told Aunt Gully I'll take your morning shift tomorrow."

"Oh. Thanks." I stretched my legs on the chaise, inhaling the calming scent of Aunt Gully's basil plants. I could already imagine those wonderful extra hours in bed.

"A little something to celebrate our catering venture!" Aunt Gully set a tray with shortcakes, strawberries, and whipped cream on the table.

"My favorite!" I sat up. "Thanks!"

Lorel waved it away.

"Who was on the phone, Aunt Gully?" I heaped my shortcake with fresh strawberries and whipped cream.

"I've lined up helpers for the night we're working the Stellene Lupo affair." Aunt Gully grinned. "Harmony Harbor, here we come."

When I finished my shortcake, I set my plate on the tray with a sigh.

Lorel's phone buzzed. "Gotta take this."

She went inside, no doubt heading to the small downstairs guest bedroom. Growing up we'd shared one of the bedrooms upstairs under the eaves but now she slept in the little room on the first floor that had been Uncle Rocco's study. Since our mother had died giving birth to me, Aunt Gully had been more than an aunt to us. When my dad was out lobstering, we lived with her and Uncle Rocco.

"Probably Patrick." Aunt Gully pressed her lips together in a little red lipsticked downward bow.

I frowned. "Aunt Gully, I can't help it. I know she's a grown woman and all, but her dating Patrick again makes me furious."

Aunt Gully shook out the tablecloth. "Everyone has to make their own mistakes, Allie." Her eyes were worried. "Maybe she'll meet someone new in Boston. Take her mind off Patrick."

"Guys as hot as Patrick aren't exactly a dime a dozen." Though hotness alone didn't explain Patrick's allure, did it? Why did Lorel keep taking him back? He always hurt her. He always had another woman. It always ended in tears. My eyes met Aunt Gully's and I realized it was simple. For all his faults, despite them, Lorel loved Patrick.

"Oh, I forgot." Aunt Gully folded her tablecloth. "Bertha asked if one of you girls could help her on her boat tomorrow morning. Her sciatica's flaring up and her doctor told her to get some help with her lobster traps. Lorel said you needed a break from work and that she was taking your morning shift. So you wouldn't mind helping Bertha, would you?"

I let my spoon clatter onto the tray. *Thanks a lot, Lorel.*

Chapter 3

Wednesday, July 1

A few minutes after chugging out of Mystic Bay Harbor, I forgot to be mad at Lorel. Bertha's boat, *Queenie*, headed into the sunrise. Those who make their living on the sea start work in early morning, while it's still dark. Our six A.M. start was pretty late, a concession to me.

Sunrise at sea is breathtaking. Watching the sun kindle an orange and pink fire in the water, listening to the seabirds, feeling the freshening wind on my face, I felt alive. Plus, the ocean's beauty made it easier to ignore the reek of the bait bags that we would stuff into Bertha's lobster pots.

A slick cabin cruiser cut us off and *Queenie* bounced over its wake. The hull smacked the water as we crested each wave and dipped over the other side. Bertha winced and flipped them the bird.

I couldn't help smiling as the boat bucked but

Bertha pressed a hand into her lower back and adjusted her weight. She turned to me. "Just remember to wear your gloves when you handle the lobsters."

"I was helping my dad haul pots on *Miranda* practically before I could walk," I said.

"You lose a finger, Gully won't let me eat at the Mermaid anymore. Don't want anything coming between me and your aunt's lobster rolls."

Bertha was in full lobstering regalia, gray-green rubberized overalls over a Bruce Springsteen and the E Street Band T-shirt, feet in black rubber boots. Her pewter hair was braided into two thin plaits. I, too, wore heavy rubber boots and I'd put a rubber apron over my shorts and T-shirt later. I hate wearing rubber, especially as the day grows hotter.

Bertha's gold hoop earrings caught the light and she'd knotted a red paisley scarf around her neck. Bertha's ancestors had made their living from the sea for hundreds of years, mostly honestly. When we were little girls, Lorel and I used to think Bertha was a pirate. I was pretty sure Bertha also thought she was a pirate.

Queenie chugged past Cat Island. Storm-stunted trees and bushes ringed a two-story, gray-shingled cottage. Movement on the lawn caught my eye and I leaned past the wheelhouse for a closer look.

"I thought that house was empty," I said.

"Sometimes the Lupos let friends stay there," Bertha replied.

The Lupos owned everything in this part of Mystic Bay. There were many grand houses in Mystic Bay, many with their own guesthouses. Leave it to Stellene Lupo to have a guest island.

"I'll take you out there sometime," Bertha said, "if Stellene un-fires me."

"Un-fires you?"

"Last year I started doing some housecleaning, to make some extra money. Worked for Stellene last year. I contacted her about cleaning again this year, but she, well, her estate manager said she didn't need me this summer. And would let me know when my services were required. Said it in that voice, you know, sounded like she'd been sucking on lemons."

Bertha fished in her chest pocket and handed me a business card.

COTTAGE CLEANERS
Bertha Betancourt, prop.
Specializing in island properties

"See, the maids at Harmony Harbor didn't like having to go out on the boat to get to the cottage. So I offered my services."

"What's it like inside that house, Bertha?" I slipped the card in my pocket.

"Well, Cat Island used to be a real artist's retreat. Old Mr. Nuttbridge lived out there alone, painting. When he died, Stellene's husband bought the island and house. 'Course it looks all run-down and ramshackle on the outside but inside it's all renovated." Bertha whistled. "Like a magazine picture."

"I wonder why she didn't fix up the outside?"

Bertha shrugged. "It wasn't a lack of money, that's for sure."

I squinted toward the island, just big enough for the cottage, some sheltering trees, and a small beach. Bertha nudged binoculars into my hands. "Thanks." I trained the binoculars on the house and adjusted the lenses.

"I swear I just saw someone go around the house." I swept my eyes over a tumble of rocks to a pier, its rotted wood sagging into the waves. "Stellene's got to take care of that old dock or it's going to crumble into the water." A rocky beach was next. "There's a kayak on the beach. Bright yellow."

"Brand-new dock on the south side." Bertha said. "That island's a good place for a hermit. Nobody to bother you out here. Lots of excitement during a nor'easter, though, water'd wash right over." She jutted her chin. "Maybe it's just somebody out kayaking who wants to check out the house. But you can be sure Stellene has top-of-the-line security."

I put the binoculars back in the wheelhouse.

The sea grew choppier as we left the sheltered water of Mystic Bay. *Queenie* rolled with the swells but Bertha walked the deck as if she were crossing Pearl Street. Actually, Bertha's step was steadier on the boat than on dry land.

"So, what's the real reason you want to get out here and help an old gal with her pots? Don't get enough fresh air at the Mermaid?" Bertha said.

I didn't want to admit I hadn't exactly volunteered. "Good to get away sometimes, right, Bertha?"

"Don't I know it, I was married three times, wasn't

I?" She threw a look toward my ankle. "I see you're out of that big boot contraption you had on your ankle."

My ankle had broken in two places in a fall down the basement steps of a house I shared with other dancers in Boston, setting in motion my move back to Mystic Bay to help Aunt Gully at the Mermaid. "Yes, now I just have to wear this wrap." I slid my foot out of my boot. "It's made of some space-age stuff, light and waterproof. The wrap's so light sometimes I forget I have it on. Doctor says I'm about ninety-five percent. I can go back to full-on dancing this fall if all goes well." I hoped. I was desperate to dance again.

Bertha raised her rubber-gloved hand, fingers crossed. "But didn't I hear you're dancing at the Jake this summer?"

The Jake was what locals called the Jacob's Ladder theater complex that hosted Mystic Bay's Broadway by the Bay. I had a role in a new experimental musical. "Yes, I'm Queen of the Mermaids in *Ondine*. I get to work in a harness, you know, like Mary Martin in *Peter Pan*. But mostly I sit on a rock and wave my arms." I put my boot back on.

Bertha patted my arm. "You'll be back on your toes again soon, my girl. And I'll be in the front row to see you."

"Thanks, Bertha."

We swung up to one of Bertha's buoys, weathered orange and red stripes barely visible over the ocean swells. Like most lobstermen and women, Bertha knew where her spots were. Buoys marked the end of lines that held several lobster traps. Many didn't even use buoys any longer, instead using GPS coordinates to keep track of their pots, but Bertha did things the old-fashioned way.

Long Island was a smudge on the horizon. Far-off boats resembled bathtub toys. The boat swayed as Bertha cut the engine. The thunk and rush of water under the keel was our accompaniment as we readied to pull up the pots. Bertha whistled a Springsteen song as I reached out with the hook and snagged her buoy, pulling the line connected to the lobster pots toward the boat. I threaded the line up and over the lobster hauler and pushed the lever. A metallic whine filled the air. Water splashed as the hydraulic winch raised the lobster trap, a three-foot-long black metal cage. When the pot was level with the side of the boat, I stopped the winch.

Bertha grunted and her powerful arm muscles bulged as we moved the pot into position on the rail so we could open it. I flipped open the cage and cleared out the things that were not lobsters—crabs that had wandered in, small fish, seaweed, other debris from the sea floor—and tossed them overboard.

One small, brown-mottled lobster waved its crusher claw in a tiny show of defiance, but we wouldn't have kept it anyway. Young lobsters with a carapace smaller than just under four inches or females with eggs were returned to the water to keep the lobster population healthy.

Bertha tossed the little fighter back into the water. "Adios, amigo. Catch you later."

Two lobsters remained. I pulled them out of the cage and measured their bodies with a gauge. "Keepers." I put them in a large plastic bucket as Bertha baited the trap and tossed it back into the water.

We fell into a rhythm. The repetitive motions—hook, loop, winch, lift—and the tangy sea air lulled me into a contented calm.

Bertha squinted at the sun. "It's eleven o'clock. One more stop and then we'll head back. Get your aunt to cook up one of these lobsters for me."

"Sounds good." Though I'd started daydreaming about hamburgers. After almost two months cracking claws and picking lobster meat every day, lobster rolls were losing their appeal.

We chugged back toward Mystic Bay, again passing north of Cat Island. Now that Bertha'd mentioned lunch I couldn't think of anything but hamburgers. My stomach growled.

"Last stop," Bertha said.

I reached out and hooked Bertha's red and orange buoy, looped the line into the winch, and pushed the lever. The engine whined, then coughed. The line went taut, jerking the boat to starboard. Bertha and I both stumbled and grabbed onto the boat to steady ourselves. The boat turned and listed closer to the water.

"Whoa!" I shouted.

Bertha hurried over. "Didn't expect that."

I checked the line. "It's caught on something."

Bertha tugged on it. "We'll wait a second. Sometimes these things fix themselves." A gull shrieked overhead then scudded across the water. *Queenie* drifted and swayed, then righted herself.

Bertha started the hydraulic winch. The engine groaned but nothing happened. "Ornery old gal." She swore and banged the winch with the flat of her hand twice, then tried again. It ground back to life.

"Maybe it's a good catch, Bertha!"

We leaned over, eager to see what was in the pot as the line rasped.

The dull metal trap broke the surface of the water, covered with debris, seaweed, and—fabric? I leaned forward. A heap of black fabric. A sweat jacket, a flash of pink. I reached to pull it in, but what I saw made me stop. It made no sense.

"What the?" Bertha reached for the trap then jerked her arm back as if she'd touched a flame. She grabbed my arm. "What the devil's that?" Her hand on my arm was a vise.

A sweatshirt and jeans. A tangle of black hair cut close and jagged, slick with seaweed.

My mind formed a thought: *A body.*

Chapter 4

Suddenly I was choking. I couldn't get any air.

Bertha screamed. She was right next to me but the sound seemed far off, as if coming from Cat Island. She screamed and screamed and pulled my arm and stumbled backward.

"Bertha!" I grabbed her shoulders, but she thudded to the deck.

"Oh, Allie!" Bertha's breath came in little gasps. "She's dead, she's dead, isn't she?"

I fell to my knees next to Bertha and squeezed her shoulders.

"Bertha. Stay here." *Of course Bertha wasn't moving.* She clutched her chest and winced, her skin purpling above her gray T-shirt.

"I'll call for help." My rubber boots made me stumble to the wheelhouse. I keyed the radio mic. Thank goodness it was the same kind of radio that my dad had on his boat. My hands worked the mic automatically to call for the Coast Guard.

"I'm." My mind blanked. *Pull yourself together, Allie.* "We're on *Queenie.* Just northeast of Cat Island. We've found a body. And Bertha looks awful." I lowered my voice. "I'm afraid she's having a heart attack. Please hurry."

I rushed back to Bertha's side and helped her onto the bench seat along the side of the boat. She slumped against me, her stocky frame a dead weight. I eased her down, tucking a life preserver under her head. *This can't be real.* But it was, as real as the slick deck under my feet, the seabirds circling, the sweat on Bertha's brow.

The body and the trap dipped as the boat gently rocked and I made sense of what I was seeing. A woman, a young woman. The figure was slight, the jeans were gray with pastel flowers embroidered on the side from waist to hem. My eyes moved to the sweatshirt, dripping, flecked with sand and seaweed. Her arm was stretched over her head, a bright pink band around her wrist. I pushed myself to my feet, drawn to her by some strange magnetism. Could she be someone I knew?

I can't look at the face. I know it won't be there. There will be spots where things have been eaten away.

Still, I couldn't help myself. My blood pounded in my ears as I pulled aside a scrap of seaweed. Her hair was black and plastered to the side of her head. The girl's eyes were closed, thank God. A silver ear cuff gleamed. Her skin was ashen, her mouth drooped, like a melted wax mask had slipped. My stomach lurched.

I cut my eyes to the pink leather band caught on the

pot. A bracelet. A black smudge ran underneath. No, it was a tattoo. My hand trembled but I pushed up the cold, sodden fabric of her sleeve. A tattooed line branched into three tines. A trident? A pitchfork?

There was another tattoo under the cuff. Seawater smeared black letters on her cement-gray skin. I turned my head to read them: HELL.

The boat rocked and dipped. My stomach dipped with it. I squeezed my eyes shut and stumbled to the back of the boat, praying I wouldn't get sick.

Gulls screeched overhead and landed on *Queenie's* bow, fretting and watchful.

Bertha sat up. We huddled together. I sat for a few minutes with my head between my knees. We drifted and rocked while the unspeakable thing caught on the lobster trap hung off the side of the boat.

I squeezed my eyes closed and tried to take slow, deep breaths. The face of the girl persisted no matter how tightly I closed my eyes. Small nose. Small ears. Silver ear cuff. I didn't recognize her. For that I was grateful.

Bertha clapped one of her big calloused hands on mine. "I'm okay, now. Just had to catch my breath. Oh, Allie, that poor, poor child."

I raised my head and faced Bertha. The color of her skin had subsided from purple to its normal sunburned ruddy hue.

"Do you recognize her, Bertha?"

She shook her head. "The sea's cruel, Allie. Who knows how long the poor child's been in the water. Who on earth could it be?"

Who could it be?

I hadn't recognized her, but I hadn't looked carefully. I was too afraid of what I'd see. But something again pulled me to my feet.

"You're going to look at her again?" Bertha tone was querulous, but had a disapproving edge.

"I saw something unusual."

I edged along the side of the boat, keeping my eyes trained on the pink bracelet, a cuff of leather, wide and studded. Seaweed coiled around her arm and hand. I was glad I couldn't see her fingers because I was pretty sure some were missing. Somehow the cuff had caught on the trap so one arm was raised over her head. Pink leather banded the gray wrist above the tattoo. Centered on the band was a carved medallion.

An engine's sputter and voices, Bertha's and a man's hailing us, edged into my consciousness. The medallion caught the sun and came into focus. The image carved into it was a wolf's head.

The Coast Guard boat brought Bertha and me to the Lazy Mermaid dock. A small group of people waited, Aunt Gully front and center, easy to spot in her bright pink Lazy Mermaid apron.

Customers buzzed around the door to the Mermaid. Red, white, and blue bunting draped one side of the building. Two cardboard boxes spilling over with decorations stood next to a ladder propped against the roof.

Aunt Gully surged forward and wrapped me in an Ivory-soap-and-lobster-scented hug as I stepped onto the dock. Behind her, Lorel twisted her hands. Bit

Markey and a lanky boy with buzz-cut brown hair leaned their skateboards against their knobby, scabbed knees. A Mystic Bay ambulance nudged through the crowded parking lot as Bertha stepped from the Coast Guard launch.

A man wearing the beige Mystic Bay police uniform pushed through the crowd—Officer Petrie, a regular at the Lazy Mermaid. His face turned serious when he got closer to Bertha and me.

"Allie," Officer Petrie said. "Too crowded here. Why don't you come up to the Plex to make a statement? Won't take long." Mystic Bay's police station, the Community Public Safety Complex, was called the Plex for short.

I squeezed Aunt Gully's arm and forced a smile. "I'll be back soon, Aunt Gully. You and Lorel hold the fort here."

"Sorry you won't be back on *Queenie* till the staties get the body." Officer Petrie nodded toward the ambulance. "Bertha, we'll get EMS to check you out."

Bertha reared back. "No need. I'm fine. Fit as a fiddle."

"Bertha, just let them check you out. It'll only take a few minutes," Aunt Gully said. Bertha snorted, but let Aunt Gully lead her to the ambulance.

Officer Petrie turned to me. "Heard about the body. Sorry you had to see that."

Me, too.

Bit Markey edged forward and wrapped his skinny arms around my waist. "I'm sorry you found another dead person, Allie."

Bit's friend elbowed him. "Well, remember, the first one she found wasn't dead yet."

"Oh, yeah, that's right."

Tears welled, but I blinked them back. "Thanks, Bit."

Chapter 5

An hour later I returned to the Lazy Mermaid, thankful that many of the usual staff at the Plex were at the Police Academy in Meriden for training. None of the subs had made the connection between me and the disaster that followed the Mystic Bay Food Festival in May. I filled my lungs with fresh air, glad to escape the Plex's suffocating beige walls, dusty fake plants, and fluorescent lights.

Hilda and Aunt Gully hovered around me like mother hens on speed. They made me sit at the splintery picnic table behind the lobster storage shed, away from the customers. Most were tourists and had no idea about my grisly discovery out by Cat Island, but locals would've heard the news by now and would be dropping by, angling for details. Gossip in Mystic Bay traveled at light speed.

Aunt Gully had somehow read my mind. Even though the lobster shack didn't serve hamburgers, she'd grilled up a huge double burger with everything for me—cheese, pickles, lettuce, and tomatoes.

A yellow hybrid Mystic Bay taxi drew into the lot and Bertha got out. She shoved money at the driver then gingerly settled onto the picnic bench across from me.

"Gosh darn worrywarts. Blood pressure this and stress that. Though it did give me a turn, Allie." Bertha shook her head. "By God, pulling up that girl gave me a turn."

Aunt Gully bustled from the shack and set a lobster roll in front of Bertha.

"Just the ticket, Gully." Bertha sighed.

Hunger overwhelmed me. I gobbled half the hamburger, but then images of the girl's face surfaced. Dread settled on me like a weight. I swallowed hard and set the burger aside. Aunt Gully rubbed my back.

Hilda brought mugs of tea.

"Thanks, Hilda." I wrapped my hands around the warm mug.

"Thank you kindly, Hilda, but I'll need something stronger than tea." Bertha dabbed her lips. She rooted in her baggy jacket pocket and tipped a flask into her tea mug. The flask was decorated with a skull and crossbones and the words "Surrender Yer Booty." She held my eye and raised the flask. I shook my head. God only knew what Bertha had in there.

Hilda patted my shoulder then returned to the kitchen.

A long gray De Soto complete with fins rounded the shed and pulled up within a foot of our picnic table.

"Hell on the half shell, that nut almost hit us!" Bertha shouted.

The driver leaned from the window. "Allie! Are you okay?"

My best friend, Verity Brooks, jumped out of the car we called the Tank. She didn't bother closing the door before she threw her arms around me so hard she almost knocked me over.

"I just heard! Some lady came in and started talking about how some guy's body had been pulled up by a lobsterman and how the same girl who solved the last Mystic Bay murder was hauled in to the police station, so I knew it was you." Verity's eyebrows arched over large, round Gucci sunglasses that matched her vintage seventies burnt-orange pantsuit and neck scarf. She took a deep breath. "Hello, everyone." Verity parked the sunglasses on her head in her thick black curls. "Oh, Bertha. Lobster *woman*. What happened? Are you okay?"

Aunt Gully raised a hand. "Now, now, Verity. Give Allie a moment."

Verity's presence was so real, so soothing. "No arrest, I just gave a statement. Who's watching your shop?" I sipped my tea.

Verity took a bite of my hamburger. "Can't remember her name," she mumbled. "They never stay long. Some college kid I hired. Told her I'd be back in ten." Verity owned Verity's Vintage Shop by the town green.

"Your customer got it wrong. It was a girl." Bertha knocked back her tea and poured more murky brown liquid from her flask into her empty mug.

"Did you recognize her?" Aunt Gully said quietly.

It was hard to find my voice. I noticed I was wrapping the same strand of my coppery red hair around my fingers over and over. I tucked my hair behind my ear and took a deep breath. "Well, young woman, twenty-five to thirty? Maybe our age or Lorel's age. Petite. Short black hair, in kind of a pixie cut."

Lorel ran out of the shack and wrapped an arm around me. "Sorry, sis, had customers. This is ghastly." For a second, I was glad to see her. But then part of me wanted to shout, *It's your fault! You should have found her. Not me.* I let my cheek rest briefly against her shoulder and felt my anger deflate. *Shake it off, Allie, it's not Lorel's fault.*

"Poor, poor thing." Aunt Gully tidied the plates.

"Do you think maybe it was a tourist who drowned?" Lorel asked. She put her phone on the table.

"That's a good point. They don't know the waters here and all the riptides," Verity said.

Bertha nodded. Her black eyes and square jaw made me think of her recently deceased bulldog, the Boss. "Especially the one off East Point, past Cat Island."

I shook my head. "But she wasn't wearing a bathing suit or a wetsuit. She had on a sweatshirt and jeans. With flowers embroidered on the legs." The river behind us slid unhurried and peaceful into the Sound. "She must have fallen off a boat."

Verity hugged me. "I wish I didn't have to leave but I have to get back to the shop. I'll talk to you later." Verity hurried back to the Tank and peeled out of the parking lot.

"Best get going." Bertha stood and dropped one of her heavy hands onto my shoulder. Her black eyes glistened. "At least we got her out of the water, Allie." Bertha's words slurred. "Now she can be reunited with her family." For all her tough talk and no-nonsense ways, Bertha was surprisingly weepy. Though probably it was the alcohol.

"That's a good thought, Bertha." I gave her a hug. Bertha stiffened, then relaxed and patted my back. She turned to Aunt Gully. "Stand-up girl, Gully. She took charge when I took a bad turn on the boat."

The creases in Aunt Gully's forehead relaxed. "She's a keeper."

Our chef Hector hurried out the kitchen's screen door and wrapped his muscular, tattooed arms around me. "Just got a free minute. What rotten luck, Allie! Are you okay?"

"I'm fine." I love Hector, but all this concern was starting to get on my nerves.

Bertha said, "I'd best head home."

"Would you like Lorel to give you a ride, Bertha?" Aunt Gully said.

Lorel's head jerked up from her phone.

"No, thank you kindly, Gully. My nephew's coming to get me. I want to get in my rocking chair with Bruce, Rosalita, and Big Man and then get a good night's sleep." Bruce, Rosalita, and Big Man were Bertha's cats. "And I have to unload the lobsters I caught today. The Coasties left the buckets on the dock."

"I can help with that." Hector whistled. Bit Markey stuck his head out of the kitchen door. "Hey, Bit, give us a hand."

"Okay." Bit waved and joined Hector as they walked down to the pier.

"I'll walk with you." Aunt Gully and Bertha followed.

Hilda emerged from the kitchen door of the shack, carrying another mug of tea.

"If I stick around here, I'll get tea poisoning," I muttered. I was itching to move. I checked my phone. Three o'clock. I had a costume fitting before rehearsal. No time for a swim.

I crossed my arms on the picnic table and laid my head on them. The girl's profile, speckled with sand and water droplets, surfaced in my mind. "Ugh." I rubbed my eyes. "I've got to go."

"I'm sorry this happened to you, Allie." Hilda set down the tea. "You must be exhausted. Going lobstering so early this morning, then finding a body, then talking to the police this afternoon. Maybe you should go home to bed."

"Thanks, Hilda. But if I close my eyes—" I shuddered. I didn't want to see that girl again. All I could do was hope that word of my discovery hadn't made it to the Jake yet.

Maybe the news would take longer to reach the theater complex, set among farms north of town, where most of the cast were out-of-towners keeping in touch with friends in Boston and New York. Maybe I'd get through my fitting and rehearsal without anyone mentioning this girl or looking at me with big sympathetic eyes, like Hilda. I just wanted, no I needed, to dance.

After a quick good-bye, I took Aunt Gully's van to the Jake.

I pulled behind the Box Barn, our smaller theater building where *Ondine* would play. The big red barn hosted the Broadway by the Bay performances of crowd-pleasing musicals.

Ondine was different. Really different. The show had been created for a German opera singer none of us had ever heard of. Our artistic director, Mac Macallen, actually called it a happening. It was scheduled for three days only. Sales were surprisingly good for something so far out of the box.

I shouldered my dance bag and hurried into the Box Barn.

Throughout my fitting, warm-up, and rehearsal my body moved without conscious thought. My mind was numb. As we stepped onstage, I relaxed. Well, as much as I could. Most of my "dancing" took place in an aerial harness. It was a blast—after I'd gotten over the fear of dangling a dozen feet above the stage and flying even higher on entrances and exits. Tonight I was glad that my role required me to be alone on a giant fake rock. I just didn't want to talk about what Bertha and I had found.

Instead of hanging out with friends after rehearsal, I threw on a sweatshirt and hurried to the van. As soon as I stepped out of the theater into the dark parking lot, the warmth and camaraderie of rehearsal evaporated. The van started with a shudder and a plume of smoke. I headed home.

The night flowed by my open window as my mind replayed scenes from early morning: Bertha at the wheel, the boat listing to starboard, the water streaming off the girl's body, the gulls shrieking overhead.

For a moment on the dark road along the shore, the sea was flowing in the window instead of air. The wind through the window that stirred my hair was the hand of the girl on the lobster pot. I shivered and threw a look at the rearview mirror, but the backseat was empty. I rolled up the window.

Suddenly I was in the driveway at Gull's Nest, unsure how I got there. I put the van in park, staring at the reflection of my headlights on the garage door's windows.

Aunt Gully banged through the screen door, trailed by Lorel. "Allie! Are you coming in?"

My legs and arms felt like lead. "I'm so tired, Aunt Gully."

Aunt Gully opened the door of the van. Lorel reached over me and turned off the ignition.

"And I bet you haven't eaten anything," Aunt Gully muttered. "Bowl of soup and then up to bed, young lady."

I didn't argue. But after only a spoonful of soup I let Aunt Gully and Lorel lead me to my bedroom. I curled onto my bed, praying that the awful images of the girl on the lobster pot that flickered through my mind would stop.

Chapter 6

Thursday, July 2

The next morning I crawled from bed exhausted. I pushed myself through my usual workout, stretching on the floor, and through a modified ballet barre, not seeing the purple and pink braided rug Aunt Gully had made for my tenth birthday, the poster of Mikhail Baryshnikov over my bed, or the row of Trixie Belden books on my old bookshelf. Just foaming gray seawater the moment the girl's body broke the surface.

The aroma of coffee brewing drew me from my reverie. I headed downstairs.

"Are you sure you want to go to work?" Aunt Gully set a plate of blueberry pancakes and scrambled eggs in front of me.

Suddenly, I was ravenous. I nodded and dug in.

"Remember Hilda, Hector, and I are going to Harmony Harbor to train Stellene Lupo's staff today." Aunt Gully bustled around the kitchen tidying the pink

Formica countertops. "Lorel's over at the shack doing prep work and has plenty of help, so you take your time."

"Full report when you return, okay?" I said through a mouthful of eggs.

Aunt Gully hung her apron on a peg. Instead of her usual Bermuda shorts and polo shirt work combo, she was wearing a light pink shirtdress with a lobster-print scarf and pearl studs, not her usual dangling earrings.

"Are you sure you're okay, honey?" she said.

"I'm over the shock." The familiar warmth of Aunt Gully's kitchen and her presence calmed me. "I just feel so sorry for that girl. I hope her family finds her soon."

"They will." A car horn honked. "Oh, that's Hector and Hilda." Aunt Gully poufed her gray bob and slid on cherry-red sunglasses. "I wish I didn't have to run."

I didn't want to spoil Aunt Gully's excitement about visiting Harmony Harbor. I pasted on a smile and pushed her toward the door. "Scoot! Nobody keeps Stellene Lupo waiting!"

"Oh, don't forget, your dad's renting out the Mermaid Motel for the Fourth of July weekend. A nice military family's taking it," she called as she hurried down the front walkway. "If you want anything you'd better run over now."

Hector held the door for Aunt Gully as she squeezed into the back of Hilda's green VW Bug.

Hector folded himself back into the car. Hilda waved.

"Have fun!" I called as they took off.

I returned to my half-finished pancakes, but my appetite had disappeared. I'd forgotten that Dad was renting our house, which we all called the Mermaid Motel.

Another change.

My mother, Miranda, died giving birth to me. My dad, Robert, whom everyone called Bibb, had never seriously dated after that. But a few months ago, he'd met a Brazilian widow named Esmeralda Lima who'd made a grand entrance to Mystic Bay on a ninety-foot yacht. Lorel and I called her the Firecracker.

At Esmeralda's suggestion, Dad was renting out our family home while they went on a dream trip to the Galápagos Islands. Renting generated extra cash. The Firecracker was good with money.

I'd moved most of my stuff to Aunt Gully's since I was working at the shack. Living with Aunt Gully meant never having to cook a meal. Lorel had her condo in Boston. I'd shared a house in Boston with other dancers before my injury. We'd both flown the nest.

With Aunt Gully gone to train Stellene's staff, my calm evaporated as I tidied the kitchen. Maybe feeling the beach sand under my toes would calm my jangled nerves.

I slipped into a swimsuit and walked down the road to what we called the Kiddie Beach—a broad half-moon of sand with shallow water perfect for children. A mom was setting up a camp of beach chairs, blankets, and umbrellas as her two little boys gathered pebbles by the water's edge.

I took off my high-tech cast. It was waterproof, but felt smushy if I did get it wet. I stepped carefully into the water and dived in. I didn't push it with any serious swimming. I let my body and my mind float for a few minutes, until a strand of seaweed laced around my ankle. Images of the dead girl flashed through my mind. I shook off the seaweed and hurried out of the water.

A stone breakwater jutted from the beach. I walked out to the end and sat on the last boulder, already warm from the sun. A cormorant tilted its head at me then beat its wings to rise from the water.

I've been a short walk from the beach all my life. My dad said I could swim before I could walk. I'd never feared what lay beneath the waves. All the ocean creatures I'd ever encountered, even the occasional shark, held only fascination for me. The dead girl was the only horror I'd ever found beneath the waves.

Who was she? How did she end up at the bottom of the bay, fully dressed, snagged onto a lobster pot?

Had she jumped into the water?

A thought chilled me. Had someone pushed her?

I hurried back to Gull's Nest, showered in the outdoor shower, dressed, and headed for the Mermaid.

Chapter 7

My jaw dropped as I pulled into the Mermaid's parking lot. Sometime after I'd left yesterday, Aunt Gully had finished decorating the shack for the Fourth of July. Bunting looked especially charming and old-fashioned against the weathered gray cedar shingles. A red, white, and blue wreath hung on the door. Silver stars sparkled from the windows. An inflatable Uncle Sam flanked the door across from our mermaid figurehead.

On the roof, a giant inflatable lobster waved a flag in its claw.

A patriotic lobster. Now I've seen everything.

Over the top was how Aunt Gully did things. Hilda had planted half barrels by the door with red geraniums, ivy, white snapdragons, and blue violets, but Aunt Gully had added red, white, and blue tinsel garlands and patriotic whirligigs that spun in the breeze. Almost lost among all the decorations was the American flag that Aunt Gully put out every day as her remembrance ritual for Uncle Rocco.

Two guys took selfies with Aunt Gully's mermaid figurehead, complete with a Lady Liberty crown and red, white, and blue sash. I squinted. Sequined letters on the sash spelled out "Miss Crustacean Sensation."

It was barely eleven A.M., but customers sunburned lobster red streamed toward the door, and our lot was almost full.

I hurried inside. The TV hung in the corner of the dining room ceiling was usually tuned to cooking shows and local news. The yellow tape scrolling across the bottom of the screen blared LOBSTER BOAT FINDS BODY IN MYSTIC BAY. My heart thudded.

A black-and-white sketch of a young woman with short black hair filled the screen. Everything around me disappeared. That was the girl Bertha and I had found. I stepped closer to the television. The police artist's pencil sketch stared from the screen—the full lips expressionless, large almond-shaped eyes giving away no secrets. There was little resemblance to the pallid body Bertha and I had pulled from the water.

A guy in a Harbor Patrol polo shirt stood, coffee cup in hand. "Hey, weren't you with Bertha when—"

Lorel took my hand and pulled me behind the counter and into the kitchen. "No comment," she said over her shoulder.

"Thanks, sis." I fumbled as I put on my apron then joined several women at the large stainless-steel kitchen table. They sported clamshell bikini T-shirts that said GULLY'S GALS and hairnets decorated with sequined lobsters.

Gully's Gals were Aunt Gully's friends from the neighborhood, her former job at Mystic Bay Elementary's cafeteria, church ladies' circle, Girl Scouts, crafts group, book club, Zumba class, Mystic Bay Historical Society, and the League of Women Voters. Aunt Gully had lived in Mystic Bay all her life and had an inexhaustible supply of friends who thought it was fun to pitch in at the shack. If they knew about my role in the discovery of the girl on the lobster pot, they hid it well. Actually, I was sure they knew but they were trying to keep my mind off it. We laughed and gossiped and talked about everything but the news as our gloved hands separated cooked lobster meat from the bright red shell.

An hour later, I took my shift at the counter. Usually the wooden screen door banged shut after each customer like an exclamation point, but now the customers were coming in such a steady stream that the door never really shut. Tourists stood half in and half out the door. The July Fourth invasion was in full swing.

A young African American woman in a navy blue sheath dress edged in the door past a guy in a Hawaiian shirt and cargo pants. He watched her appreciatively.

Her thick dark hair was sleeked into a chignon. She wore a jaunty red gingham kerchief tied at the neck. A straw purse was slung over her shoulder and she juggled a phone and clipboard. She looked like she'd just stepped out of the window of Fashions by Franque, the chichiest boutique in Mystic Bay.

Her perfectly arched eyebrows lifted as she scanned

the jumbled shelves of Aunt Gully's mermaidabilia. Her mouth dropped open as she tilted her chin to take in the ceiling, painted in iridescent green scales, as if a magical sea creature swam overhead. She wrinkled her nose.

Hmm, not a fan of Aunt Gully's "primitive aesthetic."

She skirted the line with a big-city strut. *Who wears stilettos to a lobster shack?* She leaned toward me at the counter. "Hi, I'm Zoe Parker."

"Hi. The line's over there." It was early so I didn't roll my eyes. Line cutting gets my goat.

"Zoe Parker," she repeated. "Assistant to Stellene Lupo."

I took a deep breath, then realized who it was. "Ah—"

Lorel hip-checked me aside, wiping her hands on a dishtowel. She held out her hand. "Lorel Larkin. Welcome to the Lazy Mermaid."

"This place is amazing! I love it!" Zoe smiled wide and looked directly into Lorel's eyes as they shook hands.

Liar. I shifted to Lorel's right. "Next."

There wasn't a seat to be had inside the shack. Zoe and Lorel went out into the parking lot, Zoe's designer heels clicking on the wooden floor. She wobbled in the gravel.

An hour passed like five minutes. I relaxed into my work, picking lobster meat, making rolls, waiting on customers, only jarred when I heard the word "body." My discovery was a big topic of conversation, but nobody had asked me about it. My name hadn't been mentioned on the news. My shoulders relaxed. Maybe I could end my shift without anyone mentioning it to me.

From the kitchen, excited conversation and laughter bubbled above the sound of tourists oohing and ahing over Aunt Gully's mermaidabilia.

Hilda joined me at the counter, slipping her apron over her hair, which she'd coiffed into a bouffant. Hilda usually wore little makeup, but today she sported bright red lips and a pearl necklace and matching earrings.

"You look fabulous," I said.

Hilda grinned. "Had to look my best for Harmony Harbor."

"How was it?" I handed a customer a bowl of chowder. "Did you meet Stellene?"

"No Stellene." Hilda paused to take an order. "Her staff said she's had very important meetings all week in New York and won't be here until the Fourth. She's relying on her assistant to do the legwork."

Zoe Parker. "Must be nice to have a personal assistant." I poured coffee.

"Allie." Hilda's big brown eyes sparkled. "Harmony Harbor's just like one of those Newport mansions. Marble floors and walls. The garden's huge, like at a castle. They have a conservatory full of orchids. Oh, they should call it Heavenly Harbor."

"How did they manage the lobsters?" I grabbed an overflowing plate from the pass-through and handed it to a guy with a handlebar moustache in a Patriots T-shirt. He winked.

"Get this," Hilda said. "Hector knew the chef they

brought in from Maine! Stellene, well, her assistant, found the same steamer we use in an abandoned shack up in Rockport. She found a man who worked there. Turns out he was in the navy, just like Hector."

"Small world," I said.

"They bonded. He's coming for dinner next week. Anyway, Hector and Gully say it's under control. All I can say is"—Hilda sighed—"it's impressive."

Zoe Parker's and Lorel's voices came through the kitchen pass-through. I watched them talk. The heat from the lobster steamer made Zoe's hair frizz out of place but a smile curved her glossy lips. This time her smile looked genuine.

Zoe smoothed her hair and Lorel did the same. I sighed. Lorel'd found a match. They did the air-kiss thing and Zoe waved good-bye.

"Allie. Psst." Through the pass-through window, a young woman with a spiky short haircut stage-whispered. My friend Bronwyn Denby raised her eyebrows and gave me a curt "come here" gesture. What was she doing in the kitchen?

I went into the kitchen.

"Hey, Bron."

Bronwyn and I have been friends since preschool at St. Peter's Church. She worked as an intern with the Mystic Bay Police Department while she finished a degree in criminal justice. She exchanged glances with Aunt Gully.

"You've done a wonderful job holding down the fort, Allie. I think it's time for a break," Aunt Gully said.

Gully's Gals waved gloved hands. "Have fun!"

"You need some ice cream, Allie Larkin." Bronwyn tugged me out the kitchen door.

"No argument from me."

Bronwyn yanked me behind the lobster shed and then flattened her back against the buoy-covered wall.

"Bronwyn, are you okay?"

She peered around the side of the shed into the parking lot. "Just in time."

I leaned around her. A news truck hulked by the entrance to the parking lot. A guy jumped out of the passenger door.

"Leo Rodriguez," Bronwyn said.

"God, he's relentless," I moaned. I'd met Leo, a star reporter with the Hartford TV station, during the murder investigation centered around the Mystic Bay Food Festival in May. He'd gone to what I considered extreme and unethical lengths to get his story.

Zoe Parker gave the news truck a quizzical look as she beeped open the door of a gleaming Range Rover. Leo Rodriguez brushed back his glossy black hair and pushed through the line at the front door of the Mermaid.

Bronwyn and I ate ice-cream cones and swung our legs off the pier at the Town Dock, a couple of blocks down Pearl Street from the Lazy Mermaid. Death by chocolate for me, strawberry with sprinkles for her.

"Thanks for rescuing me from Leo Rodriguez. Finding that girl was awful." I shuddered. "I don't want to rehash it on camera. Besides, it's best for Lorel to handle Leo. She'll turn my finding another body into positive publicity for the Mermaid." I shifted my bottom on the sun-warmed, splintery wood.

Bronwyn chuckled. "Lorel's something else. Miss Perfect."

I grimaced. "Her personal life's not so perfect. She's back with Patrick Yardley."

"That sounds perfect to me. Isn't he the hottest guy in Mystic Bay?" Bronwyn said. "Owns the coolest nightspot in New England?"

"You know how many times they've broken up and gotten back together," I said. "He's always got another girl in the picture somewhere. I wish she'd just—"

Bronwyn held up a hand holding the last of her ice-cream cone. "Her life. Her rules."

Everyone kept saying that but they hadn't listened to Lorel's heartbroken weeping. "It's awful when someone that buttoned up breaks down." I licked the drips on my ice-cream cone.

"Forget Patrick. How're you doing?" Bronwyn's forehead wrinkled. "Finding that girl. That's rough. I wish I'd been at the Plex when you gave your statement. I was at training in chain-of-evidence stuff."

I watched boats stream unhurried upriver toward their slips at the marina. "It still doesn't seem real."

As I told Bronwyn what had happened on Bertha's boat, images flashed through my mind. The girl's hand. Her hair, tangled with slimy seaweed. The flowered embroidery on her sodden jeans. This saddened me, this feminine, bohemian touch. The girl probably loved those jeans.

"Do the police know who she is?" I asked.

Bronwyn crunched the last of her cone and licked her fingers. "Not many details yet. She didn't have any identification on her. Nothing special about her clothes except for the jeans, which were designer, pricey, like you'd get at a fancy boutique. No matching missing persons reports from here to Maine."

With a sigh, I finished my cone and licked my fingers. "She had a tattoo. What was it? A trident?"

"They're going to release all that soon. When there's a missing person like this, the department will do a press release with details like that, trying to get an ID. Actually, that tat was a pitchfork."

"A pitchfork?"

"And underneath that it said 'hellion.' In all capital letters." Bronwyn frowned. "Poorly done. Kind of jailhouse."

"Jailhouse?" Hard to see a person who thought of herself as a hellion in the pathetic corpse I'd seen. A girl who thought of herself as a hellion but wore feminine, kind-of-hippie bell-bottoms. "Those jeans didn't look jailhouse."

Frustration and sadness surged through me. "I feel so bad for her, Bronwyn. How could she have nobody? How could her family and friends not be looking for her?"

"Some people don't have a family." Bronwyn shrugged. She had four brothers and used to sleep over with me and Verity to escape them.

I pulled my knees to my chest and wrapped my arms around them. "It's so strange, but I feel responsible for her."

"I get it." Bronwyn squeezed my arm. "I feel that

way, too. Maybe we're the ones who have to help her since she doesn't seem to have anyone else."

"What are the police doing?"

"Bringing in the state police," Bronwyn said. "Our department doesn't have the expertise for this. The staties have an expert who's worked a lot of drowning cases. Chief Brooks has been a basket case just coordinating it." She gave me a rueful smile. "This hasn't been an easy summer for him. We've never had all this serious stuff happening in Mystic Bay before."

"He's a nice man." Chief Brooks was Verity's uncle and a father figure since her own parents had retired to Florida. He'd coached Lorel's softball team. His wife and Aunt Gully were in the ladies' guild together at church.

"How long was she in the water?" I said.

Bronwyn considered. "Two or three days. Long enough for certain changes to occur, such as—"

I held up my hand. "I'm not sure I want to know." Sometimes Bronwyn sounded just like her criminal justice textbooks. After graduating from high school, Bronwyn had gone backpacking in Europe, working in hostels to fund her travel. She joined AmeriCorps when she returned and used her stipend to pay for her criminal justice studies.

"Sorry. Anyway, we're doing a lot with this case. Checking hotels, motels, contacting other jurisdictions, asking for help from the media. Checking tide charts and currents. Trying to figure out where her body went into the water."

I thought back. "Two or three days before we found her there was a storm, remember?"

"Yeah." Bronwyn nodded. "So that might've changed things. Made the currents faster, stronger."

"Moved her farther away from where she went in?" I asked.

"Possibly. Depends. You said she was caught on the lobster pot. That might have anchored her to that spot right away."

"Maybe."

Bronwyn stood and brushed the seat of her khaki police shorts. She gave me a hand up. "Time to get back to work."

We headed back to Pearl Street. "What happens now?" I asked.

"The autopsy. A lot depends on how she died." Bronwyn slid on her aviator sunglasses. "If it was a natural death or a murder."

Chapter 8

I shouldered through tourists crowding the uneven brick sidewalks, the word "murder" hovering over me like a shadow.

Back at the Mermaid, the news truck was gone. I exhaled and went in the kitchen door.

Aunt Gully and her friend Aggie Weatherburn worked at the long metal lobster-picking table.

Aunt Gully winked. "Lorel took care of him."

"Thank goodness." I smiled. "Hello, Mrs. Weatherburn."

"Allegra." Aggie was our neighbor and Aunt Gully's best friend. She squinted at me over her half-moon glasses. "Looks a bit peaked to me." That was an Aggie word—"peak-ed."

"We're okay here. Things have slowed a bit," Aunt Gully said. "Why don't you take a bit more time off?"

No encouragement needed. "See you later."

I had an hour before rehearsal, so I took the van and

headed to Main Street by the town green. Tourists clogged the narrow sidewalks, oblivious to everything except the gleaming wares in the gift shop windows and the beautiful view of the harbor.

All I could see was the police sketch. *Who was that girl?*

The artist's sketch had been, well, sketchy. Drained of personality. In the sketch, her hair had been smoothed down, but most girls I knew with short pixie cuts, like Bronwyn, wore their hair tousled, carefree, and punk.

I had no way of knowing what was under her clothing, but with the pitchfork and hellion tattoos, the girl was sending a message. She was tough. Badass. Edgy.

But something about those feminine embroidered pants didn't seem edgy to me. They were more girly, bohemian, and fashion conscious.

The green and gold sign for Fashions by Franque hung a block down from the pink sign for Verity's Vintage. I squeezed Aunt Gully's van into the tiny Staff Only lot behind Verity's building and hurried down the sidewalk.

Mystic Bay's stores were geared to appeal to summer tourists: ice-cream parlors, fudge shops, souvenirs, all with nautical flavor. Fashions by Franque kept customers coming all year by offering high-end designer clothes. No T-shirts with mermaids in clamshell bikinis here. The window was full of expensive, glamorous dresses for parties I'd never be invited to.

Two giggling teenage girls looked in Franque's shop window. A slender man with fashionable heavy black frame glasses, obviously dyed black hair, and fake-bake tan arranged a sea-blue chiffon dress by the front door, while wordlessly sending "don't come in here with those ice-cream cones dripping" vibes.

A woman with two bulging apple-green shopping bags pushed by me as I went inside the store with walls tinted the same color.

The man took in my Lazy Mermaid T-shirt, cargo shorts, and flip-flops. He gave a deflated little sigh but pulled himself together. "How may I help you?"

"Are you the owner?" I said.

He spread his arms. "The one and only, Franque!"

The woman behind the counter stifled a laugh. He stepped closer and held the blue dress in front of me. "This was made for you! That red hair! Those blue eyes! Venus on the half shell!"

"It's gorgeous." I didn't bother to look at the price tag. "Sorry, I'm not shopping today."

Franque shrugged and hung it up. "Looking for a job?" A hopeful note.

"No, it's—" How did I start? I wasn't a cop. He'd probably think I was some ghoul. But still, I had to ask.

He stuck out his hand. "Franque Delacour."

We shook.

"Allie Larkin," I said.

"Ooh, I thought I recognized you." Franque snapped his fingers. "I saw you on TV last month! And now there's that new body that was found. Was that you, too? With the lobster lady? Involved in another suspicious death?"

Maybe this would be easier than I thought.

The woman behind the counter said, "Franque watches all the shows. *CSI. CSI New Orleans, CSI Special Victims, CSI—*"

"*CSI Mystic Bay.* Well, one can hope." He tilted his head then pulled me back toward the counter. The woman nodded. "Hello, I'm Donna, Franque's long-suffering sister."

"Hi."

"You found that girl," Franque said. "Lazy Mermaid Lobster Shack. You were lobstering with that lobster lady and found the body."

"Actually, yes," I said.

Franque's sister shook her head and went to help a customer.

"Come back here." Franque waved me to a back corner of the shop next to a display of sun hats. "Don't want to upset the shoppers with any juicy forensic details. So, how may I help you?"

Franque made this too easy.

"The girl that I found was wearing very unique jeans. Gray denim bell-bottoms with embroidery down the leg."

Franque nodded. "For that boho-hippie look that was big. The floppy hats, low-slung belts, off-the-shoulder tops. You'd look killer in that!"

"The police think the pants were from some high-end designer and I thought maybe she bought them here," I said. "Do you remember carrying any pants like that?"

Franque drummed his nails on the counter. "Yes, yes, I did carry something like that. Sold out in no time. Not that they were the same pants, mind you, I don't know. Maybe the police'll come in with photos." Franque's eyes shone. "Well, if they were the same pants, they were adorable and they flew out of the store."

"Is there any way to check who bought them?"

Franque frowned. "Maybe . . . we'd have to dig into receipts. If she paid by credit card, no way to do that without going to the credit card companies, that's something the cops would have to do."

And I'm not a cop. My heart dropped. "And if she paid cash there'd be no record at all."

Franque waved it away. "You said girl, so she was young? Maybe your age?"

I nodded.

"The young people don't use cash," Franque said.

"The police did a sketch." I scrolled on my phone.

Frank frowned. "Those sketches never look like a real person."

My mind went back to the morning on the boat. "She was petite, not very tall, short black hair. She had a tattoo."

Franque scoffed. "They all have tattoos."

Not me, I thought. My ballet teacher had forbidden it. "Do you see swans with tattoos?" she'd said.

I searched my phone for the police photo. "The police haven't mentioned it yet, but it was a pitchfork. Her tattoo."

Franque's eyes lit up. "I remember! Because she didn't look like the tattooed type to me at first. She was wearing a sexy sundress, lots of bangle bracelets. A big black straw sun hat."

My heart leaped. "So, how would you describe her?"

Franque didn't hesitate. "Confident. Some people wear the clothes and some people, the clothes wear them, know what I mean?" He nodded toward a woman in a too-short leopard-print minidress leaning over a jewelry case. A broad-brimmed hat swooped over her face, multiple scarves wrapped her neck along with several necklaces. She tottered on sky-high platform sandals.

Frank tilted his head. "That girl was petite. Strong chin. Blond?"

"Blond?" My heart plummeted.

Franque shook his head. "Can't remember. Her hair was pulled up under the hat. But I remember when she paid I said something about the tattoo. She looked at me over her sunglasses. Dark eyes, dramatic eye makeup. The look she gave me. Saucy. Paid cash. She matched, outside and inside."

"Matched?"

"When a person's clothes match their inside. Their personality. Their being. That's when it works. Otherwise it's just a costume."

I shifted uneasily, imagining his judgment on my shorts and Lazy Mermaid T-shirt.

I finally found the police sketch and handed my phone to Franque.

Franque held the phone at arm's length and squinted over his glasses. "Honestly, that doesn't do that girl justice. Could be her? Maybe? And something else she did struck me." He stroked his chin. "It'll come to me."

I took the phone back and thanked Franque. I wanted to stop at Verity's before rehearsal. "Sorry, I've got to run."

"Come back any time!"

Could Franque's customer have been the girl Bertha and I found? It would be too easy. But how many women in Mystic Bay had a pitchfork tattoo? I'd have to call Chief Brooks and let him know. My spirits lifted. This was a lead, I was sure of it. It wasn't much, but maybe it would lead to the girl's identity and reunite her with her family.

Sleigh bells on the back of the door jingled as I pushed open the door to Verity's shop. My spirits lifted even more.

Verity's Vintage was an Aladdin's cave of vintage fashion. Racks with clothes from every era jammed the former hair salon, which had originally been a parlor in a three-story Victorian-era building.

Verity had started collecting vintage clothes back when she was in Mystic Bay High School and had to find poodle skirts for our sophomore class production of *Grease*. She got hooked, so much so that her parents' garage, den, and spare bedroom filled with boxes labeled *Fichus, Corsets, fifties, Bombshell, mod*. She'd started selling online and last year saved enough to open the shop.

Verity rushed to hug me. "You didn't return my calls!"

"I'm sorry, I just couldn't handle picking up the phone last night, Verity." I hugged her back. "I'm okay now but I have to find out who that girl was. And I think I found a lead." I told her about my visit to Fashions by Franque.

"I saw you going in there. I was going to ask if you'd won the lottery." She handed me her phone. "You have to call my uncle and give him this info right now."

The call went to voice mail. I left a brief message for Chief Brooks and hung up.

"I wonder if that girl came in here. I saw the police sketch on TV," Verity said.

"That picture didn't seem right to me. But maybe the clothes will be the lead."

Verity nodded. "Tell me what else Franque said."

I shrugged. "Not much. He has this theory about people's outsides and insides matching."

Verity straightened a basket of lace-trimmed handkerchiefs. "Well, that's a nice theory but sometimes people don't look like what they are inside because they can't afford the right clothes. Take me for example. I'm Chanel in my soul but not in my pocketbook. You're a sparkly sea-sprite fairy inside a total artsy weirdo who should be wearing Alexander McQueen and you're disguised as a lobster roll slinger."

I threw a handkerchief at her. "Gee, thanks."

"Plus, you walk around like a duck with your feet turned out."

I laughed. That was true of most ballerinas. "Got me."

"Lorel's inside and outside match. Money does that." Verity rubbed her fingertips together.

I thought of how together Lorel appeared and how messed up she was over Patrick Yardley. "Looks can be deceiving."

One of the clothing racks was empty. "Wow, did you sell out?"

"Get this," Verity said. "Today this girl comes in—sheath dress, pumps, hair pulled back like Lorel . . ."

"Zoe Parker," I said.

Verity touched her nose. ". . . with photos of a picnic at a seaside cottage circa 1955." She pointed to the empty rack. "All my fifties casual, poof! Said 'her employer'"—Verity made air quotes—"is doing a vintage picnic photo shoot."

"Big sale! Awesome!" We high-fived.

"She's dressing a cast of thousands."

"Lucky for you."

Verity grinned. "Nice start to the holiday weekend."

"For you, too. I heard Aunt Gully's catering Stellene's party."

"Yes. Oh, I've got to get to rehearsal."

Verity clasped her hands by her chin. "Allie, can you please, please, please get me in to the party? I can serve lobster rolls."

"Lorel said just me, Aunt Gully, and her, but I'll ask."

Chapter 9

"Allie!" a tall guy with sun-streaked brown hair and hazel eyes called as I walked onto the stage at the Box Barn. "Why didn't you tell me you were the one who found that girl?" Cody Walton's eyebrows knitted together and he wrapped me in a hug. "How terrible for you."

I blew out a breath. I should've known the news would reach the theater eventually.

"Cody, I was going to tell you. It's just—"

Cody swept his arm around the stage. "This is your escape."

"I knew you'd understand."

Techs, dancers, and actors swirled past us. I tugged him into the wings and told him what happened on Bertha's boat.

"It must've been awful," he said.

I nodded. "In a weird way, I feel responsible for her. How did she end up there? Who was she?"

Cody crossed his arms, his biceps bulging. He still

had the broad shoulders he got slinging hay bales on his family's Wyoming ranch. "What about that lady you were with? How's she?"

"Bertha's tough but the shock hit her hard at first." I sighed. "Hit me hard at first, too."

Margot Kim strode over, her long silky black hair scraped back into a high ponytail.

"Hi, Margot," I said.

Margot Kim, Cody, and I had lived with several other dancers in a sprawling Victorian in Boston, the house where I'd fallen and broken my ankle this spring.

"Allie! You finally do something interesting. Give us every juicy detail." Margot's ponytail swung as she laughed.

Cody ducked his head and shifted his weight away from her.

"Honestly, Margot, it wasn't cool or juicy," I said. "It was awful."

"Oh, come on, you'll get yourself in the news again." She pressed the tips of her pointe shoes into the rosin box. Rosin is a sticky substance to help guard against slips on the wooden stage floor. She spun away on pointe, then bourréed back toward us, taking tiny steps that made her look like she was floating on air. "Free publicity for your shack."

The simple movements stabbed a knife of jealousy into me. Since my injury, the question of whether or not I could regain my place in the company was open. Margot had already replaced me in some of my roles.

"I heard some reporter was looking for you," Margot said. "Leo Rodriguez."

My stomach dropped. "Now? Here?"

She shrugged. "One of the techs said he was asking for you."

I peered into the darkened audience, but didn't see Leo. Maybe I could get through rehearsal and get out the door without having to talk to him.

"Not the kind of publicity I need," I said. "I don't want to be associated with more deaths."

Margot tsked. "Don't be naïve, Allie. There's no such thing as bad publicity. It just means more business for that little lobster shack where you work." Margot's smile showed sharp little teeth.

"That reminds me," she continued, "I was at the casino the other night at the high-rollers tables. Saw your sister with that hot guy who owns New Salt." She tapped her chin with her finger. "I thought it was odd because I heard he was still living with some waitress who moved in with him back in May."

Hot guy who owns New Salt. Patrick Yardley.

Margot looped her hair into a bun and walked back onstage.

Usually I brushed aside Margot's mean little pricks, but my emotions were raw.

Fury rose so fast inside me I thought I'd choke.

Could Patrick be living with another woman at the same time he was dating Lorel? I balled my fists and started after Margot.

"Allie?" Cody put a hand on my shoulder. "Don't worry about Margot. She's a witch."

I forced myself to take a breath. "Agreed."

The stage manager called, "Places, everybody!"

I took another deep breath. "Back to work, right, Cody?"

But I knew what I was doing after rehearsal. Going to New Salt to confront Patrick Yardley.

Since Margot had warned me about Leo Rodriguez, I prepared evasive action: when rehearsal ended, Cody would make sure the coast was clear outside the dressing room. Then I'd hustle over to the costume shop. There was a door directly into the parking lot there. Then I'd make a break for Aunt Gully's van.

Well, it sounded simple. Once out of my harness and mermaid tail, I waved to Cody and dashed down the dim hallway leading to the costume shop. The darkened space was lined with stage decorations: gigantic clams, eight-foot-high plywood kelp, and fake coral reefs coated with glittery paint in garish fairy-tale pinks and purples. I ran to the costume shop door and turned the knob.

Locked.

"Mac!" A voice familiar from the television news rang out. Leo Rodriguez.

The lanky frame of Mac Macallen, the director of Broadway by the Bay, stepped into the hallway, and then turned around. "Leo Rodriguez, my friend!"

Footsteps rang on the linoleum floor of the hallway. One more step and Leo would see me.

I ducked inside a six-foot-tall, shocking-pink papier-mâché conch shell, curling myself up as small as I could. I peeked around the side and realized my dance bag stuck out far enough to be noticed. *Rats.* I eased back inside the shell and held my breath.

"Leo, how's it going?" Mac said.

The two men exchanged pleasantries. They both

had performers' voices—loud, precisely enunciated—so I could hear everything they said. My calf cramped. I winced and kneaded it.

"What brings you here?" Mac said.

"We're covering the body found out in the bay," Leo replied.

"I just heard. Such a tragic, terrible thing. Have the police identified that poor soul? It was a young woman, wasn't it?"

"Yes, a woman in her late twenties," Leo said. "No one's stepped forward to identify her yet."

"Tragic, tragic." Mac coughed. "Have you found out anything else?"

"Not much." Leo said. "The State Medical Examiner has to process the body. Police, Coast Guard, and Harbor Patrol didn't have much to tell us. Lobster lady who found her told me to go to hell."

Mac chuckled. Leo didn't join in. I imagined his chiseled cheekbones, perfect for TV news, his broad, white smile, the way his eyes bored into you.

"Do you know if Allie Larkin's here?" Leo asked. "I stopped by the lobster shack and her house but I keep missing her. Her sister told me she was rehearsing."

Lorel. That rat.

"Allie Larkin?" Mac said. "What does she have to do with this?"

"She was with the lobster lady when she found the body."

"Oh, that must've been a terrible shock for her." Mac was silent for a moment. "They just finished up rehearsal. We're doing this new experimental piece called *Ondine*. The director specifically asked for her."

"Easy to see why," Leo said. "She's stunning."

Leo Rodriguez thinks I'm stunning?

"Indeed. She plays the Mermaid Queen. It's a very small part but we're lucky to have a dancer of her caliber," Mac said. "She may still be onstage or in the dressing rooms. You can go down that wing."

"Okay, thanks, man. See you opening night."

"Definitely. Have a good night, Leo."

Footsteps rang and receded. I uncurled from my crouch and peeked around the shell. Right at Mac Macallen.

"I thought that was your dance bag, Allie," Mac whispered. He grinned.

I jutted my chin toward the end of the hallway. "Thanks. I don't want to talk to Leo."

"Ah, we'll make our exit through the costume shop." Mac hefted my dance bag and pulled a ring of keys from his pocket. He turned the key in the costume-shop door and we slipped inside. Light from the parking lot cast a gray glow on racks of clothing, wide worktables, and sewing machines. Mac closed the door softly then relocked it. "Should I put on the lights?"

"No, I can see well enough with the light coming in the window."

"Leo Rodriguez is one determined reporter," Mac whispered.

"Tell me about it."

Light reflected off Mac's horn-rimmed glasses as he handed me my bag.

"Thanks, Mac. I'm just going to slip out this door and then go home." With a stop at New Salt.

"Ah, yes." Mac rubbed his hand along his chin. "I'm

sure you're tired of talking about it, Allie, but—" Even in the dim light I could see Mac's frown.

"What is it, Mac?"

Mac was the epitome of sophistication and discretion. His thick silver hair truly did deserve the term "mane." He was dressed casually for him, in a button-down shirt and chinos with a sweater vest I was sure was cashmere. His shoes had a shine I could see even in the half-light, not a wrinkle on his custom-made shirt. But Mac had a pencil stuck behind his ear.

I smoothed my hair behind my ear, hoping he'd imitate the gesture.

Mac did. He looked at the pencil as if seeing one for the first time and put it down on a worktable. "The young woman you found—"

I shifted my weight and inhaled. Mac Macallen was the last guy I thought would be nosing for details.

He cleared his throat. "Just hoping it wasn't anyone who'd worked here. You know how we theater people travel. After *Mame,* lots of the actors joined a road show, some actors left for school, some for other jobs. It's hard to keep track of everyone."

Mac had a warm heart for all the boys and girls of the theater. I exhaled. "I didn't recognize her. She was . . ." I suppressed a shiver at the memory of her waxy skin. "Petite, my age maybe—"

Mac nodded.

"Black hair, cut very short," I said. "I don't know the color of her eyes," I said carefully. Or if there were any.

Mac relaxed. "Short black hair. Well, I don't think that's anyone who was in the cast of *Mame.*"

Voices carried in from the hallway.

Mac led me to the door. "Perhaps it's best if we both make a swift exit."

Mac waved as I drove out of the parking lot. In the rearview mirror I watched him fold his tall frame into his sporty red Mini Cooper. He was a sweet man.

Unlike Patrick Yardley. Aunt Gully's van screeched as I swung the wheel toward the waterfront.

Chapter 10

New Salt was on the waterfront at the marina just past Mystic Bay's historic district. Patrick and his partners had taken Ye Olde Rusty Scupper Bar and Grille and turned it into an upscale nightspot, half restaurant and half bar. Boaters could dock at the marina and stroll a few yards to enjoy fresh seafood and trendy cocktails. New Salt was jammed every night. It was Mystic Bay's meet market.

The line to get in was out the door. I ignored dirty looks as I cut to the front. I didn't care. Anger and adrenaline buzzed through me.

Inside, music thumped so loud the hostess had to shout. "May I help you?" She frowned at my sweaty rehearsal clothes. I recognized her from Pilates class.

"Hey, Kate."

"Oh, hi. Allie, right? Are you having dinner here?"

"Nope. Just looking for Patrick."

"He's not here." Her eyes cut to the stairs down the hallway by the bathrooms.

"Thanks, Kate." I darted up the stairs.

"You can't go up there!" Kate shouted.

I ignored her and the twinge in my ankle, thinking only that if Patrick had another girlfriend with him I'd throw him out the window. At the top of the stairs, I pounded on the door and threw it open.

Patrick Yardley spun around, a cell phone to his ear. His expression flashed from confusion to recognition and back again. He held up a hand but continued talking.

I was determined to keep the embers of anger fanned and not let Patrick's animal magnetism sway me. Patrick shut the door, muffling the music and bar noise below. He threw me a puzzled look, then turned to his desk, distracting me with the long lines of his muscular back and shoulders. His jeans fit him extremely well and his T-shirt was like a second skin. No wonder Lorel couldn't stay away.

Lowering his voice, Patrick continued his conversation, flicking through some papers on his desk.

Nervous energy coursed through me as I stalked around the room, looking for signs of female occupation.

I could see a bed through a doorway. I leaned in, not caring that I was invading Patrick's privacy. The bed was made, a navy blue comforter smooth across it.

It was all so tidy. No women's clothing, no cosmetics. What had I expected? Lacy lingerie tossed everywhere and a round platform bed topped with a tiger skin? My anger sputtered. If a woman were living here, there was no indication.

There was a black backpack tossed into a corner. I swung around. No yoga mat or pink running shoes by the door, just a pair of men's black sneakers.

Everything was stripped down, with the feel of a rarely used dorm room. The only thing on the wall was a print of New London's historic Ledge Lighthouse.

Patrick threw me a look and murmured into the phone. "Yes, yes. On the boat. I'll be there. Don't worry." His voice turned cajoling. "It's taken care of. Okay. Bye." He slid the phone into his back pocket. For a moment he stood in profile, his chiseled jaw reminding me of Verity's Jim Morrison poster. He grasped the edge of his desk and took a deep breath.

Patrick turned to me. "Hi, Allie. What's up?" His eyes moved slowly from my sweaty yoga pants to my bodysuit. "To what do I owe the pleasure?"

Heat rose in my face. "What's up? I just heard that you're living with some girl, one of your servers."

Patrick's expression didn't change but he folded his arms and smiled, a little crooked on one side, a little sly.

"That's news to me, Allie. Who's telling you this stuff?" His voice was warmer and deeper than I remembered, probably because the last time I had an actual conversation with him was in high school. His voice had a caressing tone. I could see how a woman could believe everything a man said in a voice like that.

I wasn't that woman.

Patrick opened his arms. "Look around. As you can see, I'm the only one here. Rumors, you shouldn't believe rumors, Allie."

My stomach twisted. Who'd told me about Patrick's

other woman? Margot. Was she playing me for a fool? Margot lived to hurt others, but I thought she was telling the truth.

"May I remind you that you're dating my sister? Patrick, I know Lorel wants to be with you but for heaven's sake—" My voice shook. I hated myself when the words came out in a whisper. "Don't hurt Lorel."

Patrick held up his hands in surrender, but his eyes were hard. "Allie, it's between me and Lorel. None of your business, little girl."

He reached for a strand of my hair and tucked it behind my ear. Instead of letting it go, his fingers slid along the strand and he moved closer, too close. He looked down at me, his green eyes ringed with impossibly thick lashes, his voice low. My knees went weak. The word "smolder" slid into my mind.

Patrick leaned close to whisper, so close his breath stirred my hair. "Got it?" His voice had an edge.

I was done. I slapped away his hand. Through gritted teeth I managed to say, "Leave Lorel alone."

By the time I was halfway down the stairs, my anger turned into remorse and embarrassment. How could I have believed Margot? I'd humiliated Lorel and myself.

By the time I pushed through the whispering crowd at the bottom of the stairs, tears blurred my vision, my face flamed. What a fool I was!

I cried all the way back to Gull's Nest. Lorel was going to kill me.

Verity sat at the kitchen table at Gull's Nest, a bowl of rocky road ice cream and Aunt Gully's *People* magazine in front of her. She dropped her spoon into the bowl as I walked in. "Where have you been? I thought you got out of practice at nine."

I tossed my keys on the table. "Verity, you won't believe what I—"

Lorel walked into the kitchen carrying a coffee mug. "Believe what?" Lorel rinsed it and put it in the dishwasher.

I froze. Lorel would kill me if she knew I'd gone to confront Patrick. "Believe what I did. I, ah, evaded Leo Rodriguez. That's right. Leo Rodriguez was at the theater," I said.

"He wants to interview you about finding the body." Lorel rolled her eyes. "Talk to him, for pity's sake. Honestly, it's like you're allergic to publicity."

That was Lorel—anything for publicity. She and Margot should be sisters. They'd understand each other. "I just want to be Allegra Larkin, dancer. Not Allie Larkin, who found the dead girl on the lobster pot."

Lorel's phone dinged. She walked out, scrolling on her phone. *Please don't be a text from Patrick.*

Aunt Gully bustled into the kitchen with an armful of kitchen towels. She pulled up short when she saw me. "Allie! You've been crying! It's all been too much for you finding that girl's body and all."

She wrapped me in a hug. I took the towels from her arms and put them in the drawer. "It's not the body." I whispered. "Well, maybe it's partly the body." I leaned around Aunt Gully to peek in the living room. Lorel sat in Uncle Rocco's recliner, channel-surfing.

"I just did the dumbest thing." I lowered my voice.

"I went to Patrick Yardley and told him to leave Lorel alone."

Verity waved her spoon. "Whoo boy, she's gonna kill you!"

Aunt Gully pursed her lips.

"I know, I should tell her what I did. I made a mess of things." I swallowed hard.

Aunt Gully threw a look into the living room. Horses' hooves thundered and horns blared from a battle scene on the television. That would be a tea party compared to the battle royal Lorel and I'd be having if she heard about my visit to New Salt.

"I know," I said, "tell the truth, and let Lorel live her own life—"

Aunt Gully's eyes softened. "Allie, you've had enough trouble for one day, for a week, for a year. Doctor Gully prescribes a hot bath and a good night's sleep. And"—she lowered her voice—"not saying a word to your sister tonight."

Aunt Gully reached into the cabinet by the sink and pulled out the bottle of her book club brandy. "Or this. Here, if you girls would like some."

Verity and I exchanged glances. Aunt Gully's book club brandy tasted like cough syrup with a hint of motor oil. "No, thanks, Aunt Gully."

"Suit yourselves. Good night, girls. Get some sleep." Aunt Gully headed upstairs.

The television snapped off. Lorel called good night. I reached for the red wine that Lorel kept stocked in the dining room breakfront. This day called for more than just rocky road ice cream.

"I'll get the wineglasses," Verity said.

I grabbed the carton of ice cream and a spoon. Verity and I curled up on the couch.

From the fireplace mantel, Aunt Gully's husband, Uncle Rocco, looked down on us with his broad movie star smile. So much had changed in the year since he passed away. Aunt Gully'd used his life insurance money to fulfill her dream of owning a lobster shack.

Next to Uncle Rocco's picture was my mother and father's wedding photo, my dad in a suit that he still had in his closet, my mother in an ivory silk gown that had been her mother's, little ballet flats peeping from under the skirt, the dress a bit too short for her willowy frame.

Verity patted my arm. "Aunt Gully's right. You've had a bad stretch this summer."

"I wish I could turn back the clock. Back to before I broke my ankle. Before I came back to Mystic Bay. Then I could be more like Lorel, popping in on the occasional weekend to help at the shack." I lowered my voice. "Don't get me wrong, I'm glad I can help Aunt Gully. But up to my elbows in lobster meat isn't how I saw myself after all those years of dance class."

Verity and I finished the ice cream. No sound came from Aunt Gully upstairs or Lorel in the downstairs bedroom.

I tossed my spoon in the empty carton. "It's actually worse than I told Aunt Gully," I whispered. "I heard Patrick's living with another girl, a waitress from New Salt."

"What!" Verity shouted. She winced and whispered, "No way!"

"Why am I surprised? Why did I even bother? He's been juggling girls since fifth grade."

"How long do you think it'll take for Lorel to find out you talked to Patrick?" Verity sipped her wine.

Half of Mystic Bay had been in the line at New Salt. "Not long. I'm doomed." I thought of Patrick's sly smile. A thought made me sit up straight. "Wait a minute. Maybe, just maybe, Patrick won't tell Lorel I went to talk to him."

"Because it's probably true, he is seeing another woman." Verity nodded. "Who told you about the other woman?"

"Margot." I sipped my wine.

Verity grimaced. "The ballerina you lived with in Boston? The one with the stick up her—"

"Yep."

"I bet Patrick won't say anything. Don't tell Lorel," Verity said. "You might be able to escape her wrath."

"Maybe."

Aunt Gully's snores drifted down the stairs. Verity and I shared a smile.

"The sleep of the just," I said.

Verity gathered her things and left. After cleaning up, I showered and fell into bed.

For a while I tossed in the dark. Through my open window, the waves whispered on the sand of the beach, a sound that had always been comforting white noise. I pushed away images of the girl on the boat, of Patrick Yardley's sly smile. Just when I thought I'd never be able to relax, I fell asleep.

Chapter 11

Ten o'clock! I threw back the covers. A note was propped on top of my phone. "Didn't have the heart to wake you this morning. There's plenty of help for prep at the Mermaid. Just come for lunch rush. Be sure to eat." Signed "Aunt Gully" and a heart.

I ran through an abbreviated workout, showered, and grabbed a bowl of cereal. I pulled my bike from the garage and rode over to the Mermaid. By the time I propped the bike behind the lobster shed, the bell at Christ Church chimed eleven and a rusty orange Volvo took the last parking space in the lot.

I hurried inside, tied on my apron, and went to the counter. As usual, the television was on. Onscreen, Leo Rodriguez walked Mystic Bay's Town Pier.

My mouth went dry.

"Leo Rodriguez in Mystic Bay. The town's full of tourists eager to enjoy the charm for which this normally peaceful town is famous, but a grisly discovery earlier this week has chilled locals and visitors alike. That's when the body of a young woman was pulled from the deceptively calm waters off Mystic Bay."

The camera pulled in tight on Leo's face. "They're calling her the girl with the pitchfork tattoo."

The camera cut to Bertha, squinting in the sun, pointing from the town dock toward Cat Island.

Leo's voice-over played over Bertha's image. "The young woman's body was pulled up by Bertha Betancourt, captain of the *Queenie,* the morning of July second. Bertha's been fishing these waters for over fifty years. And she's never seen anything like it."

"Of course I've never seen anything like it," Bertha said onscreen. The image jumped where some footage had been cut. "Do you think I pull up dead bodies all day?"

The camera turned to Leo who nodded encouragingly. I could imagine what was cut out. Bertha had a salty tongue. "We just pulled her in, poor thing"—Bertha sniffed—"and called for help."

Leo said, "Do you have any idea who the young woman could be?"

The camera turned back to Bertha. Her voice took on a tart, exasperated tone. "Of course I have no idea who she was. Never saw her before." The film jumped here, too. "Poor thing was just some unlucky soul who fell off a boat."

"Do you think that's what happened?" Leo prompted.

"How else would a fully dressed girl end up in the

water, I ask you." The disgusted glare Bertha gave Leo said his ignorance was beyond belief.

"You tell him, Bertha," a customer in a Mystic Bay windbreaker said. His friend laughed but dipped his head.

"The police have released an artist's sketch of the young woman," Leo continued. "They're asking anyone with any information to contact the Mystic Bay Police Department at the phone number listed on the screen."

The police sketch of the girl's face flashed onscreen, the same one as yesterday. Hilda stood beside me and rubbed my back. Conversation in the Mermaid hushed further, as if a volume knob had turned it down. Several people craned toward the television.

I'd been too upset to *see* the drawing the other day. Now I stepped closer to the screen, intent.

There was another silver ear cuff in the ear I hadn't seen. The girl's face was broad, the large eyes wide set. Before I hadn't noticed her high cheekbones, pert nose. She'd probably been attractive. But I still didn't recognize her. My shoulders relaxed.

"The police released these photos of the young woman's tattoos," Leo continued.

The tattoos flashed onscreen. The pitchfork. The tattoo had been partially hidden under the bracelet—the word HELLION in all capitals, the *E* curvy.

"That's funny," I said. The *H* and *E* were slightly larger and lighter than the other letters. Why?

"Do these tattoos hold the clue that'll lead us to the identity of this young woman? At Mystic Bay Town Dock, I'm Leo Rodriguez."

The screen door banged and broke the spell. Chatter resumed.

Hilda's big brown eyes glistened as she changed the channel to a game show. "Maybe now someone will identify her."

After the lunch rush, I took a lobster roll and drink outside to the picnic table behind the shack. A breeze found its way from the river and cooled my sweaty neck.

Bit put a tray with a lobster roll and bag of chips on the table across from me. He flopped onto the picnic bench, his skinny shoulders slumped.

"Are you okay, Bit?"

I could hear the toes of his sneakers dig into the gravel.

"What's going on?" I said.

Bit shrugged with one shoulder and averted his gaze.

"You can tell me anything. You know I'm not going to tell your parents." That was one promise that was easy to keep with Bit's no-show parents.

His chest heaved as he exhaled. "I got in trouble."

Bit Markey? In trouble?

He turned the colorful knot-work friendship bracelets he wore on one arm. "Harbor Patrol yelled at me. I don't want them to tell my dad. Sammy and me took his dad's Boston Whaler over there." Bit mumbled this last part.

"Where?"

"Past the Hummocks and Cat Island. The Harbor Patrol said Sammy was going too fast and we should just move along and go home. What if they tell my dad? He'll tell me to stop hanging around Sammy. Sammy's dad's in the navy and my dad doesn't like that either. He said it's too militaristic."

What was Harbor Patrol doing out past Cat Island? Harbor Patrol managed the yachts and powerboats traveling in and out of Mystic Bay marina. They mainly helped boaters find their slips at the town dock and occasionally towed boaters who broke down.

They probably assumed that Bit and Sammy were in trouble or— I hesitated. Two kids near a private island. Maybe Harbor Patrol thought they were trespassing.

"Did you guys land somewhere?" I said.

Bit kicked at the gravel. "Nope. But we wanted to. We wanted to explore Cat Island but they stopped us and told us to go back."

Things were different now. When Lorel and I were young, kids in Mystic Bay sailed, kayaked, and sailboarded all over the bay, freely exploring the tiny islands not far offshore. Some had cottages on them and so we avoided them, preferring to play on the uninhabited ones, most little more than rocks covered with gull poop, sand, and stubborn scrubby trees.

"When did this happen, Bit?"

"Early this morning. The Harbor Patrol guys were mad."

A thought jolted me. "Maybe they were looking into the girl that Bertha and I found."

Somehow Bit had managed to eat his lobster roll without my noticing. "Here, have some of mine, too." I split mine in half and gave it to him. We finished the roll and then licked our fingers.

"I don't think Harbor Patrol's going to tell your dad," I said. Why would they? Bit wasn't doing anything any other Mystic Bay kid hadn't done a thousand times.

"All hands on deck!" Sunlight glinted on Hector's bald head and gold earring as he called from the kitchen's screen door. "The Fourth of July weekend invasion has commenced."

Bit rushed off to the shed to get more lobsters. I tossed our trash and ran to the kitchen.

A line of hungry customers streamed in the door the rest of the day so I had no time to think about anything beyond lobster rolls. As the afternoon wore on, I realized I hadn't seen Lorel in a while. "Where's Lorel?"

At the stove, Aunt Gully stirred a pot of her secret-recipe Lobster Love sauce. "She had to go to Boston for a meeting, then she's going to meet Patrick at the casino for dinner."

Lorel's job was intense, so it didn't surprise me that she'd have meetings during her vacation. "Funny how Lorel says she hates the casino but she's up there all the time with Patrick."

Aunt Gully started singing and stirred her sauce faster. I sighed. I didn't want to talk about Lorel and Patrick, either.

Two Gully's Gals came into the kitchen. "Gully, we want to play restaurant!"

"Allie, why don't you take a break?" Aunt Gully avoided my eyes. It dawned on me that she'd been giving me a lot of breaks. I wasn't going to argue about taking a break from picking lobster. I washed my hands, waved, and pushed through the screen door.

Without conscious thought, my footsteps followed the uneven brick sidewalk. The sights that usually cheered me—the sparkling water on the river, the gaudy pink-and-orange color scheme of Bit's family's rambling Victorian, the colorful shop windows—were a blur. All I could see was water streaming off the body of the girl hooked on the lobster pot. The Girl with the Pitchfork Tattoo.

Why hadn't she been identified yet? Who were her friends? Her family? Hadn't anybody been looking for her? So many people were thinking of her and working to find her family. Even Mac Macallen had seemed concerned and he didn't even know her.

Mac. There had been something about our conversation in the costume shop that made me uneasy. His home wasn't far from the shack, so I decided to head over and see if he was around. People who work in theater have irregular schedules and Mac sometimes went home during the day to tend his garden.

My footsteps took me into the neighborhood just past elegant Christ Church on the hill. Roses tumbled over the black iron gates of houses that had been expensively renovated and restored. Mac Macallen lived in number 30, a former sea captain's house painted a soft yellow with black shutters.

Two urns of red geraniums flanked the front door, matching the red Mini in the driveway. Mac's license plate showed his commitment to the theater—THEBAY1. I lifted the old-fashioned lion's head door knocker and rapped. And waited. No answer, no sound except birdsong and a lawnmower farther down the block. I walked down the porch, leaning past a potted palm to peer in the window. No dice. Mac had plantation shutters covering the tall windows.

I'd attended a cocktail fund-raiser here in the spring. Mac had celebrated the renovation of a small red barn/ garage behind his house into a guest cottage. Perhaps he was there or working in his garden. I walked down the drive to the backyard.

Mac's yard sloped down to Harris Cove, which flowed into the Micasset River farther to the west. Mac's waterfront backyard had a million dollar view. There was a small lean-to at the back of the garden with boating equipment, and a small motorboat was tied up at the dock. I trailed my fingers over some crimson roses and marveled at their scent.

On the back of the house, slate steps led to a patio that ran the length of the house. I ran up the steps to French doors and knocked. I shaded my eyes, peered in, saw an elegant mahogany table topped with a vase of red roses. No Mac.

Suddenly, I felt watched. I swung around. The red barn looked closed up tight. The neighbors' view of Mac's backyard was blocked by tall arborvitae.

I realized that anyone watching me might assume I was a burglar casing the joint. People in Mystic Bay didn't worry about crime. Jaywalking, double parking, noise, overenthusiastic tourists helping themselves to plants and historic gewgaws, yes. Theft? Many residents didn't even bother to lock their doors.

Skirting a black cast-iron table, I moved to the next window. The kitchen. Past that was another set of French doors.

I peered in, breathing fast. It was clear Mac wasn't

home. What was wrong with me? Some feeling was driving me to peek inside.

This room was an art studio. An easel in one corner had a large painting on it, covered with a white sheet. I tilted my head and mashed my cheek against the glass to get a better angle.

Larger-than-life faces with exaggerated planes, some with eyes or noses out of proportion, slashes of white or red paint for highlight, glowered from the walls. Some were female nudes. They looked like work done by Picasso. Terms from a long-ago art history class surfaced. *Cubist. Impressionist.*

None of the faces in the portraits looked happy. The heavy diagonal lines of color, the thickly applied paint rendered the figures disturbing. Ugly. Strange.

One portrait showed a young woman with long white-blond hair against a backdrop of orange flame. Her wrists were covered by heavy black and pink slashes. Or were they handcuffs? TMI. Still, I pressed closer to the glass.

In the next portrait, heavy slashes of black paint formed a black ponytail. The subject's chin tilted up and the lips turned down atop an elegant, long neck.

Margot. I gasped. That was Margot, though I wasn't sure it was a portrait that she'd appreciate. Was Mac painting all of us? My eyes went to the covered easel. Could he be painting—me? Would I find my hair rendered with awful orange clumps of paint under that sheet?

I had to see what was on the easel.

I turned the handle on the French door.

It was locked. Drat. I rattled it.

A dog barked down the street. I jumped.

What am I thinking!

Far off on the river a yellow kayak knifed through the water. *Please don't be Mac.* I couldn't just go down his back steps as if I were making an entrance in *Mame.* I edged across the patio and swung a leg over the railing. Careful of my almost-healed ankle, I dropped between two laurel bushes then bushwhacked to the front of the house.

What had come over me? If that had been Mac in the kayak, he just saw me dive into his bushes.

I hurried back to the Mermaid, feeling foolish. Those portraits were unnerving, but maybe Mac was trying a new technique. Or maybe he was just not very good at painting portraits.

Plus, there was probably only an eighty percent chance that he was the kayaker who saw me leave the house. How many women with long red hair did he know? My shoulders slumped. Probably one. Aunt Gully had always warned me about my curiosity getting the better of me.

A gust of hot exhaust from a green motor coach blasted me as it muscled down the narrow street. I coughed. The bus was emblazoned with a five-foot-tall lobster wearing a tricorn hat. YANKEE LOBSTER TOURS. I rushed into the Mermaid. "All hands on deck! A tour bus is coming!"

The hours flew by. When it was time to head to rehearsal, I waved to Aunt Gully and took the van to the Jake.

* * *

I perched atop my rock as stagehands prepared the grotto scene, the scene written especially for the no-show German opera singer Dara Van Der Witz. Her understudy swore and hurled an empty water bottle into the wings.

"Sorry." She pressed her fists to her forehead. "It's just so frustrating. This Dara what's-her-name hasn't shown up for any rehearsals and we open next week. I've talked with Mac, I've talked with anyone who will listen, and they just tell me to be patient."

"It is weird." I shifted carefully. My mermaid tail made balancing tricky. "But it's only one scene. Sometimes performers just walk on." Unusual, but I'd seen it happen. Rules and professional standards that applied to ordinary performers were bent for divas.

"I looked her up online," she said. "There's no record of any opera singer, German or otherwise, named Dara Van Der Witz. It's all a bad joke."

I gave my tail an experimental flip. "Maybe it's someone who's trying something new and doesn't want anyone to know about it."

She snorted. "Nobody in this business does anything in secret."

Mac crossed the stage and gave me a cheerful wave. I relaxed. Obviously he hadn't seen me snooping around his house.

After rehearsal, a group of us went out for drinks. I texted Aunt Gully to let her know I'd be late. Afterward, the group decided to go dancing at New Salt. There was no way I was going back after my scene with Patrick. I headed home.

Chapter 12

As I swung into Aunt Gully's driveway at eleven, Lorel was getting out of her BMW sedan. Lorel's caramel leather miniskirt and white silky top glowed in the porch light. Lorel slammed the car door.

Light from the living room window flickered. The curtain twitched—Aunt Gully was sneaking a peek.

Lorel glared at me.

Warily, I got out of the van. "What did I do now?"

Lorel looped the chain of her purse over her shoulder. She leaned back on her car, pressed her hand to her forehead. "Nothing. I've got a headache."

An engine rumbled and a white sports car screeched into our drive. The driver slammed the brakes and barely missed the rear of Aunt Gully's van. The engine cut and Patrick Yardley burst out. He stopped short when he saw me. "Allie."

"Patrick."

A Harbor Patrol SUV rolled by the house. What were they doing over here? Lorel, Patrick, and I froze but it didn't stop. Too bad they weren't really cops. They could have arrested Patrick for driving recklessly. He'd almost rear-ended Aunt Gully's van.

Lorel and Patrick didn't notice. Waves of unspoken emotion twanged between them. I didn't want to get caught up in this, especially if Patrick was here to tell Lorel that I'd gone to New Salt to talk to him.

Lorel swore under her breath. "Allie, just go in the house."

I hurried in the front door, tossing my dance bag on the couch. Aunt Gully looked up from a ball of green nylon netting that she crocheted into sink scrubbies and sold at the church holiday bazaar. Her face was pink.

"What's going on?" she stage-whispered.

"You tell me. I thought they were going on a date." I sidled toward the window.

"They were supposed to meet at the casino." Aunt Gully sighed. "Where they always seem to go."

Patrick's voice, urgent and low, flowed in on a breeze that lifted Aunt Gully's curtains. I strained to hear.

Aunt Gully put down her crocheting. "Come on, young lady. Let's give them some privacy. Nice night for a walk."

"Stop being so decent, Aunt Gully. Besides, didn't I just see you by the window?"

"Who, me?" She led me out the back door.

We cut across the backyard and scooted down the

road, skirting puddles of light thrown by the street-lights.

Aunt Gully glanced back toward Gull's Nest. "That's some sports car Patrick has. New Salt must be doing well," she whispered.

I looked back. Patrick folded his arms and looked at the ground. Lorel faced him, a shadow, her words indistinct, but her tone strident.

"Or he's doing well at the casino," Aunt Gully said.

I doubted it. Nobody did well at the casino. "Mr. High Roller." Margot had told me she'd seen Patrick and Lorel in the special high rollers area. At least one thing she'd said was true.

Aunt Gully and I took the narrow strip of sand between two cottages, one dark and one with windows glowing, that led to Kiddie Beach and the breakwater. The occupied house was a rental named Fast Times. A late-night talk show blared inside.

We turned south, along the beach. I kicked off my shoes and my ankle wrap and let the cool waves curl over my toes. Aunt Gully took off her slippers and did the same. We didn't speak as we walked. I knew she was thinking about the same thing I was— Lorel.

A group roasted marshmallows over a bonfire. The smoky scent was sweet. One guy strummed a guitar as we passed. A thin band of moonlight striped the water.

After a few minutes Aunt Gully and I turned and headed back.

"They should be done by now," Aunt Gully said as we approached the path back to the street. "I hope."

Arguing voices made me stop short. I tugged Aunt Gully's arm as two shadows emerged from the same narrow path between the cottages we'd taken earlier. The pale moonlight shone on smooth blond hair. Lorel and Patrick. She stomped barefoot in the sand, holding her strappy shoes. Instead of heading down the beach as we had done, they turned toward the breakwater. Thank goodness they were so intent on each other that they didn't see us.

We stopped where Fast Times fronted the sand and peered around the cedar-shingled wall. Patrick's voice was urgent, but I couldn't make out his words.

"Whatever line he's giving her, I don't think it's working," I whispered.

They stepped onto the breakwater.

The sliver of moon gave stingy light but Lorel knew every rock on that breakwater. She could walk it with her eyes closed. So could I. Patrick, on the other hand, took his phone out of his pocket and turned on the flashlight. A beam of light bounced slowly along the stones as Patrick stepped from one rock to the next. Lorel sat on the rock farthest out. Distant. Remote.

Typical Lorel.

Aunt Gully whispered, "Do you think they're breaking up?"

"I can only hope."

Patrick left his phone flashlight on. He crouched behind Lorel and reached for her. Lorel lashed out, backhanding him, then covered her face with her hands. He fell back on the rocks. I was glad I couldn't hear what they were saying. I was pretty sure the laugh track from the television in Fast Times covered the sound of Lorel's sobs.

Aunt Gully grasped the heart-shaped locket at her throat. "Allie, that boy's been nothing but trouble for your sister."

"Lorel thought she could change him."

Aunt Gully sighed. "Leopards don't change their spots."

A shred of cloud crossed the moon and blacked out everything on the breakwater except the flashlight beam of Patrick's phone.

The kids down the beach shouted. A dog barked. The waves hissed on the sand. These were the normal sounds of summer for as long as I could remember. Normal. That's what Lorel should have—some nice normal guy with a nice normal job with an exceptionally nice income.

Farther down the street, a string of firecrackers crackled. Aunt Gully and I jumped.

"We should go back." Aunt Gully tugged my arm. "I don't know what got into me."

"We want to protect her." I turned to go, but the breeze shifted and carried their voices toward us. Lorel's voice shrilled. Aunt Gully and I froze.

The cloud passed and again the gray moonlight outlined Patrick and Lorel on the breakwater. Patrick held out both arms like an offering.

"Don't you take him back, Lorelei Larkin," Aunt Gully whispered.

Patrick's phone rang. Lorel shouted, "Damn cell phone!"

Lorel snatched at Patrick's hand and threw the phone. There was a small splash.

Aunt Gully squinted. "Did she just throw his cell phone in the water?"

"Ha! I believe she did." *Go, Lorel.*

Lorel pushed Patrick aside. His arms pinwheeled as he fought to regain his balance, but he tumbled off the rocks. He shouted something I was glad Aunt Gully probably couldn't make out. Lorel stormed off the breakwater.

Patrick, in the water up to his knees, splashed with both hands, searching for his phone.

"And don't ever speak to me again!" Lorel stomped off in the sand.

"Oh, God, here she comes. Go!" Aunt Gully and I scampered down the path and hustled across Fast Times's front lawn. We dashed down the street to Gull's Nest, keeping away from the streetlights, our bare feet slapping on the pavement.

"Oh, dear Lord," Aunt Gully gasped. "I hope she doesn't see us."

We hurried into the house. I threw myself on the couch and arranged myself into what I hoped was a casual pose.

Panting, Aunt Gully scurried into the kitchen. A few moments later she flopped beside me on the couch, mopping her brow with a dishtowel. I hit the TV remote and the screen came to life with the loud laughter of the late show.

A few minutes later Patrick's powerful engine

roared down the street. I went to the window. "Where's Lorel?" I muttered.

The back door opened and closed quietly. I dove back onto the couch.

Aunt Gully put her feet up on the coffee table and crocheted placidly. Her face was bright pink. "Lorel?" she called. "Gonna eat something, honey?"

Lorel walked slowly into the living room, her head bowed.

"Not hungry." Lorel put her purse on the side table. "You two will be happy to know that I've broken up with Patrick."

"What!" Even I didn't think I sounded convincing.

Aunt Gully put down her crocheting and started to get up. "Let me—"

Lorel held up a hand. "I don't want any tea or book club brandy. I don't want to talk about it. I'll let you know when I want to talk about it. If ever. He's just not the man I thought he was."

He was exactly the man I thought he was. Aunt Gully and I shared a guilty look.

"See you in the morning. Big day tomorrow," Lorel muttered. I listened to her bare feet pad down the hallway to her bedroom.

For a few minutes I wrestled with my emotions, then got up to follow her. Aunt Gully put a warning hand on my arm. "Let her be, Allie, let her be."

Chapter 13

Saturday, July 4

There'd been talk about making Aunt Gully and me grand marshals of the Fourth of July parade, in recognition of our roles in solving the crime that had roiled the town just a month earlier. But since the high school girls basketball team had won the state championship, the honor went instead to the Mystic Bay High School Lady Mariners.

Thank goodness. Their banner read: STATE CHAMPIONS. I could only imagine what the banner on the Lazy Mermaid float would've said: "Serving Up Murder"? "Lethal Lobsters"? "Claw and Order"?

Lorel had been surprisingly calm this morning, composed but distant. I hoped this would be the last we'd hear of Patrick Yardley. I texted Verity to share this news, plus break it to her that Stellene Lupo had sent only three passes for her Fourth of July event—for Aunt Gully, Lorel, and me.

I'll Drown My Sorrows in Uncle Emerson's BBQ,
Verity texted back.

We cheered as floats and bands passed by the Mermaid. Per tradition, kids with bicycles decorated with red, white, and blue streamers were the penultimate group, then the Pup Parade brought up the rear. Bit and several friends pulled a wagon of mutts sporting powdered wigs and a sign that read: THE DOGCLARATION OF INDEPENDENCE. We laughed as pooches dressed in star-spangled hats, bows, sweaters, and tutus trotted by, then we hurried back to open the Mermaid's doors.

The day passed in a blur of lobster rolls, red, white, and blue T-shirts, and selfies with lobster-loving tourists. At five o'clock, Lorel and I helped Aunt Gully make last-minute additions to the equipment we were bringing to Harmony Harbor for Stellene Lupo's Fourth of July bash.

"You'll get to see the Extra Fireworks from Harmony Harbor," Hilda said.

Like most locals, I'd been spoiled by the Extra Fireworks. Mystic Bay had a fireworks display every Fourth of July. Stellene had one on the Saturday night of the weekend closest to the Fourth. Mystic Bay kids knew that if the Fourth fell on a Saturday, all you had to do was find a vantage point—a boat on the bay worked best—and you'd have fireworks to the east and west—two spectacular displays of dueling fireworks. Just like this year.

A parade line of Aunt Gully's friends in matching red, white, and blue T-shirts bedazzled with GULLY'S GALS streamed in. When had Aunt Gully had time to make them? "Here we come, Gully! The cavalry's here!" Half of Mystic Bay was taking a shift at the Mermaid.

One friend had a megaphone programmed with various excruciatingly loud soundtracks. He aimed it at the ceiling and sounded the bugle call played at the racetrack, the "Call to Post."

"And we're off!" Aunt Gully laughed and waved.

Aunt Gully, Lorel, and I got into the van. I turned the ignition. Gray smoke plumed from the rear and the van shook. Aunt Gully and I exchanged glances. After a few seconds, the gray smoke subsided and the shaking stopped. We breathed a sigh of relief.

Harmony Harbor! Excitement surged through me. Sure, I was going there as waitstaff and not a guest, but I'd be inside the doors of one of the most exclusive parties in New England.

"Do I have everything?" Aunt Gully rummaged through her tote bag. She turned to Lorel in the backseat. "I have my basket, right, Lorel? With your fresh Lazy Mermaid T-shirts?"

"All taken care of, Aunt Gully." Lorel scrolled on her phone.

I eased the van through the parking lot. Aunt Gully's friend with the megaphone ran alongside the van. The first bars of "The Stars and Stripes Forever" blared and reverberated in my chest. Customers in line laughed and pointed. Some kids covered their ears.

"Harmony Harbor, here we come!" Aunt Gully said.

Chapter 14

It had never rained on Stellene Lupo's fireworks display. Mother Nature herself wouldn't dare disappoint the woman known as the Star Maker, whose modeling empire put gorgeous faces on magazine covers and reality TV shows around the world.

Harmony Harbor was a short drive from Mystic Bay, but another world, tucked within the Mystic Bay Nature Preserve well away from envious eyes. It wasn't the biggest or the most secluded home in Mystic Bay—that was the mansion on Orion Cove—but Harmony Harbor was easily the most expensive. Stellene's husband, media mogul Kurt Lupo, had styled it on Rosecliff in Newport. He'd not only founded the Harmony Harbor Yacht Club, but also poured millions into charities, including the local libraries, Broadway by the Bay, and Mystic Bay Hospital.

In the rearview mirror I saw Lorel smile. I caught Aunt Gully's eye.

"Well?" Aunt Gully turned to Lorel.

Lorel shrugged. "I feel pretty good. Breaking up with Patrick was the right thing to do. I'm starting a new chapter."

"Do you want to tell us—"

"No." Lorel turned her head. "And no I-told-you-sos, okay?"

I told you so. Aunt Gully and I shared a guilty look.

We drove past vibrant green parkland hemmed in by the gray stone walls of the nature reserve. The scenery was calming. I felt myself relax.

Soon the stone walls grew taller, the trees thicker. The road narrowed and twisted. We passed a line of luxury cars stopped by broad-shouldered men at a towering black iron gate, the kind you'd find at a palace. This was the main entrance to Harmony Harbor.

We craned our necks as I drove slowly past. The gate guards scrutinized the drivers' invitations before letting them enter.

Lorel scanned the papers Zoe Parker had sent. "We have to go on another half mile and turn for the trades-man's entrance." The road curved and forked. "Go left here."

I pulled up to a guard shack by another black iron gate, this one half the size of the other.

"Papers." A beefy, clean-shaven man in sunglasses, dark jacket, and white shirt took Lorel's papers. His handheld scanner beeped. Two black boxes mounted on the gateposts caught my eye. Security cameras.

"Papers," I whispered. "You'd think we were cross-ing the border to Austria."

"Crossing into the land of the one percent." Lorel's

lovely face glowed. "The security's unreal." Security was a turn-on for Lorel.

"Follow the drive to the left. Park under the porte cochere," the guard said. The cast-iron gate swung open. We rolled past emerald-green lawns smooth as a golf course to a gleaming white marble mansion. "It's like a fairy tale." Aunt Gully sighed. I pulled under the porte cochere covered with red climbing roses.

Two women, one tall and angular, the other short and plump, in black dresses and immaculate white aprons, stood on the stone steps. Their hair was parted exactly in the middle and slicked back into a low bun. Each had a small red, white, and blue rosette pinned to her bodice.

"All these special conditions. I'm surprised they didn't ask for a blood sample," I muttered. "That reminds me, Lorel, you never did say why Stellene wanted me and you to serve—"

"Oh, that." Lorel cleared her throat. Aunt Gully and I turned to face Lorel. "Stellene thought it would be, ah"—Lorel reddened—"fun for us to dress up in special costumes."

"Special costumes?" My voice rose. "What special costumes?"

"Don't make a scene, Allie." Lorel avoided my eyes as we got out of the van. "It'll be fine." She greeted the two women as I hefted Aunt Gully's plastic laundry basket.

"I don't mind not wearing this T-shirt," I said. "I'm used to the dumb clamshell jokes." Our Aunt Gully-designed T-shirts had two strategically placed clamshells on the front and NO FUSS FINE FOOD across the back.

"Stellene's known for her wonderful taste." Aunt Gully's eyes widened as she took in the marble statues and ornate lamps under the portico. I shook myself. *We were all drinking the rich lady's Kool-Aid.* What on earth kind of special costumes would we have to wear? Was that even legal? Maybe she wanted us in the maid's uniforms. That was better than a clamshell bikini T-shirt.

The taller woman spoke. "Welcome to Harmony Harbor. I'm Yasmin. This is Tara." Tara, plump and smiling, bounced on her toes. "Please come with me to the kitchen, Mrs. Fontana. The footmen will unload your van. Young ladies, please follow Tara."

"Footmen. She said footmen!" Lorel's eyes sparkled. My sister and I don't have much in common, but we're fans of any British crunchy-gravel television show set in a stately home.

"This is truly a stately home," I whispered.

Two guys in understated navy blue suits hurried toward us. Stellene's footmen were handsome, their trousers skinny, their hair perfect. Probably off-duty models from her stable.

"Let me take that, miss." One of them took the laundry basket from my arms.

I leaned toward Lorel. "When she said footmen I expected powdered wigs and knee breeches." I was almost ready to forgive Lorel. "I wonder what she wants us to wear. We look all-American in our T-shirts and shorts. That's as all-American as it gets."

"Stellene's party has a vintage carnival theme." Lorel smoothed her hair but looked away.

Lorel's evasiveness was getting under my skin. "Did you tell me that before?"

"Didn't I?" Lorel was busy taking in the sweeping view across the emerald lawn to the water, the expensive vehicles parked by the eight-bay garage, the marble statues of stalking wolves, jaws agape, flanking the entrance. Lorel was used to wealthy tech people but this was a whole different level of wealth. She was dazzled.

Heck, I was dazzled.

We followed Tara through broad carved wooden doors. At the end of the hall, palm trees and white-painted metal furniture glowed under a tall glass ceiling. A pyramid of white boxes tied with red, white, and blue ribbons towered on a table.

I nudged Lorel. "A conservatory! Mrs. White with the candlestick in the conservatory."

All this wealth would be balm to my sister's soul. Couldn't have anything better happen to get over Patrick Yardley than spend time with the one percent.

Lorel and I followed Tara down a narrow corridor to the right. Tara's black rubber-soled shoes whispered along the marble floor. She pushed through another carved wooden door into a narrow whitewashed corridor.

Tara opened a plain oak door and waved us in. "Costumes and crowns are on the bed."

Crowns? Costumes?

Tara closed the door quietly behind us. A single bed with a white chenille coverlet, a simple oak bureau with a mirror, and a straight-back chair were the only furnishings.

"No expense spared in the staff quarters." Lorel opened the box on the bed.

"Did she say crowns?" I turned the box so I could read the label. SIDESHOW MERMAID. "Lorel! Sideshow mermaid?"

I lifted the lid and my jaw dropped.

I looked at Lorel.

She looked at me.

We burst into giggles.

Stellene's fashion-designer friends had confected fantasy mermaid costumes for Lorel and me. The headpieces weren't bad. Who was I kidding? "This is absoutely gorgeous!"

I lifted a wreath of sea-green wire netting sprinkled with miniature jewels, shells, and pearls, then a matching glittery bra top. Mine was turquoise, Lorel's pink.

Next I unfolded a length of shimmering green fabric. At least Stellene wasn't putting us into real mermaid bottoms. Iridescent fabric fish scales wrapped like a sarong. I put it on. Tight but manageable.

"Nothing says Fourth of July like a clamshell bikini top and a mermaid crown," I said.

Lorel hooked her top and sighed. "We're sideshow mermaids."

"I kind of like it." I turned side to side in front of the mirror. "Except for the bra. You fill your shells better than I do."

Lorel rummaged in the top drawer of the bureau and pulled out a pair of scissors.

"Come here." Lorel snipped my straps and knotted them into a halter. "Better."

Lorel's gold scallop-shell earrings caught the overhead light.

"You knew about this costume business, didn't you, Lorel?"

"Hmmm." Lorel looked away, placing the scissors on the bureau.

I folded my arms. "Spill."

Lorel shrugged. "When someone like Stellene Lupo wants something, you give it to her. Besides, I've seen you wear a lot less than this onstage in front of hundreds of people."

Well, that was true. And I did like the costume. I wound my hair into a loose braid.

"It's great contacts and publicity," Lorel said. "I thought it was worth a few hours in a mermaid getup."

"Two hours of creepy rich guys leering at my clams and scales?" I asked.

"Enough for a new van for Aunt Gully?" Lorel knew she had me.

I caught sight of my reflection. The costume was, I had to admit, beautiful. Maybe it would be fun. "Pass me my crown."

Chapter 15

Two humid hours carrying a heavy silver tray of lobster rolls made me glad I was wearing little more than a bathing suit. Sweat dampened my chest and back. I longed to dive into the water off Harmony Harbor's beach or into the spectacular marble pool.

Off the beach, Stellene's fleet of vintage wooden Chris-Craft motor launches ferried guests from their yachts to the estate. On the vast green lawn, revelers whooped on carnival rides. There was even a miniature Ferris wheel. Guests ducked in and out of several white tents—a fortune-teller, arcade games, feats of strength. The strongman was an actor from Broadway by the Bay. He twirled his moustache at me.

In the throng of Stellene's New York friends were models from her agency, pop stars, sports figures, a TV doctor who couldn't keep his hands off my fish-scale sarong, and pro athletes. At first the guests played it cool, but then everyone was taking selfies with everyone else.

A jazz combo provided background music as I went from group to group among the carnival rides and tents, offering my tray and lingering when conversation interested me. Most of Stellene's party guests were used to being waited on. They just kept talking when I materialized with my tray of lobster rolls.

"You going to Stellene's big fund-raiser for organ donation in September?" A tall woman by the shooting gallery signaled me for a roll.

"Never miss it. It's her husband's foundation. Kurt's life was saved by a kidney donation all those years ago." A man with her scooped up two rolls. "Using a living donor made all the difference."

The woman continued. "Remember how he insisted that some teenaged boy take a kidney that had originally been meant for him? The boy would have died without it. Kid was a nobody, but Kurt believed that organs should go to the sickest first. He said he'd wait his turn. Almost died, but he stuck to his principles."

Screams of laughter rang from the Tilt-A-Whirl.

"That's why they called him Saint Kurt. You know how Stellene and Kurt met? Stellene was his nurse after a skiing accident in Tahoe. A man of his age shouldn't have been skiing but he never took no for an answer."

"That's one thing he had in common with Stellene." The man's eyes followed Lorel appreciatively as she hurried past then ducked behind the fortune-teller's tent. A few moments later, a muscle-bound bald guy followed, head swiveling. He continued down the lawn. Was that guy stalking Lorel? I hurried after him, but was stopped by a crowd of hungry partygoers.

The sky deepened with lush shades of purple and orange, setting off strings of fairy lights that lit paths between the white tents. The carnival rides glittered like jewels in the dark.

Guests gathered by the torchlit pool deck and under the marble colonnade that ran the length of the mansion. Zoe Parker, glowing in a white sundress, sat at the center of a circle of admirers. She beamed as they raised champagne flutes to her. "Congratulations to our new director of marketing!" Zoe smoothed her hair and smiled.

From running Stellene's errands to director? She'd sure flown up the career ladder quickly.

I caught sight of Lorel, but didn't see her stalker, thank goodness. We circled the pool several times. I longed for a quick dip but reminded myself I was working. I consoled myself with the scenery. Many of Stellene's exceptionally good-looking male and female modeling clients ringed the pool.

One young man stood out, not just because of his wiry, tattooed frame and sun-streaked blond hair. He cannonballed off the side of the pool and dog-paddled over to me as I offered lobster rolls to two skinny women who waved me away. In one smooth motion, he climbed out of the pool.

"I'll take 'em all!" The young man swooped the tray out of my hands, showering us with droplets of cool water. The women shrieked but laughed.

"Henry Small! You're crazy!" one said.

A gorgeous guy who took a shortcut to the food by swimming across the pool? Just my type.

He handed my tray back and took a lobster roll in

each hand. He winked. Drops of water slid from his broad shoulders to his sculpted pecs. I was too dazzled to speak.

"Thanks, gorgeous." He sprinted back to his friends playing corn hole on the other side of the pool.

"You know him? Is he taken?" one woman asked.

"Forget it. He's with Eden," her friend said. "Plays guitar in her band. I think they're an item."

"Musicians are always trouble."

Some are worth it, I thought.

"How can they be an item?" the friend said. "She's built like a bowling ball. Plus what about that other guy? Lars. I thought they were together?"

"Doesn't matter." The first woman shrugged. "Eden's a big star. She can have anyone she wants. Come on, let's go to the gypsy fortune-teller tent."

I scanned the crowd. Eden! Was Eden here?

Eden was a singer as famous for her mysterious origins as for her amazing voice. Even though she refused all interviews, her face was on the cover of every magazine in Mystic Bay Drug.

I threw one last glance at Henry Small and continued my circuit through Stellene's sleek guests: actors, models, a couple of Bollywood stars, even politicians. The mayor of Mystic Bay, Keats Packer, and his wife, Blythe, sat poolside. Keats smiled. His wife turned her back on me.

A towering NBA star swooped my last three lobster rolls in one hand and asked me to pose in a selfie. I obliged.

After refilling my tray, I circulated on the patio, daydreaming of handsome Henry Small and listening for interesting gossip.

"Tinsley launches her new jewelry line this fall. They're doing a big splashy debut. Took oodles of advertising."

Stellene's daughter was designing jewelry? Interesting.

The voice lowered, conspiratorially. "You know what happened to her in Greece, right?"

I tacked right and silently offered my tray to the group. A tiny woman with cornrowed hair languidly waved me off with a hand sparkling with diamonds.

"Tinsley always was the wild child. She was at a party, a rave they call them? On some island in Greece on spring break." Diamonds sipped her gin and tonic as I moved slowly around the group. "Well, some creeps gave her some local stuff called a bombe. It's like drinking ethanol. She almost didn't survive."

Someone said, "Poor little rich girl."

Diamonds threw me a look and I moved on to a group wearing Mystic Bay Yacht Club blazers.

"You know Stellene had a whole medical suite put in here when she renovated," a sweaty, red-faced man slurred and waved his drink. "For her face-lifts."

"Shut up," a woman with him hissed.

"Common knowledge." The drunk man winked at me. "Hey, fish girl, how about one of those lobster rolls?"

I angled the tray between us, pasting on a smile. He leered and tried to pick up two rolls in his free hand, spilling lobster on the platter. As soon as he had them,

I spun away with my now empty serving tray. I didn't want to be around when the lobster hit the floor.

Instead of returning to the kitchen to replenish my tray, I pushed through the heavy wooden door near the conservatory. To the right was the hallway leading to the servants' quarters where Lorel and I had changed.

My feet were killing me. The muscles in my face were frozen in an unconvincing smile. I stood in front of a grandfather clock. Eight forty-five. We were supposed to stop serving before the fireworks began a little after nine P.M. Close enough. Five minutes with my feet up would be heaven.

The sound of water trickling in a fountain beckoned me to the conservatory. I started down the marble hallway past an open door. The room beyond was dark, but light from the party spilled in through a tall window. A gleam caught my eye.

I stepped into the room. To my right was a table with a lamp. I switched it on.

I gasped. Instead of what I expected—artwork, crystal, marble—weapons covered the walls: swords, guns, and rifles. Long guns and short guns, some with bayonets affixed. Hunting scenes on the wall broke up row after row of guns. What on earth was this door doing open? My skin prickled, but I slowly circuited the room, making my footsteps soft. This room was certainly supposed to be off-limits.

Color photos on the fireplace mantel were the only nonweapon items in the room. One photo caught my eye. A girl with long honey-colored braids waved from a double kayak. I picked it up.

The girl in the front grinned so wide her braces and orange elastics were visible. Behind her a woman with white-blond hair held her paddle over her head. Her chin was lifted, regal. Stellene Lupo. Behind them was Cat Island and beyond that Fishers Island. I set the photo down carefully. The guns made me nervous. I turned off the light and left the room, closing the door firmly behind me.

I went into the conservatory. Much better—the air was humid and fragrant with the scent of dozens of tropical plants. The glass walls framed the patio where guests stood under strings of fairy lights glowing like stars. The room was instantly soothing, lovely as any stage set.

White-painted metal garden furniture surrounded a large marble table. I set down my sterling serving tray. Leave it to Stellene to use old-fashioned, heavy silver trays. I kneaded my aching arms, settled on one of the couches, and put my feet up. The plush cushions cradled my body. I sighed.

"I know. They're so comfortable," a soft voice said.

I sat bolt upright. A girl about my age emerged from the shadows behind a fountain, one of those old-fashioned ones with a draped nymph pouring an urn of water.

"Sorry—"

The girl laughed and flicked on a wall sconce. "Scared you, huh?" She was dressed in a vibrant red and pink Lily Pulitzer sundress with a red scarf loose around her shoulders. She tilted her head, sending her honey-colored wavy hair cascading over her shoulder. Her striking light blue eyes were circled with heavy mascara and green eye shadow. It was the girl in the gun room photo, grown up.

I swung my feet to the floor. "I'm Allie Larkin. With the Lazy Mermaid."

The girl laughed, a sparkling sound like the water splashing from the nymph's urn. "With that getup I never would have guessed. I know. I'm Tinsley. I asked my mom to have you guys cater. I was at the shack earlier this summer. Loved it. I just had to have my own sideshow mermaids for the party."

What Tinsley wants Tinsley gets.

She laughed again, a short bark. "Sorry about the whole mermaid getup. You do know you're auditioning?"

"Auditioning?" My eyes flicked to the corners of the room. Were there cameras? "For what?"

Tinsley leaned a hip against the table. "My mom and I saw you dance last year in Boston. You did *Swan Lake*."

"One of my favorite roles." I suppressed a pang of regret.

"You were one of the four swans," Tinsley said. "You stood out."

As a principal dancer, I'd had a role in the famous *pas de quatre* called the Dance of the Little Swans. With three other dancers, I did the difficult and precise traditional choreography with cross-linked hands.

"Yeah, the red hair." I shrugged.

Tinsley shook her head. "No, it was the way you moved. You had me believing you were a magical creature."

A warm blush crept up my neck. "Thank you."

Tinsley pulled an orchid close, let it snap back. A couple of purple petals fluttered from her fingers.

The clink of glassware, a shout from the pool, and laughter from the party filtered in through the room's glass walls but now I felt as if I were under a microscope.

"What do you mean, auditioning?" I said.

Tinsley tilted her head and looked down her nose, hawklike. Her dress and petite frame made her appear very young, but her look was knowing. The secretiveness annoyed me. I stood so she had to look up at me.

Tinsley arranged her scarf high on her chin. "My mother had this idea about using real people for models. But only special real people. Eden's guitarist, Henry Small. A couple of my friends for a shoot in Montauk. She thinks you'd be a great model." She smiled, then tipped her chin and mouth behind her scarf. "I think so, too."

My hand flew to the mermaid crown. "No one's told me anything about this."

"My mother doesn't realize how much I know," she said.

Footsteps squeaked in the marble hallway. "Miss Lupo?"

A sturdy woman in a nurse's uniform, complete with white stockings and white rubber-soled shoes, rushed into the conservatory. Sweat shone on her upper lip. She took a deep breath to compose herself. "It's time to go upstairs."

Tinsley rolled her eyes. "Okay, Olga. Gotta go. Nice to meet you, Allie."

"Nice to meet you," I parroted, taken aback. A nurse?

"I'll see you soon." She said it like a statement of fact. The nurse held an arm just behind but not touching Tinsley as the women walked out of the room.

A nurse? What was that about? What had I heard while serving lobster rolls? Something about Tinsley in Greece?

And modeling? Sure, it was flattering, but talk about out of left field. I already had one job I was dying to get back to, I didn't need another.

Still, modeling could be fun.

I slinked toward a gilt-encrusted mirror over a marble bench. Looking in the mirror was a mistake. Dark gray circles ringed my eyes. *Just get through the night, fish girl.* My bed was going to feel fantastic after this.

Footsteps whispered along the hallway. Lorel poked her head in the conservatory door. "There you are." She joined me in front of the mirror and squinted at her reflection. "Ugh."

"Maybe it's the lighting in here."

"Just one very long day," Lorel said.

Footsteps thudded down the hallway.

"Oh, no, I hope it's not that Australian tennis player," Lorel whispered. "He's an octopus."

We crouched behind the fountain.

The very tan, muscular bald man I'd seen following Lorel earlier jogged into the room, looked around, then exited through the French doors to the colonnade. He left the doors open.

Lorel exhaled. I laughed.

"How can you laugh? Plenty of hungry sharks were after you, too."

I pulled on the straps of my mermaid top. "These outfits are way too alluring. Let's put our work T-shirts back on."

"What'll Stellene say?" Lorel twisted her hands. "Stellene'll be angry."

A mosquito buzzed on my bare shoulder. I smacked it. "We're done. Stellene can walk around in a clamshell bikini and see how she likes it."

Chapter 16

Fireworks blossomed over Harmony Harbor, tendrils of white ice arcing across the sky. Bursts of red, green, and gold followed, huge chrysanthemums of light one after another.

Looking down on the bay from the patio of Harmony Harbor, the effect was one of two fireworks displays: one in the sky for the earth dwellers and a mirror-image show for those beneath the waves. At the point the sky met the surface of the water, dozens of shadow boats, from satellite-topped yachts to fishing dories and a few suicidal kayaks, bobbed on the light-dazzled sea.

In the distance, Mystic Bay's fireworks rumbled and thundered, the lights a miniature version of the ones shot from Stellene's hired barge out in the bay.

The last starburst boomed and fizzled into the ocean. Smoke and the pungent scent of spent explosive rolled toward us. Lorel and I had slipped our Lazy Mermaid T-shirts over our clamshell bikinis and squeezed into a tucked-away spot next to an urn on the low wall enclosing the patio. The Australian tennis player was nowhere to be seen.

After the grand finale fireworks, Stellene's guests whooped and cheered. Applause carried on the warm night air. Then the thin note of a violin threaded its way through the chatter. Voices hushed and heads swiveled as guests tried to find the source of the music.

I traced the sound high up on the west wing of the mansion. A blue spotlight bloomed on an ivy-covered marble balcony. A woman stepped into the light holding a jeweled half-mask on a stick in front of her face. She was dressed in—light. Her dress, with a high ruff behind her head like Queen Elizabeth I, glowed and strobed with rainbow hues. She lowered the mask. The crowd gasped.

Lorel squeezed my arm. "I can't believe it! That's Eden!"

Eden! Eden! The name traveled through the crowd. Cell phones and cameras were lifted.

As Eden sang, the crowd danced and I lost myself in the music. Even Lorel, usually a stick in the mud, swayed with me, her eyes shining. Many revelers held giant sparklers and twirled them in the air in time to the music.

Henry Small sat on the edge of a table by the pool, his face raised, the torchlight hollowing his cheekbones, his blond hair long and curling over his ears. Two women sat on the table on either side, their arms looped around him. Two more women sat in chairs by his legs. One woman rested her hand on his knee. Their stillness made a statue of a careless god surrounded by worshipful goddesses. All four women looked at Henry, not the woman singing from the balcony. Henry sang along, indifferent to his audience. With difficulty, I turned my gaze back toward the singer.

Eden moved stiffly, with almost robotic movements, but the deep tone of her voice made me think of honey, golden, dark, sweet.

Out of the corner of my eye, I noticed a tall, striking woman on the patio. Her long, straight silver hair shone like the sterling candelabra on the table behind her. Her chin was lifted, her back straight. Regal.

Stellene Lupo. She was rapt, her hands folded and held to her lips, but she smiled broadly. Once again she'd cemented her reputation of giving the party of the summer. Who else could get Eden?

Then it hit me. The song Eden had just sung was one I'd heard dozens of times at rehearsal. All week we'd been blocking a show for an opera singer no one had ever heard of, who would be slotted into the show at the last minute. Some names had been floated, but suddenly I was certain that *Ondine* was meant to be a showcase for this woman who was casting a spell over the crowd at Stellene's party. Eden.

A tall man moved next to Stellene, bent close to speak to her. Mac Macallen. He was dressed in a navy blazer over an open-collar shirt with an ascot. An ascot! On anyone else it would look ridiculous, but Mac owned it. Stellene leaned into him and he put one arm around her waist. With the other hand he raised a flute of champagne in a toast toward the balcony. Ah. Their friendship made sense. Their worlds overlapped. Modeling. Money. Music. Theater.

I turned back to Eden. Just outside the ring of light encircling her, farther down the façade of the mansion, two shadows moved on another balcony: one stocky, dressed in white, bent from the waist then straightened. The other figure was seated.

The song ended, Eden waved, the light blacked out. The audience exploded in applause and a last barrage of fireworks shot from the barge offshore. This time the fireworks were all silver and white, a fountain of diamonds that showered the partygoers with glittering light.

For a moment, these fireworks illuminated the two people on the balcony, Olga the nurse and Tinsley. Why weren't they downstairs at the party?

Stellene and Mac headed into the conservatory. Her laughter rang on the marble walls.

Moments later, Stellene's footmen moved through the crowd with trays of sparklers. House music by a DJ on the patio amped the party energy. Strings of fireworks popped by the waterfront. Guests whooped and cannonballed into the pool, some wandered down to the private beach. Couples drifted into the long shadows of the gardens on either side of the house.

Henry Small and his goddesses were gone.

Lorel and I went to the kitchen, passing servers hefting platters of all-American desserts: miniature pies, chocolate chip cookies the size of a dinner plate, stacks of brownies.

I snagged a pie as I passed.

Lorel shot me a disapproving look.

"What?" I bit into the pie. Gooey cherries filled my mouth. Bliss.

"We're staff, not guests." Lorel folded her arms.

I licked my fingers. "This staffer is starving."

In the massive kitchen, caterers packed equipment while Stellene's servants cleaned, their traditional black dresses and frilly white aprons standing out among the colorful chefs' jackets. Aunt Gully tucked a wooden spoon into the plastic laundry basket holding her cooking essentials: her pink Lazy Mermaid apron, her lucky utensils and pots, and her secret ingredients in large glass canning jars.

"Note to self," Lorel muttered. "Get rid of Aunt Gully's crummy old laundry basket."

"You girls ready?" Aunt Gully hugged Yasmin. "Thank you for your help, Yasmin. Anytime you want to come to the Mermaid, you're welcome."

"Wait, we have to get a photo in our costumes." Lorel and I removed our mermaid crowns then pulled off our T-shirts. Everyone crowded closer to admire the intricate beading on our crowns and clamshell tops.

Zoe Parker strutted through the kitchen door carrying a small gift bag. Her beautiful sky-high stilettos clacked across the tile.

"I have a little surprise for you, Mrs. Fontana, to thank you for the wonderful job you did tonight. And for you, Lorel and Allie." Zoe reached into the bag and pulled out three gift boxes tied with red, white, and blue ribbons—the party favors I'd seen stacked on the table in the conservatory. Excitement buzzed through me.

"Tinsley and Stellene wanted you to have them." Zoe handed Aunt Gully a long, thin box and gave Lorel and me two identical square boxes.

"Well, isn't that the nicest thing? Thank you. Please thank them for me." Aunt Gully admired the wrapping. It was beautiful, but I tore into mine, revealing a pink velvet box. I lifted the lid and tilted it. Underneath in curling gold script it read *Treasures by Tinsley*. Inside was a baby-blue leather bracelet, woven through with little silver medallions, like the coins on a belly dancer's belt. The coins shimmied and caught the light.

Lorel's was the same as mine.

"Oh!" Aunt Gully pulled out a necklace with a large hammered-silver medallion on a chain strung with crystal beads. "Really, this is too much."

"These are designs from Tinsley's new line of jewelry," Zoe said. "Won't be made available to the public until the fall."

"They're wonderful. Please thank Stellene and Tinsley for us." As I slipped mine on I almost forgave Stellene for making us wear mermaid costumes. Aunt Gully and Lorel put theirs back in the boxes. Neither Lorel nor I had brought purses, so Aunt Gully tucked the boxes in hers.

Stellene, tall and elegant, and a short, broad-shouldered blonde in an oversized T-shirt entered the kitchen. Everyone went silent and then Zoe's voice shrilled. "Eden!"

Eden! Right here in the kitchen!

Tara and Yasmin shared a wide-eyed glance and melted back toward the pantry.

Stellene's arms were crossed and her jaw set as she walked alongside Eden.

The pop superstar was shorter than I expected, curvy and square jawed. She wore white yoga pants and an oversized, stained Mets T-shirt, so oversized the neckline slipped over her shoulder revealing the broad strap of a red sports bra. Her bare feet moved soundlessly over the kitchen floor.

"I didn't get a chance to eat before I sang." Eden's voice boomed. "Time to raid the kitchen."

Aunt Gully reached for her basket. "Well, we'll take care of that right now. I'll make you a lobster roll."

"Oh, hello, you're still here, Gina." Stellene used Aunt Gully's given name, which no one did. She must have seen it on the contract.

Eden grinned. "That's so sweet of you. You're the Lazy Mermaid lady."

"I'm Gully Fontana, but you can call me Aunt Gully. Everyone does. And these are my nieces, Lorel and Allie." Aunt Gully waved the staff and caterers forward and introduced them as she started preparing the rolls. Eden shook hands with everyone and posed for some selfies. "And this is Tara and Yasmin," Aunt Gully said.

Stellene shifted from one foot to another. She probably didn't have any idea what her servants' names were. Suddenly Stellene looked like a guest in her own house. She glanced at us as Aunt Gully and the staff resumed working.

"You two looked perfect," Stellene purred.

I glanced down. I'd forgotten I was still wearing the mermaid costume.

"Thank you so much for the beautiful bracelet." I raised my wrist.

"Yes, Stellene, thank you. They're gorgeous," Lorel said.

Stellene blinked, then caught Zoe's eye. I wondered if Tinsley had disobeyed her mother or meant for us to have these at all. Maybe Zoe was just getting rid of some leftover party favors.

"Tinsley asked me to make sure you all received a gift, with her compliments," Zoe said.

Stellene's shoulders relaxed. "You're very welcome." Stellene talked with Greenwich lockjaw, her lips hardly moving, all the planes of her face smooth and sculpted. Her eyes were a pale light blue that made me think of February ice on Harris Core.

Zoe's phone buzzed. "Sorry, gotta take this. Good night, all." She strutted from the kitchen.

Aunt Gully bustled over, a wooden spoon in one hand, her gray hair frizzing. "The jewelry's lovely. You and your daughter are so thoughtful."

"It's a new business venture for my daughter," Stellene said.

"How exciting! Tinsley's a talented girl," Aunt Gully said.

"I'm so very proud of her." Stellene's cheeks pinked.

Stellene's phone buzzed. "Excuse me, I have to take this." She hurried from the kitchen.

Eden pulled a chair up to the long wooden table that looked right out of a French château. She turned the chair backward and straddled it, curling her bare feet over the rungs. Her black nail polish was chipped. On her neck and wrist were tattoos that looked like bar coding.

Aunt Gully hummed at the stove and everyone else pretended to be cool about having one of the most famous pop stars in the world eating in the kitchen. I sat at the table with her and Lorel joined me. We chatted about the party and Mystic Bay. I couldn't bring myself to ask the one question I was dying to ask: Are you singing in *Ondine*?

Aunt Gully set a lobster roll in front of Eden.

"Ooh, that looks good. Thanks, Aunt Gully." Eden took a bite, moaning. "So good! You're the real deal."

Stellene strode back into the kitchen with her arms crossed, rubbing her upper arms. A tiny line creased her smooth forehead.

Eden swallowed and turned toward Stellene. "Like I was saying, Stellene, thanks for asking me to stay. But I gotta tell you, I'm spooked. Some girls were hiding in my closet. I took some selfies with them, and security escorted them out, but I've got to get back on the yacht. I don't feel safe here."

Stellene's expression was pained. Lorel and I shared a look and melted away from the table. We joined Aunt Gully as she repacked her basket.

"What do I pay that security team for?" Stellene fumed. "They're supposed to be the best—"

Eden raised a hand. "No worries, Stellene. But if I could go back on *Model Sailor*, that would be great."

Model Sailor was Stellene's yacht. Everyone knew *Model Sailor*, one of the biggest yachts to cruise Mystic Bay.

"Nobody would think to look for me there," Eden said. "And I loved being able to swim off the boat."

Stellene waved it away. "Nonsense. I'll have the team sweep the house again."

Eden shook her head. "Stellene, I just feel safer on the boat."

"Too bad I let my crew have the night off. Really, I think you'll be more comfortable here in the house." Stellene's voice was more clipped, more intense, uncomfortably so. The kitchen staff turned away. Lorel and I busied ourselves helping Aunt Gully tidy up, but from the corner of my eye I watched the two powerful women spar.

"I'll be fine on the boat. Just have one of your boat guys take me out." Eden licked her fingers.

Stellene's lips whitened. She looked toward me. I jumped and pretended to pack Aunt Gully's already packed basket.

"I know you like a hearty breakfast. You'd do better here where my staff can cook for you." Stellene's laugh was shrill. "Even I don't know how to cook on the boat."

"I've cooked on a boat," I said. "I'd be happy to show you." I couldn't believe the words flew out of my mouth. I froze, afraid that Stellene would look at me with those icy eyes again.

"Would you?" Eden smiled. "That would be great. See, Stellene, Allie—it's Allie, right?—will help me out. Allie, would you mind staying overnight with me on the boat? I know it's weird and you just met me and all, but that would be great. I can't just walk into restaurants these days."

"Those stoves can be tricky. Maybe Lorel could help you, too." Aunt Gully took off her apron and folded it, smiling innocently at Eden. Lorel's mouth opened but she didn't say anything.

Eden laughed. "See, a party. With mermaids. Awesome. And didn't your chef say he stocked the yacht? So I'm all set."

Did I just invite myself onto Stellene Lupo's yacht with Eden?

"Oh, no, I couldn't let you." Stellene's carefully modulated tone disappeared. Two red spots blotched her cheeks. "You must stay here in the suite. You'll be more comfortable. It's more secure."

"The boat'll be fine." Eden put her plate in the sink. "It's not your fault your guests got past security."

Oh, *your guests*. Eden twisted the knife. How could Stellene make Eden stay here with guests like that?

"I insist—" Stellene's voice faltered.

"Thanks, Stellene," Eden said. "You're the hostess with the mostess, I know, but the boat'll be fine."

"Of course." Stellene shrugged. "Well, okay. I'll have Jackson take you to the dock in one of the golf carts. It'll take a few minutes to arrange. He'll meet you at the conservatory entrance." Stellene pulled her phone from her pocket and hurried from the kitchen.

"Well, you kids have fun." Aunt Gully gave everyone a hug. "Whenever you're in town, come in for a lobster roll, my dears."

Dazed, I watched Aunt Gully carry her basket to the padded door of the kitchen, followed by Yasmin and Tara. Before she went through, Aunt Gully turned and winked at us.

"How could this night get any better?" Lorel breathed.

The kitchen door opened and Henry Small walked in. "Hey, it's the mermaids."

My mind went blank as he approached. Then he swung into the seat next to Eden. "There you are, my love."

I remembered the gossip I'd heard on the pool deck. Of course a superstar like Eden would have such a handsome boyfriend.

"Guess where we're spending the night?" Eden crowed.

Chapter 17

Lorel and I changed back into our T-shirts and shorts. We met Eden at the same door where just hours earlier I'd parked the van. A golf cart drove up.

"Good evening, I'm Ken Jackson." The driver helped us into the cart. Henry hefted a duffel into the back of the cart and sat in front. Eden sat in the back of the cart with Lorel and me.

Eden's song rang in my mind. "Eden—"

"Allie—" She turned to me just as I spoke.

"You know Dara Van Der Witz, right?" I whispered.

Her smile flashed in the dim light. "Yes, yes I do." She chuckled. "Don't I look like a German soprano? And I recognized your name. And that outfit." She shook her head.

Ken Jackson started the cart and we rolled forward.

"Wait!"

The driver braked.

Stellene ran up to us, holding two champagne bottles aloft. "Take the party with you. This is some of my best champagne. Promise me you'll drink every drop!"

She handed the open bottles to Henry and Lorel.

"Stellene, you're the best," Eden crowed.

Stellene smiled, kissed her fingertips and blew a kiss.

All is forgiven, I thought.

Lorel sipped and passed the bottle to me. I took a swig. *Ah, delicious.*

"That's a promise we can keep." Henry chugged the champagne and howled as Ken Jackson drove along a darkened path to the waterfront.

Henry passed the bottle to Eden. She and I clinked bottles. "To *Ondine*!"

Several powerboats were tied up at Stellene's dock. One was a vintage Chris-Craft, a sleek wooden powerboat that looked like it should be ferrying the Rat Pack to a party with Doris Day and Marilyn Monroe. Ken stowed the bag in it, then helped us board.

"She's a beauty," I said as Ken took the wheel.

The engine purred to life. We slid out in the dark sea, leaving the thumping music and sparkling lights of the party at Harmony Harbor in our wake.

Several strands of Lorel's hair worked their way from her chignon. She giggled as she sipped from the champagne bottle and then passed it to me. I offered the bottle to Ken. He waved it off with a laugh. "No, thank you, miss."

People say champagne goes to their head, but champagne goes to my head and my feet. After just a sip, I couldn't help dancing. The boat's ride was smooth, but after two steps I fell on my bottom on a pile of life preservers.

This set off uncontrollable giggles. Henry helped me up and I sat with Lorel on the bench seat. Eden sang, her powerful, throaty voice riding on top of the engine's roar. The boat sped to a sheltered inlet, smoothly slaloming through a darkened flotilla of sailboats, powerboats, and rowboats, all heading home after the fireworks. Red, green, and white running lights scudded on the water. A Harbor Patrol boat hovered nearby, keeping a watchful eye.

Ken took it a bit fast, but he was showing off for Eden. She stood next to him, her loose white T-shirt and peals of laughter flowing behind her.

Henry dropped between Lorel and me.

"Do you live in New York?" I asked.

He sat back and looped his arms around us.

"New York and L.A. when we're not on tour. Which we are all the time. I barely live anywhere except hotel rooms." In the dark, lit only by some inboard lights, Henry was a silhouette, and the scent of chlorine and masculine sweat and champagne, and a voice with an appealing rasp. "Yep, I'm a city boy now. But where I grew up there were more cows than people."

I caught the white flash of Lorel's smile in the darkness. It had been a long time since I'd seen her so relaxed. Of course, as a method of relaxation, drinking champagne on a motorboat with a handsome guy couldn't be beat.

"How long have you known Eden?" Lorel said.

He chuckled. "Eden? Since before she was Eden."

He stood and lurched forward as the boat slowed and approached the yacht. Lorel leaned over to me.

"How on earth did we end up on a motorboat with Eden?" She laughed.

Hearing Lorel laugh made me happy. Maybe she'd truly left Patrick behind.

Stellene's massive white yacht loomed out of the darkness, three stories tall and topped with satellite dishes.

"Whoa!" Lorel said. "This thing's big enough to qualify as a cruise ship."

Ken throttled down and brought us alongside *Model Sailor.* As we approached, the yacht lit up with LED lights along the rub rail.

Two men stepped onto the swim platform at the rear of the yacht and helped us board. "Anything else we can get you?"

We shook our heads. The men got into the launch. "Madam wanted you to have complete privacy."

"Tell Madam thanks a bunch!" Eden crowed. We waved them off.

Henry lurched to get his footing as the yacht rocked gently on the tide.

Lorel headed down a passageway and Henry climbed a ladder to the upper deck.

Eden grabbed my arm. "We won't drift anywhere, will we?" Her famous dusky voice was urgent.

"We're at anchor." A momentary worry flickered—the crew had taken off. "The weather's calm. We'll be fine." I smiled, but I wondered about a question she didn't ask. Who could come out here at this time of night?

Eden's crazy fans, a little voice reminded me. Maybe it was the champagne, but I dismissed the thought. No one knew we were here. Besides, Stellene's security detail was probably watching the boat. She wouldn't want a repeat of the incident with the fans sneaking into Eden's room.

"Come on up!" Henry called. Eden clambered up the ladder.

I hurried down the passage after Lorel and found her lying on a queen-sized bed in a stateroom.

"That looks great but shouldn't we be in the crew quarters?" I asked.

"I'm not sleeping in those two guys' beds," Lorel said.

"Good point. Just don't snore too loud."

Lorel giggled and passed me the champagne bottle. We went up to the galley. The kitchen was all granite and teak, with real crystal and china in the cabinets.

"Unreal. On a boat." I shook my head.

Eden waved us into a spacious glass-enclosed space with modern furniture and a huge television screen.

"We came over on this boat with Stellene today. I love that this room is called the saloon." Eden laughed.

"Just like the old West," Henry said. He sprawled on a dove-gray leather sectional couch. Lorel and I sat next to him. His forearms were covered with tattoos. One was a face. I looked from the tattoo to Eden.

"That's Eden." I laughed.

Henry's eyes were bright. "I get a tat for every band I play with. Check this out." He flexed and a coyote moved on his bicep. "Blue Coyote was the band. See, it's blue?"

I sighed. I could look at his tattoos all night. I pointed at one on his left arm. "Sunrise?"

"Dawn of Rock. Lame name," Henry said.

Lorel pointed to a small one on his forearm.

He chuckled. "Kinda rough, huh? That's 3H. Everyone in the band had a name that began with *H*."

"And be sure to show them your scales," Eden said.

"Scales of justice." He pulled down the neck of his shirt and turned so I could see the tattoo. Words in Latin crossed his upper back underneath scales at the base of his neck.

Eden sipped from the champagne bottle. "Henry studied criminal justice for a while. You have to read the Latin for her, Henry."

"*Fiat justitia ruat cælum* is a Latin phrase. It means 'Let justice be done though the heavens fall.'"

Eden fanned herself. "Talk Latin to me, baby!"

"A little bit dramatic, don't you think?" Lorel laughed. I sipped from my champagne bottle and passed it to Lorel.

Eden handed Henry the other champagne bottle. "Want the last bit?"

Henry swigged from the bottle then tipped it upside down. "One dead soldier." It fell to the floor. I picked it up and tossed it into the trash bin in the galley.

"Will we be safe out here?" Eden rubbed her eyes and slumped next to Henry. Lorel handed me the champagne bottle.

"We'll be safe. Nobody knows we're here except for Stellene." Henry patted her hand.

"And her crew." I yawned and rubbed my eyes,

forgetting I still held an almost empty bottle of Stellene's champagne.

Lorel shrugged. "And they're fired if anyone shows up here."

"Stellene picked us up from a friend's house this morning on Montauk. She said the boat's a great way to escape. I agree. Her clients use boats all the time because nobody thinks to watch the marinas." Eden's eyes fluttered closed.

"And Queen Stellene packs heat." Henry jumped up and headed to the bridge. "Don't worry, I'll protect you."

"She does what?" Lorel said.

Henry opened a compartment and turned back to us, keeping his hands behind his back. "Packs heat. Her husband was a big gun collector."

I remembered the room full of weapons.

"Stellene showed it to us on our way over from Montauk. See, I'll protect you, fair ladies." Henry brandished a gun.

"Whoa, Henry, put it back," I said. The gun was a dull black color that seemed to suck all the light in the room into it.

"Stellene's husband, late husband, collected guns and she learned to shoot. She keeps one onboard for security." Henry sighted down the barrel.

Lorel said, "Is it loaded?"

The boat rocked and Henry stumbled across the saloon. Lorel jumped up from the couch.

"Stop, you idiot," Eden slurred.

"Careful!" I shouted.

"Don't worry, I grew up on a ranch." Henry stumbled and dropped the gun. He picked it up and the gun went off.

Eden screamed. I dropped the bottle. Champagne foamed and spilled across the rug. The boat rocked. Henry missed his footing and dropped the gun again.

"Henry, what's wrong with you!" Eden shouted. She lunged off the couch and picked up the gun. "You just shot up Stellene's couch!"

Henry laughed and swore. Red crept up his cheeks. "I didn't mean to do that, honest!"

"I don't want this." Eden shoved the gun into Lorel's hands.

"I don't want it!" Lorel shoved it at me, like a game of hot potato. I waved it off.

Lorel ran to the bridge and shoved the gun back into the drawer. She slammed it shut. In the shocked silence, we looked at each other. Then we burst out laughing.

"On that terrifying note, time for bed," Henry said.

"Yeah, that was enough excitement for me." Lorel twisted her hands.

"You're a menace," I said to Henry.

"He always has been." Eden ruffled his hair.

"Yeah, but I'm cute." Henry knelt by the couch. "Bullet went through and got the floor. I'll have to get this repaired for Stellene."

Eden moved a pillow to cover the hole in the couch cushion. "See, all taken care of."

Henry groaned. "Nah, I'll have to make it right."

Eden shook her head. "Mr. Responsible. That's what happens when you're the grandson of a judge and son of a sheriff. What was his name?"

"Good old what's his name." Henry laughed.

"He was a Henry, too," Eden said. "Henry 'Eye for an Eye' Small."

I could only imagine what Henry's law-and-order grandfather would make of his tattooed musician grandson.

Eden and Henry stumbled into the master cabin. "Time to get some beauty sleep. Don't wake me before noon," Eden called. "Oh wait, I've got rehearsal at eleven. Somebody wake me around nine? Remember, I'm ravenous in the morning." She shut the door.

I grabbed a towel from the galley and mopped up the champagne. The teak flooring under the couch was splintered around a small hole. It would cost a fortune to repair. Well, Eden could afford it. I sat back on my heels, dizzy. "Why am I so tired? It's only after midnight, right?"

"It was a long day, plus all that champagne." Lorel pressed her hand to her head. "That gunshot almost gave me a heart attack."

I laughed. "Did you see Henry's face? He gave himself a heart attack."

"Let's go to bed, Allie." Lorel yawned. "We've got to get up and make breakfast."

We walked carefully down the passage to our bedroom. I pressed my hand against the wall to keep my balance. I was so tired.

"I don't think those two are getting up too early." Muffled laughter floated toward us. "I'm glad there's a cabin between us. I don't want to hear anything personal. Though don't you think there's something off about them?"

"Who?" Lorel threw herself onto the bed, not bothering to turn on a light. Pale silvery light came through the porthole.

I plopped fully clothed onto the bed and kicked off my sandals. "Henry and Eden?"

"Famous people are different." Lorel crushed the pillow to her chest and pulled out her phone.

"And who leaves a gun lying around like that? Stellene's so worried about security but she leaves a loaded gun lying around," I said.

Lorel's face was gray in the light from her cell phone.

"Are you drunk dialing Patrick Yardley? Didn't he drop his phone in the—" I stopped short.

"His phone." Lorel rubbed her eyes. "Oh, that's right."

Lorel was drunk and sleepy. I wasn't going to get her in a more vulnerable mood.

"So Lorel, why did you and Patrick call it off?"

She was quiet for a long time. My eyelids were so heavy. Just when I was about to roll over and go to sleep, she spoke so softly I had to strain to hear her.

"You have to swear you won't say anything, Allie. I think . . ." Lorel's voice trailed. "Patrick's in trouble but he won't tell me why. I mean, it's his gambling. And his backers. They keep asking for more and more money. He won't let me help. He doesn't trust me. He—" Lorel started to cry, then snored.

What was she going to say next? The champagne

and the gentle rocking of the boat made it impossible to keep my eyes open. I drifted to sleep. The dead girl from Bertha's boat surfaced for a moment, but sleep came so fast her white face faded like fog.

Great. I got up and staggered to the bathroom in the dark. When I finished I fumbled back across the stateroom and fell into my bed. Just as my head hit the pillow, a white blur passed by the porthole above my bed.

Was that blond hair? What was Eden doing up? Or was it Henry? I was too sleepy to think. I rolled over.

Pop! Pop! Pop!

My eyes flew open. My mind struggled to shape thoughts. It was the Fourth of July. Jerks tossing cherry bombs off a boat. So close. I strained to hear more, but there was nothing but Lorel's gentle breathing. I rolled over and drifted back to sleep.

Chapter 18

Sunday, July 5

It seemed that only a moment had passed when the shrieks of passing gulls woke me. I rolled over and sat up. A jolt of pain made me press my hand to my forehead. The champagne. Did I drink that much?

The gulls' screams grew sharper, formed into words.

"Help! Allie! Help me!"

Lorel?

I stumbled to the door and ran toward the sound. Lorel's screams ripped at my chest.

"Lorel! Where are you?" I shouted.

From the saloon, Henry's sleepy voice called, "What's going on?"

I didn't bother to answer him as I ran out to the swim deck.

A black rigid-hulled inflatable, the fast and stealthy boat Navy SEALs use in the movies, was tied up to the back of Stellene's yacht. What on earth was Lorel doing in that RHI?

Lorel held her hands palms out like she did when she was a little girl and got her hands covered in sand. Heat rose into my chest and my face. Her palms were smeared with something reddish brown.

Blood?

"Lorel, are you hurt?"

Henry thudded down the passage behind me, breathing hard. "What the hell's going on?" He grabbed my arm.

A man lay in the bottom of the RHI, huddled at the bow. My eye moved from jeans, a light blue shirt, mottled with red and brown stains, to tousled brown hair. My heartbeat thundered in my ears.

"Allie, help! It's Patrick. It's Patrick," Lorel shrieked.

"I'm coming." I threw off Henry's hand and swung my legs over the wide side of the RHI, pulling at the end of the rope that tethered it to Stellene's yacht. Water slicked the bottom of the boat.

"Allie, what do I do? He's dead, he's dead." My sister pressed her hands to her head, smearing her beautiful golden hair with brown streaks.

I leaned against the high sides of the RHI to steady myself. Behind me, Henry swore. I turned to him in a fury. "Call 911! Stop standing there and do something!"

His mouth fell open. "I, I don't know how to use a boat radio—"

"Your cell should work. Hurry!" I turned back to my sister. "Lorel." I tried to steady my voice. "Are you sure?"

I reached down. Patrick's beautiful hair was unmistakable. I couldn't bring myself to push back his hair to see his face, but I pressed my fingers against his neck. The stubble on his jawline rasped under my fingers. His skin was cold. There was no pulse.

Patrick Yardley is dead! How? What was he doing here? I swallowed hard and met Lorel's eyes.

Lorel screamed and again pressed her hands to her head. Suddenly I couldn't bear his blood on her hands, in her hair.

Lorel's chest heaved as if she was going to be sick.

It was too much. Patrick's blood. My sister's screams.

Lorel fell toward me and grabbed my arms so tightly her nails dug into my skin. I wrapped my arm around her and tried to help her walk past Patrick's body, but her knees buckled. The RHI started to drift and turn in the water. There was a reddish smear on the shoulder of my T-shirt. *Patrick's blood!* Sickness overwhelmed me. *I have to get this blood off us.*

I leaned over the side of the boat and pulled Lorel into the water with me.

The shock of hitting the water extinguished my panicked thoughts. The water closed over my head and roared in my ears. Lorel was motionless for a second, then she clawed for the surface.

We surfaced, gasping. Henry knelt and dragged Lorel onto the swim deck. I followed. I was numb. Lorel coughed and choked up water. The water wasn't that cold, but my legs trembled as I pulled myself up. Henry wrapped Lorel in a towel and held one out to me.

Lorel sagged and Henry and I half carried, half walked her to the saloon.

Henry kicked aside his duffel bag and lifted a wrinkled blanket from the couch. Lorel collapsed onto it and buried her face in a pillow. I covered her with my body, feeling her tremble. A warm softness covered me. Henry tucked the blanket on top of us.

I squeezed my eyes shut but I couldn't block out the image of Patrick's lifeless body. How could I ever unsee it? Worse was seeing Lorel fall apart. I pressed closer to her, trying to comfort her, trying to keep her together, trying to keep myself together.

Henry paced back and forth, running his hands through his hair, picking up a T-shirt and a water bottle and stuffing it inside his duffel. A distant voice came from his phone. "The cops are coming and said they're sending the Coast Guard, too. They said to stay on the phone but I don't know what to tell them," he said. "Just the name of Stellene's boat."

"We're at anchor off Harmony Harbor," I said. "They'll know where it is."

"Should I call Stellene?"

Not a phone call I wanted to make. I pressed my cheek against Lorel's wet hair. "Let the cops do it."

Lorel wailed and I stroked her hair as questions flooded my mind. Did Patrick come to see Lorel? Two deaths on the water in Mystic Bay in one week? What on earth was Patrick Yardley doing in a boat tied up to Stellene's yacht?

Chapter 19

Somehow I got Lorel into our stateroom and helped her into a hot shower. There were some sweatpants and T-shirts in a drawer. I pulled Lorel out of the shower and dressed her. She didn't resist, just sat on the edge of the bed staring at nothing. This scared me more than her weeping. I threw on some clothes from the same stash in the drawer.

"Lorel, let's get something to drink."

Lorel whimpered. "I have to go to him."

"No, Lorel, no. We can't help him now." I led her back to the saloon.

The television was on. Henry jumped up from a chair and we settled Lorel into it. There was a black terry-cloth robe draped on the back of the chair and he gently laid it around her shoulders.

"Damn. This is awful. Did you know that guy?" Henry said.

I nodded. "My sister's boyfriend, well, ex-boyfriend," I said quietly. "Patrick Yardley."

He didn't blink. "Doesn't ring a bell."

Eden, wrapped in a matching oversized black robe with a sleep mask pushed to the top of her head, joined us. Her eye makeup was smeared and her short blond hair stood up all over her head, like the feathers of a baby bird. "I feel like hell. What's going on? What did I miss?"

Lorel turned her face away and closed her eyes.

Henry pulled Eden into the passageway. They spoke quietly. She swore. Her footsteps thudded toward the back of the yacht. I picked up the television remote and hit the mute button as Bertha's interview with Leo Rodriguez replayed on the screen.

Eden and Henry returned. Eden's face was pale. "Some boats are coming."

Eden sat next to Lorel and rubbed her back. "How awful," she murmured. "I'm so sorry."

Henry pulled aside the saloon's curtains. Bright sunlight streamed in. I winced.

Henry nodded. "Me, too. Wicked hangover. Drank too much. I'm in no shape to face the day, forget the cops and—" He looked at Lorel, hunched his shoulders, and looked away.

"Allie, let's get Lorel something to drink." I followed Eden into the galley.

"Here." Eden found a box of tea bags. She nodded at a coffee maker. "Or maybe coffee? She looks like a coffee girl."

I took four mugs out of a cabinet. "Tea's probably better now." I filled a kettle with water while she opened the refrigerator.

"Tea for me and Henry, too." She put two scoops of

sugar and milk into two mugs. "What do you and Lorel like?"

"I'll have it plain and put some sugar in Lorel's. Thanks."

"Anything with caffeine. My head's splitting." Eden ran a hand through her cropped hair and whispered, "So that guy was a friend?"

"My sister's ex-boyfriend. Did you know him?" My mind was still spinning. Did he come to see Lorel last night?

"I mean, I didn't see his face." Eden shuddered.

"Patrick Yardley. He owned a restaurant in Mystic Bay. New Salt."

She shook her head, her large dark eyes blank, just as Henry's had been. "No, I don't recognize the name."

We brought the tea into the saloon. I helped Lorel sit up and pressed a mug into her hands. Eden handed a cup to Henry and sat on the arm of his chair.

"Try a sip, Lorel," I said.

She obeyed, but her hands shook so much I wrapped mine around hers to steady them. A Coast Guard launch pulled up to the yacht, a Mystic Bay police boat right behind. In the distance a Harbor Patrol boat approached. Everyone was coming. Everyone was too late.

"What do we do now?" Eden said.

Voices and the sound of heavy footsteps rose from the passageway.

"Stellene didn't even want me out here," Eden muttered. "I should've stayed in the house."

Chief Emerson Brooks ducked his head and stepped into the saloon. He was Verity's uncle and he'd coached

Lorel's softball team. His solid, familiar presence wiped away my last bit of composure. Tears welled and blurred my vision.

"Allie! Lorel! What—" He rushed to kneel by Lorel.

"Aunt Gully catered Stellene's party." I wiped my eyes. "We stayed out here last night."

Chief Brooks put a hand on my shoulder. "How are you doing, honey?" I hugged him and then introduced Henry and Eden. Lorel looked at him blankly, shivering.

Two Coastguardsmen entered the saloon and nodded at Chief Brooks. They knelt next to Lorel, talking softly with her.

"Allie," Chief Brooks said, "let's let them tend to Lorel. Come tell me what happened." Reluctantly, I stepped aside.

Chief Brooks, Henry, Eden, and I sat at the table. He set his hat down and ran his hand through his cropped gray hair. "Patrick Yardley. Was he here on the boat with you? Having a party?" His eyes were sad. Disappointed?

Eden, Henry, and I started talking at once.

"Maybe you'd better fill me in, Allie."

In a low voice I told Chief Brooks everything that had happened, but I kept my eyes on Lorel. She sat upright and seemed to have pulled herself together enough to talk with the men as they took her blood pressure. From below came heavy footsteps and the occasional shout. The roar of boat engines and diesel fumes drifted in with humid air.

"We'll take statements from all of you," Chief

Brooks said. "We'll get you off this boat and take you back to shore."

"I have a rehearsal this morning," Eden said.

Henry said, "Did you call Lars?"

"He's coming down from Boston," Eden said.

The silent television screen said it was nine A.M. On a normal day we'd be helping Aunt Gully at the Mermaid.

"I have to call Aunt Gully," I said.

"Give her a call. I'll get you over there as soon as we're done." Chief Brooks looked at Lorel, his brow knotted. "And get Lorel back home."

"Chief." An officer looked in from the passage.

Chief Brooks and one of the Coastguardsmen joined him. The other packed their equipment gave Lorel a reassuring smile, and also went into the passage.

They conferred in low tones but I couldn't make out what they were saying. Eden and Henry shared a look, then they both scrolled on their phones.

This simple action made my temper flare. I rubbed my aching head. Why was I being so judgmental? Eden and Henry didn't know Patrick. They didn't know Lorel or me. They'd been perfectly nice. They'd go back to their lives untouched by this tragedy. I went to Lorel.

Lorel stared out the window as a fishing boat chugged past. Without turning she said, "I said terrible things to Patrick that night on the breakwater, Allie. I didn't even get to talk to him last night. I didn't get to say good-bye." I squeezed her shoulder then I called Aunt Gully.

"Lazy Mermaid Lobster Shack," Hilda answered.

For a long moment I didn't know what to say. I took a deep breath and explained the situation.

"Oh, God, no!" she moaned.

"Hilda, put Aunt Gully on." My voice frayed.

"What's going on?" Aunt Gully said as Hilda wailed in the background.

"Aunt Gully, it's Allie. I can't say much but we're on Stellene's yacht. Chief Brooks is here." I could hardly form the words. "Patrick Yardley's dead."

Aunt Gully gasped. "Are you and Lorel all right?"

Lorel, still clutching her mug, stared at nothing.

"Yes." No need to worry Aunt Gully further.

Chief Brooks came back into the room.

"We're going to take you all over to Harmony Harbor. Just have a few questions to ask of you. Mrs. Lupo's letting us use her home then you may be able to go."

May. He said "may."

"Aunt Gully, we have to go. Chief Brooks said they're going to ask us some questions at Harmony Harbor. I'll call you when I can."

"Honey, I'll be right there."

"Okay." No sense arguing. Aunt Gully was coming over.

Chapter 20

The Coast Guard patrol boat pulled away as we left the saloon. A Mystic Bay Police boat was tied up to the yacht. Chief Brooks's crew had rigged a tarp so we couldn't see Patrick's body. My knees trembled as we walked past. Chief Brooks used his body to shield Lorel from the RHI, murmuring to her, coaxing her. "It's all right now. Just another step." Henry hovered alongside, holding Lorel's arm.

Eden stared at the team working in the RHI, her oversized T-shirt flapping in the wind. I lowered my eyes. How long had Patrick's body been out there last night? How had I slept while just feet away his life bled out into the bottom of that boat?

My mind spun. Who wanted to kill Patrick Yardley?

Eden and Henry didn't even know him.

On the other hand, I'd just had a very public blow-out with him at New Salt. How many people had seen me rush out of his room after I'd confronted him about his other woman? Only half of Mystic Bay. My stomach churned.

Lorel had had a screaming fight with him on Kiddie Beach. How many people had seen that? There'd been people on the beach. The kids having the bonfire. Renters watching television at Fast Times.

Chief Brooks helped Lorel step from Stellene's yacht into the police boat. An officer offered me a hand and I took it as I followed Lorel. The tide was going out and the wind had picked up, making the boat rock. My head throbbed and I was queasy after all the champagne and the terrible sight of Patrick's body. I couldn't bear to look back at Chief Brooks's stricken expression.

Henry handed Eden into the police boat, then he jumped in. He misjudged the boat's motion and fell to his knees. Eden sat next to Lorel and put an arm around her. Henry scrambled to his feet and stood by the rail. The wind stirred his blond hair around his forehead. He had a high hairline hidden by his mass of hair. From the side his nose was hooked, strong, like an eagle. The crew started the engine and the sharp tang of diesel fuel made my stomach twist again as we pulled away from the yacht.

In the darkness it had seemed that we were miles from Harmony Harbor, but we returned to the dock in just a few minutes. As the crew tied up I looked back at *Model Sailor*. From this distance, Stellene's yacht was a white toy on the horizon, a dream just out of reach.

Eden joined me at the boat's rail. "Last night was a million years ago," she said.

At the end of the dock, Stellene stood tall, her mouth a stern straight line of plum-colored lipstick. Over-sized round sunglasses hid her eyes. Even at this early hour, she looked chic in white trousers, a white linen sweater, and a beaded belt slung around her waist. Behind her, crews dismantled the tents and carnival rides she'd provided for her guests' entertainment. Her crossed arms dared the police to further disturb her plans.

In the distance, a man hefted a bright yellow kayak from the beach and carried it into the boathouse.

Two golf carts rolled toward the pier and parked. Two officers in tan Mystic Bay uniforms approached Stellene, trailed by a woman in a maid's uniform. Tara. She threw worried glances toward Lorel and me.

We stepped onto the dock.

"I left my duffel bag," Henry said.

"We'll get your things to you," one of the officers said. "Later."

Eden took Henry's arm. Lorel held on to my arm but she stumbled on the rough planks of the dock. Her eyes were fixed straight ahead. "Allie, I just want to go home."

"Soon." I turned to the officer. "Can we go home?"

"We need to ask a few questions first."

Another one of Stellene's golf carts pulled up behind her and a man got out. Beige suit, striped tie, horn-rimmed glasses.

Lawyer. Stellene must have him on speed dial.

Another man got out, short, with long shaggy brown hair parted in the middle, dressed in plaid shorts and a plain black T-shirt.

"Lars!" Eden ran to him and they embraced. Henry's eyes met mine, then he followed.

The other officer jutted his chin to the second golf cart. "This way, please."

Lorel slumped into the cart, her body slack against mine. I wrapped my arms around her and held her tight.

The officer nodded at the driver and the cart moved forward.

"Can we go home?" Lorel whispered.

The officer looked about my age, with brown buzz-cut hair and sympathetic dark eyes. "Chief wants to have you answer some questions, then I can take you home. Sorry."

"See, Lorel we can go home soon," I said.

Lorel muttered, "Yes, Allie, we'll stop at home right on my way to jail."

"What are you talking about?" I whispered.

"Allie." Lorel's whisper was fierce. "Look. There we were on a yacht in the middle of nowhere. We're the only two people who knew Patrick. I"—she choked—"had a relationship with him. Who do you think the cops are going to finger for killing him?"

"Lorel—"

The officer was sitting very straight in his seat. I was certain he and the driver were listening to every word. I lowered my voice and squeezed her shoulder. "Shh. You know darn well neither one of us kill— hurt Patrick."

"Well, who did?"

"I don't know. What do we know about Eden and Henry? Huh?" I said.

"That they were as drunk as we were last night."

"Lorel, maybe somebody came over on that boat with him."

Lorel's voice was shrill. "And did what? Killed him and then swam back to shore?"

The police officer threw a look back at us. He was taking mental notes, I knew it.

"We're not under arrest, are we?" I thought of the crime shows I watched. He'd given us no Miranda warning.

He shook his head.

My mind churned with thoughts of last night. When we rode over to the yacht on Stellene's beautiful wooden powerboat. Eden singing. Drinking champagne. Then exploring *Model Sailor*. Laughing in the saloon. Henry firing the gun.

The gun.

Oh, my God.

The popping sounds I heard in the middle of the night. Fireworks, I'd assumed. Could I have heard the shots that killed Patrick Yardley?

The blur outside my window. Stellene's crew had left all the security and running lights on. I was pretty sure I'd seen blond hair. Eden and Henry both had blond hair. If those popping noises had been the shots that killed Patrick I was sure Lorel was innocent. She'd been asleep beside me.

Could Eden have killed Patrick, a person she didn't even know? She hadn't batted an eyelash when I said Patrick's name, and neither had Henry. If they knew Patrick and had killed him, they were the best actors I'd ever seen.

I felt like the earth was shifting under me.

What was Patrick doing on that boat? Why on earth was he in a rigid-hulled inflatable like some kind of commando when he and his brother owned *Miranda*, my dad's old fishing boat? Why had he tied up to *Model Sailor*?

The cart rolled past the patio.

"Could you stop by the gate?" I said. "My aunt Gully's coming over."

The officer swung around. "Aunt Gully from the lobster shack?"

Lorel slumped against my shoulder. "Stop the cart!" I shouted.

The driver hit the brakes. The officer jumped from the cart and ran to Lorel's side.

"She's fainted!" I said.

The officer and I pulled Lorel from the cart, her body completely limp.

The police officer swung her into his arms and carried her to a chaise longue.

Why couldn't Lorel go for a guy like this? The police officer was tall, dark, not bad looking, and law abiding. His uniform shirt barely contained his burly muscles. He gently set Lorel down on the chaise. I lifted her legs and sat next to her. The driver ran into the house. A short time later he hurried back out with a glass of water. Yasmin, one of the maids from the night before, followed with a towel.

The officer stepped away, keyed his mic. I heard the words "medical care." When he finished, he pulled a notebook from his pocket and fanned Lorel.

Lorel's face was so pale. Blue veins traced around

her eyes and mouth. Her lips were gray. She looked awful, so small inside the too big sweats from Stellene's yacht. Seeing my sister, usually so strong, like this shook me.

Movement by the doorway drew my eye. Tinsley peered around the door frame, hunched in a pink tunic with a gauzy matching scarf.

Yasmin wet the cloth and put it on Lorel's head. The big police officer and driver hovered. A siren screamed in the distance.

Tinsley stepped close, dipping her chin and mouth behind her scarf. "What's going on?"

"I wish I knew." I squeezed Lorel's hand.

Lorel murmured and held her other hand over her eyes. The officer pulled over an umbrella to shade her face.

"Can we talk?" Tinsley whispered.

"Yes," I said. "But I have to talk to the police first."

Tinsley nodded and stepped back.

Hector, Hilda, and Aunt Gully rushed around the corner onto the patio. I jumped to my feet.

"Who's running the shack?" I said. "Bit Markey?"

"We're closed until we know you're both okay." Aunt Gully wrapped me in her arms. I felt numb, exhaustion crowded out every emotion. "Lorel fainted." I whispered in her ear, "I think the police officer's in love with her."

Hilda grabbed onto Aunt Gully and me. "Thank God, you're okay. What a nightmare! How could this be real?"

Hector also wrapped into the group hug. "Aunt Gully said she'd drive over herself, but Hilda said that

Gully shouldn't drive when she was upset, and that she would drive, and I knew that would be no good, so I took them both."

"How did you get past the gate?" I said.

Hector shrugged. "I tailgated the ambulance."

EMTs wheeled a stretcher across the patio.

Tinsley kept her distance as the police officer fanned flies away from Lorel. Hmmm. Good thing Nurse Ratchet wasn't around to see Tinsley. Where was Olga? I also wondered if Tinsley could answer the only question that mattered: What was Patrick Yardley doing at *Model Sailor*?

Everyone moved back to make room for the EMTs.

Lorel's eyes fluttered open. "What are you doing? I'm fine. I'M FINE." Lorel batted away the EMTs. One turned to Aunt Gully. "You family? We'll take her to the hospital for a bit, just to keep an eye on her."

The officer muttered into his mic again. "I'll accompany Miss Larkin to the hospital."

Aunt Gully and Hilda hovered as the EMTs helped Lorel onto the stretcher. "We're going, too."

A man in a beige suit and a buzz cut strode out the door onto the patio like a G-man from a fifties police drama, his shiny shoes clicking on the stone patio. He gestured to the police officer. They whispered together.

Tinsley stood still, arms folded, her chin tucked behind her scarf. No one seemed to notice her. She'd perfected the art of invisibility. Was she angry? Entertained?

How things had changed from last night.

The G-man walked up to me. "Detective Budwitz.

If you're all right, Miss Larkin, we have a few questions."

"Yes." I squeezed Aunt Gully's arm. "I'll talk with the detective, Aunt Gully. You go with Lorel. We'll catch up at home."

"Are you sure you're okay, Allie?" Aunt Gully's voice was strained.

"What a waste of time," Lorel snapped as the EMTs rolled her away.

Lorel would be okay. "Yes. I'll see you at home."

Chapter 21

The G-man led me through the conservatory to another hallway and into a small study. Tinsley slipped in behind us.

In the study, dark-paneled bookshelves climbed to high ceilings. Leather-bound books lined the shelves. Though no one had probably read them in decades, not a bit of dust danced in the bands of light streaming in the window. Tinsley silently pulled a sheer curtain to shade us from the sun and stepped from the room. I wondered if the police detective realized that she wasn't an employee.

Detective Budwitz asked me a lot of questions I could barely remember moments after he asked them. The only one that stood out: "What was your relationship to the deceased?"

My honest answer would've been that I hated him. He'd made my sister miserable since fifth grade. Instead I spoke the more dangerous truth: "He was my sister's ex-boyfriend."

"And your relationship to Stellene Lupo?"

I almost laughed. Mermaid? I cleared my throat. "I worked at the party last night."

His small bright eyes blinked. He printed on a yellow legal pad, the letters dark and square. The words "pinpoint accuracy" came to mind.

"And then you were a guest on the yacht?" The tiniest bit of disbelief shaded his question.

It did seem weird. What were we doing on that yacht? It never should've happened. Stellene didn't want Eden on the boat. She wanted her to stay in the mansion. Had all this happened because of a singer's crazy whim?

"We, my sister and I, were on the yacht to cook breakfast." Which we didn't even do.

He looked up when I told him about the figure I'd seen passing the window and the sounds that I thought were fireworks.

"What time was that?" he said.

I squirmed. Why hadn't I looked at a clock? "I'm not sure. After midnight? It was dark. I didn't check." And the champagne had muddled my mind.

A knock on the door. A young woman in a State Police polo came in carrying a small box.

Budwitz nodded at her.

"This is a swab test for gunshot residue," she said.

I blinked. Those popping sounds must have been gunshots. "I didn't—"

She gave me a reassuring look. "Just procedure."

Heat rose in my face. "I mean, everyone else handled the gun except me."

Lorel. Lorel had handled the gun.

"What gun?" Budwitz said.

"There was a gun. In the saloon."

Budwitz jotted notes.

His eyes bored into mine "Did you fire the gun?"

"No," I whispered.

The woman had me sign some forms I hardly looked at.

Budwitz's cell rang. He excused himself and left the room.

"Have you washed your hands?" the young woman asked. She took a swab out of a vial and rubbed it along my palm and fingers. Then she repeated the process with my other hand.

"Um, not exactly," I said. "My sister and I fell, uh, went in the water."

Budwitz returned. "You went in the water? Swimming after you found the body?"

"Not exactly." I explained, haltingly, what had happened.

Budwitz stared, his narrow lips slowly turning down as I spoke. The young woman threw him a look, packed up, and left.

Budwitz jotted more notes then stood.

He gave me his card. I glanced at it. State Police Major Crimes Unit.

"Can I go?"

He nodded, once. When I left the study, Tinsley was waiting outside. She pulled me into a little parlor and eased the door halfway closed.

A fancy china clock on the fireplace mantel read noon. How did it get so late? Detective Budwitz's footsteps clicked down the hallway.

"Are you hungry? I had Tara bring snacks," Tinsley said.

A silver tray was stacked with the same brownies from last night and a crystal carafe of lemonade. I realized I was starving. I picked up a brownie, gulped it, and took another.

"Mom's guests are absolute frigging locusts, but Tara knows I like brownies so she put some aside for me," Tinsley said. "When they heard the cops were coming all the guests cleared out. Now it's just cops and lawyers. My mom. First thing she does, call the lawyers."

Before I could say anything, voices came down the hallway. Tinsley and I went to the door and peeked around the frame. Three people approached: Eden, Lars, and a woman I recognized. My heart skipped.

"I'm not under arrest, am I?" Eden's voice rang off the high ceiling and marble floors.

"No."

Eden and Lars passed, holding hands, trailing a trim brunette in a dark gray pantsuit with professional stud earrings. Her dark hair was pulled back in a bun so tight not a single strand dared to escape. That stride. That posture. So straight it was almost robotic. A brownie crumb lodged in my throat.

Detective Rosato. I'd met her a month earlier and had given her the nickname Robo Detective for her no-nonsense, expressionless demeanor. She was a perfect partner for the G-man, Budwitz.

What did I expect? Like many Connecticut towns, Mystic Bay was too small to have special units to investigate serious crimes like murder. The state wasn't that big. How many major crimes units were there? Of course she'd show.

Thank goodness I got Detective Budwitz. Just the memory of Detective Rosato's laser look made me want to confess to something, anything.

I swallowed hard. Tinsley and I stepped back out of sight.

"Please wait outside," Detective Rosato said.

"You don't understand, Officer." Eden's voice, beautifully modulated, was peremptory. "We're a unit."

The man with Eden spoke, his voice higher pitched and nasal. "My name is Lars. We are one. We make all our decisions together. We're one being."

There was silence. I knew exactly the expressionless look that Detective Rosato was giving Lars, regarding him like a particularly unimpressive specimen under a microscope. I'd laugh if I didn't find her so terrifying.

After a few moments, the nasal voice said, "I'll wait outside on the patio." Footsteps squeaked down the hallway.

The door across the hall closed firmly.

Tinsley tugged my hand and looked both ways in the corridor. "Come with me. And whatever you do, don't make a sound, okay?"

Tinsley slid off her shoes. I did the same. We tiptoed into the hallway, the marble cool under my feet. Just down the hallway past the study door was a black lacquered screen and some potted palm trees. We sidled behind them and Tinsley eased open a narrow wooden door. Low murmuring voices filled the room, as if a radio or television were on. Tinsley held a finger to her lips.

Shelves stocked with linens ran down both sides of the room, linens and some huge old-fashioned serving pieces, soup tureens, punch bowls, and platters Verity would give her eyeteeth for. Tinsley went to the very end of the room and slid against the wall to sit cross-legged on the floor. She pointed right across from her. I sat, too. She grinned and inclined her head toward the wall.

Not a radio. Voices. Eden's and Detective Rosato's. A wooden board leaned against the wall next to a black mesh panel, a concealed opening between the two rooms.

My jaw dropped. Tinsley's smile widened.

Shock was my first reaction. Had Tinsley eavesdropped on my interview with Detective Budwitz? Of course she had. She was enjoying this.

"Did you know Patrick Yardley?" Detective Rosato's voice.

"You mean the dead guy in the boat? No, never heard of him, never met him. Ever." Eden's last word was definite.

There was a pause. The silence stretched. I remembered the way Detective Rosato's black eyes held mine, how she put her little notebook on the table but didn't write in it. Just aligned a pen with the book so it was perfectly parallel. The way she watched you during long silent pauses. For all the bravado in her voice, I wondered if Eden was squirming now.

"You told Mrs. Lupo that you wanted to stay on the boat," Detective Rosato said. "Why?"

Tinsley's chin rested on her hand, fascinated. Rings sparkled on her fingers. Her nails were painted bubblegum pink. She looked younger than me. Maybe twenty-one?

With a jolt, I remembered what I'd heard about Tinsley. Wild child. Rehab. Was that why she had the nurse?

Eden's loud sigh interrupted my thoughts. "Some kids, fans, got into my suite here. Stellene made a big deal about all the security she had but it was garbage if those kids could get in my damn bedroom. I mean they were freaking teenagers. She had picked us up yesterday from Montauk on the boat, I just thought, nobody's going to get to me on the boat. And since those kids probably told all their friends and posted pictures all over on social media that I was HERE in the house, I wanted to leave. Get it?"

Tinsley raised her eyebrows.

Detective Rosato's voice didn't change. "Last night you were on Mrs. Lupo's yacht with Henry Small and two women."

"Yeah. Two sisters. Local. They were going to cook breakfast. You should be talking to them. They're the ones who knew the guy, Yardley, whatever his name was."

My heart pounded. Yeah, she should be talking to us. And she would.

"Did you know these sisters?"

"No. Well, not really."

Silence.

Eden said, "I saw Allie Larkin dance in Boston but we didn't meet."

Tinsley made a clapping motion.

Eden's voice was tired. "Honestly, Officer, we, me and Henry, had no idea who that guy was."

"How long have you known Henry Small?" Detective Rosato asked.

"We were in a band together—"

The door eased open behind me. Stellene Lupo stopped short when she saw us.

Chapter 22

The force of Stellene's displeasure and shock filled the narrow closet. Tinsley rolled her eyes but slid the wooden panel back into place. I sprang to my feet. Tinsley winced and shifted to her knees. I gave her my hand and helped her up.

Stellene stepped aside, wordlessly, as we left the room and eased the door closed. She walked down the hall to the patio doors. Tinsley and I retrieved our shoes and followed.

Stellene held the door for us, her shoulders back, her chin high, radiating disappointment.

"Sorry, Mom, I—"

Stellene shot her a look. Tinsley dropped her chin.

Stellene smoothed her hair and sat on the chaise longue where Lorel had been just a short time earlier. Stepping from the cool marble hallways of the mansion into the humid July air was like walking into a wall. I squinted in the sun and shaded my eyes.

I groped for something to say. "I should go see my sister."

Stellene patted the seat next to her in the shade where the cop had moved the umbrella. Tinsley walked back into the house, looping her hair around her fingers. Reluctantly, I sat next to Stellene.

She turned toward the harbor and I studied her profile. Everything about her was slender and long—her nose, her neck, her hands, her feet in silver sandals. Tinsley's round face, snub nose, and full lips must have come from her father. Stellene's hair was a perfect blend of white-blond and silver. Silvery like steel. With her rigid posture, her name suited her.

"I'm sorry about all—this." Stellene waved a graceful hand. "This isn't how I thought last night would be."

I couldn't think what to say. Gee, the party on the boat was great until the dead guy showed up.

"Did you—" She turned to me. "Was everything all right on the boat when you went over?"

"Yes," I said. "Wonderful. Actually, we all had a bit too much champagne. We went to sleep early." Probably best not to mention Henry firing the gun. Oh my God, was that the gun that killed Patrick? My stomach clenched. I'd forgotten to mention to the cop that Henry'd actually fired it. How could I forget to mention that?

Stellene's lips turned up. Did she care that much about being a good hostess? I guess she did. She'd caved in to Eden's demand to stay on the boat and look where that got us.

"It's a beautiful boat." This small talk was excruciating.

Tinsley came back outside carrying sunglasses. She handed them to her mother and sat on a low marble bench. "We were talking about taking *Model Sailor* on a cruise, right, Mom? To Greece."

Words from last night surfaced in my mind. That story about Tinsley's party in Greece gone wrong, how she'd ended up in the hospital. Wild child. She didn't look wild now. She looked young, literally keeping her distance from her mother.

"We will." Stellene put on the sunglasses and looked out over the harbor, past the tidy waterfront boathouse and manicured half-moon of sandy beach, tiny Cat Island to the east.

In the distance, a Mystic Bay Police boat circled *Model Sailor,* probably to keep curious boaters away. Every boat had binoculars on board. Every beach cottage had a telescope. Everyone in Mystic Bay must know by now that Patrick Yardley's dead body was just offshore in the boat tied up to *Model Sailor.*

"Did you know Patrick Yardley?" I asked.

Stellene's jaw tightened.

Tinsley nodded. "Yeah, he was a friend of—"

"—A friend." Stellene gave Tinsley a look that said *Stop talking.*

Stellene waved gracefully, dismissing it. "Everyone knew Patrick. New Salt was the place to be, right? We went there for dinner, right, Tinsley?" Sunlight sparked on Stellene's silver jewelry, a medallion at her throat, hammered silver hoops in her ears.

Tinsley looked away.

"You must be exhausted." Stellene stood and turned back to me. "My driver will take you home. We'll show you to the car."

Tinsley stood, hands clasped at her waist.

"Tinsley, call the driver. I'll go with you." Stellene looped her arm through mine. Stellene took me around the house while Tinsley spoke into her phone.

We walked to the garage across a parking area that looked like a luxury car lot. Mercedes. Range Rovers. A red Mini caught my eye. The license plate read THEBAY1. Mac Macallan was here? He'd stayed overnight?

Stellene squeezed my arm as a Range Rover pulled up. "Give my best to your sister."

The backseat of the Range Rover was plush leather. I sank back against it, giving myself up to its cushy embrace. Tinsley stood rigidly behind her mother as we pulled away.

My phone buzzed with a text from Hilda. I'd missed several *Where are you?* texts from Verity and Bronwyn.

They sent Lorel home. Are you still with the police? Aunt Gully texted.

On my way home. Done with police, I texted. At least I hoped so.

My eyelids were so heavy. I struggled to stay awake. As I drifted, I remembered the look Stellene and Tinsley exchanged on the patio, heard the frost in Stellene's voice, the warning to Tinsley.

A friend of a friend.

What had Stellene not wanted Tinsley to say?

Chapter 23

A police car was parked in the driveway at Gull's Nest. I thanked Stellene's driver and ran to the front door where Aunt Gully was waiting. She wrapped me in a hug.

"Lorel's in bed. The doctors gave her a sedative."

I was glad Lorel was sleeping. My own shock and fatigue were enough. I couldn't bear Lorel's sorrow anymore.

"What about the Mermaid?" I asked.

"Hector and Hilda went to the shack to keep things going."

We went into the kitchen.

"What!" My mouth dropped open upon seeing the police officer from Harmony Harbor sitting at the kitchen table with a soup bowl in front of him.

Aunt Gully said, "Paul was going off duty but offered to take us home. Wasn't that sweet?"

I rolled my eyes. "So you had to feed him?"

The police officer's name tag read *Gibson*. He set his spoon down and jumped to his feet.

"He looked hungry." Aunt Gully blew her nose and patted my arm. "You poor thing. Two visits with the police in one week."

"Must be a record," I muttered. Gibson's eyes widened.

"Two? Wait a minute. You're the one who found the body in the bay? With the lobster lady?" he said.

"Yep, that's me." I sank into a chair.

The television blared. It was always on in Aunt Gully's kitchen. The face of Leo Rodriguez, my least favorite reporter, filled the screen.

"So, Paul, how about some cake?" Aunt Gully sliced into a coffee cake. Aunt Gully's friend Aggie baked amazing coffee cake, aka the Food of the Gods. There was also a tinfoil-wrapped loaf of what was probably banana bread and an unidentified Crock-Pot on the counter. With a shock I realized Aunt Gully's friends were bringing us sympathy food.

Gibson looked at me, then at the cake. He was probably picking up on my just-get-out-of-here vibes. "Thanks, but I'd better go."

"Take some with you." Aunt Gully wrapped the cake in plastic wrap and handed it to him.

"If there's anything you need, please give me a call." Gibson handed her a card and edged out of the kitchen, giving me a wide berth. "I'll show myself out."

Aunt Gully smiled at Gibson but her face was drawn, pale. Usually she had the sparkle of a Mrs. Claus, a role she often played at the Mystic Bay Women's Club

Christmas party. I noticed a wad of tissue peeking from the sleeve of her light yellow shirt.

It dawned on me. Not only was Lorel devastated by Patrick's passing, but one of Aunt Gully's best friends was Darcie Yardley, Patrick's mother. A wave of grief washed over me.

"Oh, no. Aunt Gully, have you talked with Mrs. Yardley?" I rose and wrapped her in a hug.

Her shoulders bowed. "I'll go see her tomorrow. Her sister's with her now and Hayden, too." Hayden was Patrick's brother. "I didn't want to leave Lorel alone. What a terrible thing to lose a child, Allie. That poor woman. God knows Patrick gave her enough to worry about, always in trouble that one, just like his father."

Spar Yardley was what old-fashioned novels call a ne'er-do-well. Mrs. Yardley worked double shifts as a nurse while Spar did occasional work in the shipyard or marina, but mostly spent time drinking with his buddies. His troubles with alcohol were well-known in Mystic Bay. Mrs. Yardley was the glue that held that family together.

"Poor Darcie." Aunt Gully's eyes brimmed with tears.

A weight settled on my heart. I'd been so busy thinking of Lorel and myself. Aunt Gully worried about all of us—me, Lorel, Mrs. Yardley.

My friend Hayden. He'd lost a brother.

Aunt Gully and I held each other and sobbed.

All afternoon friends visited to check on Lorel. The murmur of conversation and the aroma of brewing coffee rose from the kitchen. I'd curled up on my bed and turned off my phone, hoping to rest, but my nerves jangled. Every time a car pulled up I jumped. Lorel had spoken with the police while she was at the hospital, but even though they'd let her go, I figured she'd be the one the police would focus on.

I put on a swimsuit, grabbed a towel, and eased down the stairs, pressing close to the banister and straddling the creaky third step from the bottom so Aunt Gully's friends in the kitchen wouldn't hear me. I hesitated, then tiptoed down the hallway and opened Lorel's door.

We'd always shared a bedroom at Aunt Gully's and at the Mermaid Motel growing up. We lived between the two houses; when Dad was away on long fishing trips we'd stay at Aunt Gully's. On the rare nights we were both at Aunt Gully's, we'd share the bedroom and chat as we drifted to sleep.

I realized with a jolt that Lorel started staying in this tiny downstairs study/guest room since she'd gotten back with Patrick.

Lorel lay under the pink quilt Aunt Gully'd sewn for her when she was in her Disney-princess phase. She was so still that for a moment I almost panicked, but then she sighed and shifted under the quilt.

I eased the door closed and slipped out the front door, holding the screen door until it closed so it wouldn't bang shut. A pack of kids on bikes rolled past, towels looped around their necks. We were all heading to the Kiddie Beach by the breakwater.

I tossed my towel onto the sand by a couple of sunbathing teenagers, ripped off my ankle brace, and pushed through the waves to the deeper water. I plunged in and swam toward the raft, barely lifting my face for a breath. I had to move, to burn off the fear that felt like a rope around my throat.

Salt water burned my eyes. I pulled myself up the ladder and flung myself on the rough planks of the raft. My ankle twinged. I was pushing my luck. *Stupid, Allie, stupid.*

Two kids whooped and cannonballed off the side. My mind churned with memories of last night, a night that had begun so magically, champagne and music and a nighttime glide across the bay to a multimillion-dollar yacht with a star and a handsome musician.

And ended with my sister smeared with her boy-friend's blood.

I rested my chin on my knees, tasted the salt water on my lips. With a shock I realized I still wore the blue leather bracelet, the gift from Tinsley. Water droplets flew as I wrenched the bracelet off and hurled it away. Its sparkle dimmed as it sank beneath the dark water. I wished I could throw away every memory of what happened on the yacht.

More kids climbed the ladder, shouting, rocking the wooden raft. One little girl flung herself into the water. Her small body disappeared then resurfaced, her short black hair plastered to her face.

Just like the dead girl on the lobster trap.

I scrambled to my feet and dove back into the water.

Back at Gull's Nest, I showered away the sand and salt in the outdoor shower and threw on a bodysuit and yoga pants. I'd eat something and go to rehearsal. I was glad to have something to think about other than Patrick and Lorel.

In the kitchen, Aunt Gully stood at the stove while the television murmured about the girl with the pitchfork tattoo. She'd been shouldered aside by this tragedy. Guilt added to the emotional weight I carried.

Aunt Gully sautéed salt pork for her chowder. "May Strange is with Lorel," she said.

The door of Lorel's room shut quietly. A middle-aged woman with curly salt-and-pepper hair came into the kitchen.

May Strange had been our doctor since we were little girls. She looked at me over her half-moon glasses, looped around her neck with a rainbow beaded lanyard.

"Allegra, how are you doing, honey?" She was one of the few people in Mystic Bay who always called me and Lorel by our given names, Allegra and Lorelei. I'd always loved my name, especially since I learned it was also the name of a great dancer, Allegra Kent. Lorelei, despite being a fan of the *Gilmore Girls,* disliked her fanciful name and preferred the more professional-sounding Lorel.

"I'm okay." I exhaled. "Worried about Lorel."

"This business with your sister." Dr. Strange tsked and shook her head.

Did Dr. Strange not know I'd been with Lorel on the boat? I didn't feel like rehashing it. I stayed silent as I cut slices of coffee cake.

"She'll be up soon, Gully. I'd say make sure she eats, but I don't have to worry about that with you." Dr. Strange took off her glasses and rubbed them on Aunt Gully's kitchen towel. "Her body's fine. She's a strong-minded girl, so she'll get over the shock. Her broken heart—well, that's not my department."

"Iced tea?" Aunt Gully raised a pitcher. "Coffee cake?"

"Iced tea, please." Dr. Strange jutted her chin at my ankle. "How's your ankle?"

"Much better. The doctor in Boston made me this cool, lightweight plastic brace." I did a *développé à la seconde,* raising my leg high above counter height so Dr. Strange could see the plastic sheath on my ankle. "It's waterproof."

She nodded. "It's amazing the medical advancements possible with all this new technology."

Aunt Gully handed a glass of iced tea to Dr. Strange. "Thank you, Gully."

The term "medical advancements" made me think of a conversation I'd overheard at the party.

"Dr. Strange, what's a living donation?"

"An organ harvested from a living donor. You can do a living donation with part of the pancreas, for example, or a kidney. You can live perfectly fine with just one kidney, so, aside from the usual rigors of any surgery, it's possible to donate without too many ill effects." She tipped her head and looked at me over her glasses. "You thinking about donating to someone?"

I groped to remember the conversation. "Someone at the party was talking about Kurt Lupo. He'd had a kidney transplant. That's why Stellene does a big fundraiser for organ donation."

I bit into a slice of cake. Cinnamon and nutmeg heaven.

"Was Stellene the donor?" Aunt Gully asked.

Dr. Strange sipped her iced tea. "I remember when Kurt got his donation, years ago. No, Stellene wasn't a match. Kurt had someone lined up, but then a young man at the same hospital needed a kidney, and unless he got it right away, he would have died. The young man was a match for Kurt's donor, too. Kurt felt the neediest should go to the head of the line."

"There are some wonderful people in the world," Aunt Gully said.

"Luckily, Kurt Lupo found another donor, a living donor, shortly afterward. Recipients do better with a living donor. Personally, unless it was to save one of my sisters, you'd have to pay me a million dollars for one of my kidneys. And even then, I don't know if I'd do it. Donations can be harder on the donor than the recipient."

"That makes sense," Aunt Gully said. "It must be a new lease on life for the person who gets the organ."

"That's why some people call Kurt Saint Kurt," Dr. Strange said. "Stellene's president of his foundation."

"Excuse me, Dr. Strange." I brushed crumbs from my hands. "I've got to go to rehearsal."

"Are you sure?" Aunt Gully's forehead wrinkled.

Dr. Strange laid a hand on her arm. "That's good medicine, Allegra. Gully, can I still take you up on that offer of coffee cake? I want to talk to you about Darcie Yardley."

"Come right home afterward." Aunt Gully pointed her wooden spoon at me.

"Yes, Aunt Gully."

Chapter 24

Monday, July 6

Full sun streamed in my window the next morning. *What time is it? Ten A.M.!* Aunt Gully had let me sleep in.

My phone buzzed from deep within my bag. I let it ring. Opening my eyes was an effort I could barely manage and I didn't feel up to talking.

Instead of the escape I'd craved, rehearsal had been the opposite. Emotions were already high. The "German soprano" still hadn't shown and I knew why. Everyone had heard about Patrick Yardley's death. Even those who didn't ask questions looked at me with such pity I couldn't stand it. When Margot hugged me, her eyes glittering with questions and false concern, I'd shoved her away.

The house was quiet. Aunt Gully was at the shack. Lorel was probably still asleep. I sat up slowly. Stress had tightened my muscles. Instead of my usual exercise routine, I headed to the shower and let the steamy water pour over me. I considered crying, but I was cried out. So many questions kept running through my mind.

Why was Patrick at *Model Sailor*? Had he heard that Lorel was going there? How would he have found out? Would he be jealous that she was going to the yacht with handsome Henry Small? That didn't make sense. Patrick had never been jealous of another man. Other men were jealous of him.

As unlikely as it was that Patrick had followed Lorel to *Model Sailor,* it was even more unbelievable that someone saw him and followed him there to kill him.

It made more sense that one of us on the boat had killed Patrick. It wasn't Lorel or me. So that meant it had to be Henry or Eden.

My fingertips wrinkled. I wrapped myself in a robe and toweled my hair.

The police would zero in on Lorel, especially if they knew the truth about her breakup. Which I hadn't told them. Which my honest sister probably did.

First things first. I had to learn more about Eden and Henry Small.

Who was Eden? Just Eden, no last name. I searched online. There were thousands of results, and dozens of news stories about her stalkers. No wonder she felt hounded.

After several minutes of research, only one thing was clear. As a headline said, "Eden—Music's Mystery." Little was known of her life, especially before she began her singing career.

Why the secrecy? She didn't seem shy but she was protective of her privacy. Who could blame her? But even her name, Eden. The obvious connotation was Garden of Eden. Who named their kid Eden? Nowadays lots of people gave their children unusual names, but Eden was older than I was. Was it even her real name? Was she hiding her real identity? What could be hidden in your past that was so terrible that you'd want to hide your identity? Was she a criminal?

I shook my head. *Overactive imagination, Allie.* I looked closely as photo after photo of Eden flashed by on the screen of my phone.

One old photo captured Eden onstage at a small club, sitting at a piano in front of a mural of race cars. I looked closer. I'd been in that club. The Checkered Flag in Boston. A guitarist stood behind her at a microphone. I looked closer. The guitarist was Henry Small.

My phone buzzed. Verity and Bronwyn texted. I texted back, *Call you later.*

Next I Googled Henry Small.

The first image I found was from an ad campaign for beer: A picture of Henry, shirtless, cradling his guitar in a rusted pickup truck. His tousled blond curls, his crooked grin, the warm invitation in his blue eyes—the ad made me want to run out immediately and buy beer. Lots and lots of beer.

Aside from the beer ad, there wasn't much about Henry Small online except for a few articles noting that he was in Eden's band and a couple of old photos. I scrolled through and stopped at one taken in a low-ceilinged club, showing him playing guitar behind two young women. A banner behind them read "3H" but the angle of the photo cut off whatever followed the *H*. Three H what? Hearts? Harbors? Hamburgers? Wasn't there an organization called 4-H? Was it a play on words?

I looked closer. It was definitely Henry, skinny but undeniably handsome even in a ratty wife beater T-shirt. The two women, teenagers really, were both blond. One had a round face, her head tilted, her eyes closed, deep into the music. Eden, I was sure. I'd seen her tilt her head that same way as she sang. The other young woman was captured mid-sway, her long hair swinging, her eyes on Henry. Who could blame her?

The Web site was from a VFW hall in Wyoming. A quick search showed that the hall had closed years ago. A dead end.

I scrolled further. There were photos of a sheriff Henry Small, Jr., his father, judging from the same wiry frame and strong jaw. I found a listing for Henry P. Small III from a graduation at Wyoming Central College. Associate's degree in criminal justice. Henry the Third was Henry Small, the guitarist/model from Stellene's party.

Henry had been in a band as a teenager, had then taken a detour into criminal justice, then returned to music. Why? Family expectations? The law had been his family business, just like lobsters had been mine. A guy with a criminal justice degree seemed even less likely to be guilty of Patrick's murder.

I returned to the blurry photo of Eden in the Checkered Flag. I had a friend who'd been plugged into the Boston music scene for years. Maybe he knew Eden.

It was early but Rafael never slept anyway so I called him.

"Rafael!"

"Allie! How's my favorite dancer?"

The truth would take hours to tell. "Wondering if you could help me out. What do you know about Eden?"

"Eden? Well, I don't know her personally. She's the big mystery, right?" He laughed softly. "I know Lars, her partner, kind of. He's out of MIT. He was into really experimental music. All I know is, a few years ago he went to a family wedding out West somewhere. Eden was singing in the wedding band. And when he came back, he brought her with him. Did you meet her?"

"Yes. She's nice," I said carefully. "And I met her guitarist, Henry Small. I thought he was her boyfriend."

"Whatever floats her boat, right? Though Lars seems to be more than, you know, a boyfriend. Eden calls Lars her Creator."

Creator? "Wow, that's strange. What about Henry Small? Hear anything interesting about him?"

"Great guitarist." Rafael was silent for a moment. "Been in a few bands. Something's trying to surface. Some story about a girl leaving him at the altar? Or the other way around? Not sure."

I wondered if the girl had been Eden or the other girl in the blurry photo. I thanked Rafael and ended the call.

Chapter 25

An hour later I parked in the street near the Yardleys' house. Cars crowded the driveway. The gray-shingled Cape was built in the eighteen hundreds and had always been in the Yardley family. When Patrick and Hayden were younger, its flower beds burst with color, the lawn was tidy, the windows gleamed.

Now weeds choked the flower beds, paint peeled off the shutters, and the shades were often drawn. Darcie Yardley had gone back to work full-time at the hospital and the boys' father, Spar, had never had a taste for yard work.

I'd picked a few white roses from Aunt Gully's garden. As I passed through the garden gate propped open with a chipped brick, I felt their insignificant weight in my hand.

A man held the screen door for me as he left the house. I stepped through a mudroom lined with coats and bags hanging from pegs. Just as I remembered it when Hayden Yardley and I were in Theater Club sophomore year of high school.

Spar Yardley sat at the kitchen table, a half-empty bottle of whiskey and an empty glass in front of him. "Laughing Allegra," he said. He always called me Allegra and quoted the Longfellow poem. He rose unsteadily from the table and patted my back. As I kissed his cheek, the smell of alcohol enveloped me.

Spar Yardley was a wiry man with a head of thick brown hair shot through with white. A strong jaw that was handsome on his boys looked stubborn on him. Still, Aunt Gully said he'd been a handsome young man, until the drink got hold of him.

"I heard your sister was in the hospital." Spar's eyes were red, watery. "Is she all right?"

I wondered if the Yardleys knew that Patrick and Lorel had split. The realization that they probably thought that Lorel and Patrick were still a couple sent a wave of panic through me. What would I tell his mother?

"Lorel's home now, in bed," I said. My stomach churned. "She's okay."

"Good, good." He slumped back into his chair.

Mrs. Yardley's sister came into the kitchen and set a cake plate on the kitchen counter. She gave me a quick hug and walked me into the dining room. "Your aunt's already been here, left a pot of soup on the stove, bless her. People tend to go heavy on the cakes and breads but when there's men in the house you need a meal."

"Is Hayden home?" Already I wanted to run, away from Mr. Yardley's sad, drunk eyes.

"Upstairs taking a phone call. You young people, always on the phones." She shook her head. "Patrick was always doing business on his. His whole life was on there."

The night Patrick and Lorel fought on the breakwater flashed in my mind.

Mrs. Yardley materialized at my elbow like a ghost. Normally, she was an energetic woman who worked long shifts at the hospital. Now her eyes were blank and dull. Everything about her was gray. Her curly hair was uncombed, her eyes were shadowed with gray smudges. She even wore a gray baggy sweater over a turtleneck. I tried not to show my shock.

I embraced her bowed shoulders gently, then handed her the flowers. "Thank you, sweet girl." Mrs. Yardley handed the roses to her sister. "Sis, put these on the coffee table, will you?"

Her sister took the flowers and the hint. Mrs. Yardley steered me to the corner of the room. Over her shoulder, school photos of Hayden and Patrick marched up the stairs.

"I'm so sorry, Mrs. Yardley."

Mrs. Yardley's face crumpled. She pressed a lace-edged handkerchief to her lips. "I don't know if it's real yet." She stared through the sliding door to the rusted swing set in the backyard. "At the hospital people pass all the time. It's not real until it's you." Her eyes brimmed. "And then it's still not real. Is Lorel all right? She was admitted to the hospital before we heard about Patrick. Before the police came." Mrs. Yardley swayed. I lunged and caught her as she slumped to the floor.

"Mom!" Hayden Yardley's footsteps pounded down the stairs. Hayden's broad shoulders made the room suddenly feel small. He slipped an arm around his mother. "I'm okay, I'm okay," Mrs. Yardley whispered. She leaned on us and we walked her to the couch.

"Maybe you should lie down again, Mom." Hayden's voice was strained. One of Mrs. Yardley's friends tucked a pillow behind her head and another spread a wooly throw over her legs.

"In a few minutes. Father O'Malley's coming. I want to see him," Mrs. Yardley said.

Father O'Malley would have a challenge doing a service for a young man who never set foot in church. Lightning might strike St. Peter's, or me, for thinking that.

"Allie, hug your sister for me," Mrs. Yardley said.

"I will, Mrs. Yardley, I will."

Hayden laid his hand on his mom's. She closed her eyes. I wondered if she had taken the same sedatives as Lorel.

Hayden stood. "Allie, can you talk for a sec?"

We went out through the sliding glass door onto a wooden deck, into birdsong and heat. A wall-unit air conditioner hummed behind us.

We sat in the shade of a sun-bleached patio umbrella on two plastic lawn chairs. Hayden leaned his elbows on his knees and rubbed his face.

"Allie, I wish I could say I'm surprised. But I'm not." His eyebrows lowered over his warm brown eyes as he watched the swings sway in the breeze.

My shoulders relaxed. Hayden and I could always

talk. "I can't figure out for the life of me what he was doing at Stellene's yacht."

Hayden shook his head. "Patrick was into all kinds of trouble. And this is just between you and me so for God's sake don't tell Lorel, or especially Verity." Verity never could keep a secret. Hayden inhaled. "My brother supplied drugs to Stellene. Bit of coke. For years. Started out doing errands for her, but . . ."

I flashed back to Tinsley and Stellene. "Patrick was a friend—of Stellene's." No wonder Stellene didn't want Tinsley to tell me she knew Patrick.

Hayden continued, "Suppliers and customers coming in on yachts, going out on yachts. He was into some bad stuff. He knew some bad people."

"Hayden." I lowered my voice. "Did Patrick tell you that he and Lorel'd broken up?"

"We didn't talk about stuff like that. Honestly, we didn't talk much at all. But Lorel and Patrick, that was never going to work." Hayden shook his head. "Patrick didn't know what a good thing he had with her." He tilted his chair on two back legs. "Who am I kidding? She was way too good for him. I'm glad she broke it off."

"How am I going to tell your mom?"

"I'll do it." Hayden took a deep breath and righted his chair. "But not today."

Hayden had always had to do the tough stuff. Get his father home when he was drunk. Drive his mom to her chemo appointments. Patrick was never around.

"Have the police been here?" I asked.

Hayden looked away. "You mean after they told us

the news? No. My dad was drinking down at New Salt. My mom called me and I came down from Boston."

"I talked to the cops. Some G-man named Budwitz."

Hayden smiled. "Not your friend Detective Rosato?"

"That's probably in my future."

Hayden sat back, his dark brown eyes troubled. "Allie, did you see or hear anything important on the yacht? You or Lorel?"

A car door slamming in the driveway made me jump. Maybe I shouldn't be telling any of it but I told him everything. "And the worst thing is, Lorel found Patrick."

"She didn't deserve that."

The glass door slid open. Mrs. Yardley's sister stuck her head out. "Hayden, your mother wants you."

"I'd better go," Hayden said. "Allie, let's talk later, okay?"

"Okay." I gave him a hug and walked through the house. I could feel the eyes of the old ladies inside follow me, probably thinking, *Those Larkin girls can't stay away from the Yardley boys*. How things would change when news got out that only Eden and Henry Small and Lorel and I were on the yacht with Patrick. That Lorel and Patrick had had a screaming fight and had broken up. Would people think that one of "those Larkin girls" killed Patrick?

Chapter 26

I drove past the Seahorse, a bar/restaurant in the marina where the hardcore sailors hung out. Maybe someone from Stellene's waterfront crew would be here. It was the closest bar to Harmony Harbor. Maybe they'd know why Patrick was at *Model Sailor*.

I pushed through the door into the snug bar, wood paneled with a low ceiling and red vinyl booths. It was almost noon. Several customers already stood at the horseshoe-shaped bar. The television over the bar played a game show nobody watched.

The bartender was a chum of my dad's.

He jutted his chin. "Allie girl! How's the littlest mermaid?"

"Doing okay, thanks." I leaned over the bar and gave him a kiss.

He leaned close. "You're sure?" His troubled expression let me know that he'd heard about Patrick's death.

"Yeah, and Lorel, too."

He wiped a glass and changed tack.

"Ankle's healing fine, I hear. You're going to be in that new show, right? The missus and I will be front and center."

"Thanks."

"Having lunch?"

"No, I want to talk to somebody." I lowered my voice. "Is anybody here that works for Stellene Lupo at Harmony Harbor?"

He inclined his head toward a man sitting alone in a corner booth. "Ken Jackson. He's been surrounded by amateur detectives wanting to know what happened at the yacht. Man just wants to eat his fish and chips."

Ken Jackson had taken us to the *Model Sailor*. "I won't bother him. Much," I said.

Dad's friend clapped a hand on mine. "You sure you're all right?"

His big warm hand reminded me of my dad's. "Yes."

With a pang I realized that since my dad was still sailing with Esmeralda, *Ondine* would be the first time he'd missed one of my opening nights. Even when he was exhausted from a long day on the lobster boat, he always came to my performances.

I straightened my shoulders and walked over to the corner booth.

Ken hunched protectively around the remains of his fish and chips.

"Sorry to interrupt your lunch, Mr. Jackson," I said.

He stood, wiping his chin with his napkin. "Hi, Allie, right? Please call me Ken. Have a seat."

I slid into the booth and a server put a glass of water in front of me.

"Having lunch?" she asked.

"No, thanks."

"Another beer?" she said to Ken. He nodded.

I didn't know where to start but Ken jumped in.

"I heard someone was taken away by ambulance at Harmony Harbor. Was that your sister? Is she all right?"

"Yes, she's okay. Thank you." I didn't think she was actually okay but I didn't want to talk about it.

"What a crazy situation." Ken shoveled in the last of his fish and French fries. His sunglasses slipped and he set them back on his head. His hazel eyes were surrounded by the telltale white raccoon rings of sailors and others who spent long hours on the water in the sun. "I left you guys at the *Model,* went home to bed, came back to work in the morning, then the, well, you-know-what hit the fan."

He nodded his thanks as the server brought his beer.

"Did you talk to the police?" I asked.

"Yeah, but didn't have much to tell them, except—" He gulped his beer. "Well, it was nothing."

"What?" I asked.

"Cops asked if I noticed anything unusual. Well, yeah, some guest took out one of the kayaks after the party and left it on the beach. Some clothes left on the beach, too. And well"—Ken glanced away—"that you guys were drinking on your way over to the yacht." He gulped his drink.

Great. "You had to be honest."

"Tell the truth and shame the devil, that's what my gran told me."

I wondered what he was thinking. *Probably that I could be a murderer.*

Ken raised his eyebrows. His hazel eyes were keen.

This was an exchange. If I gave him some information, he'd give me some information. I signaled to the waitress to bring Ken another beer. I considered what to tell him, and then told him the bare bones, leaving out the gun and Lorel's hysterics. "We got up and found that RHI tied to the back of the yacht. Called the police."

"And you knew Patrick?" Ken said.

"My sister was in his class at Mystic Bay High School." I wasn't going into any more detail. "You know what's weird? Where did he get that RHI? He and his brother, Hayden, own a lobster boat, *Miranda,* they bought from my dad."

Ken nodded. "Not very stealthy, pulling up in a lobster boat. Those RHIs are quick. Maneuverable. Hard to see, if that's what you're after."

We sat in silence as the waitress set the beer in front of him.

"Like all those movies with the Navy SEALs." Ken chewed a toothpick.

"Did you know Patrick?" I said.

Ken looked away. "Seen him around, you know? Everybody went to New Salt for drinks, that kind of thing."

Maybe Ken had some secrets of his own. I wondered if "that kind of thing" was drugs. "Have you worked for Stellene Lupo long?" I sipped my water, hoping the change of subject and beer would relax him enough to let his guard down.

"Started out working for Mr. Lupo." In the bright sunshine streaming from the window, Ken's hair was shot through liberally with gray and a thin scar looped from the side of his mouth to his chin. "Took care of his sailboats. He had some wonderful vessels." Ken's expression was dreamy. "Liked to sail with his little girl, Tinsley. Nothing scared her. Little reckless, that one, to tell the truth. She capsized more times than I can count. But after Mr. Lupo died we sold the sailboats. Mrs. Lupo likes to kayak, so does Tinsley. We keep the vintage motor craft but mainly she likes those for photo shoots."

"They're beautiful."

He nodded. "Mrs. Lupo got the yacht a year or so back. Helped her sail it down to Miami. She even did a photo shoot on it. Lots of models that day." Ken's grin was lopsided, wolfish. "Mrs. Lupo has been good to work for."

"You know," I said, "I wondered why she didn't have it at the dock at Harmony Harbor. The yacht, I mean."

"*Model Sailor* drafts too much for Harmony Harbor," he explained. The water was too shallow for such a large vessel. "She's berthed at the marina usually. But for the last couple of months Stellene's kept her anchored out." He sipped his beer and looked away, again avoiding my eyes.

Ken was an old, loyal employee. Would he tell me everything he knew, even if it was something his employer didn't want known? Was his loyalty to Kurt Lupo or to the woman who sold his beloved sailboats? I didn't move, just kept my eyes on his face and let the silence stretch.

"Not mine to question. But Mrs. Lupo wants to be alone, like that old movie star. Greta Garbo. Sometimes." He hesitated.

I held my breath.

"She had visitors at the boat." Ken looked away. "Not sure who, she sent us away when she had company. But one night I was sure I saw an RHI heading over to *Model* as I returned to our dock."

An RHI. Just like the one where Patrick Yardley died.

Chapter 27

A look of relief crossed Aunt Gully's face as I stepped through the back door of the Mermaid.

I looped on my apron. "Work's the best medicine, right, Aunt Gully?"

She nodded. "Lorel called. She's up. She decided to work from home on her social media stuff."

Not picking lobster. Spreadsheets and social media, those were Lorel's medicines.

"Aggie's sitting with her." Aunt Gully stirred some spices into her Lobster Love sauce. "I didn't want her to be alone."

I hid my smile. Spreadsheets would be much more fun than teatime with Aggie Weatherburn.

Aunt Gully, Hector, and I fell into an easy rhythm: live lobster into the steamer, plunged into cold water to cool the shell, onto the stainless steel table where we separated the meat from the shell, then layered into golden brown hot dog buns and topped with Aunt Gully's Lobster Love sauce. Repeat. We were so busy that the lunch rush flew past and I was able to keep my thoughts distant from what had happened on *Model Sailor.*

But like a bad dream I couldn't shake, I couldn't push away thoughts of the Girl with the Pitchfork Tattoo. Who was she? What had she been doing in Mystic Bay?

"Okay if I take a break, Aunt Gully?"

Aunt Gully shooed me out. "Of course, honey. I've got some Gals coming in soon."

My phone buzzed with a text from Bronwyn as I got in the van: *Tox report back for drowned girl. She overdosed.*

Slowly I slid the phone back in my pocket. I'd assumed the girl had drowned. This news shook me.

What had happened in her last moments? Had she been at a party on a boat and slipped overboard, under the influence of whatever she'd taken? What about her friends? Had they noticed she was missing? Or had her friends dumped her in the water, hoping she'd disappear on the tide?

Or had she been alone, wanting to end it all?

I mulled this over as I drove to Verity's shop.

Two red beach cruiser bicycles complete with woven baskets leaned against the wall outside Verity's shop. A little bouquet of black-eyed Susans peeked from one of the baskets. Picture perfect.

The sleigh bells jingled as I went in.

"Allie!" Verity put down a handful of men's ties and wrapped me in a hug. "How are you? Why didn't you answer my calls? How's Lorel?"

I lowered my voice. "She's better. Honestly, I'm still just numb."

A guy in a tight black T-shirt and jeans peeked around a rack of men's clothing.

"Henry!" My hand flew to the neck of my sweaty work T-shirt.

Henry Small pushed his sunglasses to the top of his head. "We meet again. How are you, Allie?" He touched my arm gently. "How's your sister?"

"I'm fine. Lorel's okay." The perfect bicycles registered. "Did you guys ride over here from Harmony Harbor?"

"We're here till Eden's done with the show. Stellene hasn't kicked us out, yet. It's strained." Henry scrubbed the back of his head, tousling his hair. "Stellene blames everything on Eden wanting to go out to the boat. She said something about having a guest island but—"

"Cat Island?"

He nodded. "But Stellene says there's a problem with the plumbing. You'd think she'd just call a plumber, right? It's her way of telling us to go. We've overstayed our welcome at the mansion, that's for sure."

Verity's eyes widened as she watched us talk.

"I'm sorry you've been dragged into all this," Henry said.

"Me, too." I almost laughed at Verity's surprised expression. "Henry, this is my friend Verity Brooks."

Henry and Verity shook hands. "Nice to meet you." Verity's expression went soft and dreamy. She held on to Henry's hand a moment too long.

Eden parted the emerald drapes that enclosed Verity's dressing room. She wore a baseball cap pulled low over her forehead and large sunglasses that screamed "incognito."

She put a poufy black silk Victorian gown on the counter. Its jet beading sparkled in the light, reflecting off a huge gilt-edged mirror behind Verity's showcase of estate jewelry.

"Allie!" She gave me a quick hug. I introduced her to Verity.

"You all were on the boat together." Verity reached behind the counter for a large cardboard box, but her hands shook and tissue paper scattered on the floor. She bent to retrieve it.

"Yeah." Henry's blue eyes were troubled. "Did the cops talk to you, Allie?"

"Just one. I think they got what they needed from me but they're still gathering evidence. And when they're done they'll probably arrest Lorel."

Henry shook his head, his brow wrinkled.

Eden leaned close. "Allie, when we had the gun—"

Verity knocked the box off the countertop.

Eden pulled me away from Verity. She, Henry, and I huddled near a rack of mod minidresses.

"You didn't touch it? The gun?" Henry said in a low voice.

"No," I said.

"Just the rest of us," Eden said. "Me, Henry, Lorel."

"I heard popping sounds that night. They must have been gunshots. I wonder if that's the gun that killed Patrick," I whispered.

We shared a long look.

"Some people who were in here—" Eden took her hat off and fanned herself with it— "said that the killer had to be someone on the yacht." The sunlight streaming in Verity's shop window highlighted the multiple silver studs in Eden's ears, her round cheeks, the narrow space between her front teeth.

"Of course that's not true. We didn't even know the guy," Henry said.

I stared out into the street. Patrick's killer had to have followed him to the boat. That meant two people came to the boat in the middle of the night, Patrick and someone else. Who would want to rendezvous with Patrick Yardley?

"You're a million miles away," Eden said.

"Yeah, sorry," I said. "Just thinking that anyone with a boat could have gotten out there."

"Right? Remember when we took that beautiful motorboat out there? All those people were out there watching the fireworks." Eden folded her arms. "I mean, Henry and I were saying you and your sister were too nice to shoot someone. Plus, we were all hammered with that champagne. I don't know about you but I fell asleep like that." Eden snapped her fingers.

"Yeah, you don't drink much, so it hit you hard," Henry said.

Verity's door bells jingled and two women entered. Eden put on her baseball cap and turned her back toward them.

Verity folded the beaded dress. "I can deliver this to you." Her voice sounded hopeful.

"You've got those bikes, right?" I caught Verity's eye. "It'd be hard to carry that bulky box on a bike.

Verity and I can drive the dress over for you." Delivering the dress would be a perfect excuse to get into Harmony Harbor. I had questions for Tinsley and Stellene, especially now that Hayden had told me about Patrick being Stellene's drug connection.

Another thought made me pause. Perhaps there was another reason Stellene didn't want Tinsley to mention Patrick. What if Tinsley was another one of Patrick's girlfriends? What if Stellene was? Would that give them a motive to kill Patrick?

"Isn't this dress a bit different for you?" Verity asked Eden.

"I need a different image for the next album. I want to look serious." Eden threw me a mischievous look. "Serious as a German soprano."

Henry edged into the narrow space behind Verity's counter and reached for a top hat on a high shelf. The mirror reflected his tattooed, muscular arms and broad chest. A red blush traveled up Verity's neck and face. I smothered a laugh, but I'd been admiring him, too.

Then I had the oddest feeling I was back on *Queenie*, the floorboards rocking under my feet. I reached out for the display case to steady myself.

"Awesome hat." Henry caught my eye in the mirror and grinned. "What do you think?"

I looked down, disoriented and blushing.

"Awesome," Verity whispered.

"Awesomely ridiculous." Eden said.

"I'll take it." Henry handed it to Verity with a flourish.

"I'll see you at the theater, Allie," Eden whispered.

"We'll bring the dress and hat to Harmony Harbor."

Verity had a death grip on the box. "Please let them know."

I tried not to laugh. Verity was going to deliver that box herself come hell or high water.

"I'm texting Stellene right now." Eden bent over her phone. "Done."

Henry handed Verity a credit card. She dropped it and Henry bent to pick it up.

I shifted away from the customers and whispered, "Why did you decide to do *Ondine*?"

Eden sighed. "For Lars. He wrote the score. Don't know how the fans will take it, but it was a labor of love. We wanted to do it someplace where I could be"—she waved a hand—"not me. And that guy wanted to come to Mystic Bay." She jutted her chin at Henry.

"Oh?"

"Yeah, this whole thing started because Stellene has a thing for real people as models. She saw Henry and asked him to do—"

"The beer ad," I said.

Eden nodded. "I told Stellene Lars was writing a show for me. Stellene said Broadway by the Bay would be a perfect venue. And then Henry told me he wanted to visit"—she hesitated—"an old friend up here." She cleared her throat then chuckled. "Turns out that it was all just Stellene's master plan to get us up here to play her Fourth of July picnic. The woman's a genius at getting what she wants."

Stellene gets what Stellene wants.

Murmuring voices outside made me turn. Several faces pressed up against the window. Eden's fans had found her.

"Oh, no," Eden said. "How will we get to our bikes?"

I thought quickly. "Forget the bikes. I can drive you back to Harmony Harbor in my aunt's van."

"Oh, thank you! But first would you take us to your aunt's lobster shack?" Eden said. "If it's not too much trouble? I want to get a lobster roll before I go back. Then I can have a car come for us from Harmony Harbor."

"Sure." With handsome Henry? No trouble at all. "The van's parked just outside the back door. Hide in the backseat. I'll be right there."

"Good-bye, Verity. Thank you." Henry waved.

"Good-bye, Henry. I'll deliver the box as soon as I can." Verity sighed and waved.

Eden and Henry slipped out the back of the store.

I whispered the plan to Verity while she rang up a necklace for one of the ladies.

"Wish I was going with you." She sighed. "But I've got to watch the shop. The life of an entrepreneur."

The shop door burst open and a chattering mob of people spilled inside, cell phones at the ready.

As casually as I could, I walked to the back of the store and yanked the green drapes closed on the dressing room.

I hustled to the van. Eden and Henry sat on the floor in front of the bench seat. Henry rooted in a carton marked *Fourth of July Decorations*.

I eased the van into the street. The crowd in front of Verity's shop had swelled to a mob that spilled off the sidewalk. A police car pulled up to the curb by the fire hydrant.

"The life of a star, right, Hil?" Henry put a foam Lady Liberty crown on Eden's hat.

"Hil?" I said.

Eden elbowed Henry. "Giving away my secrets. Well, I confess. I was born Hilda. Just like an old farm wife."

I smiled. The name suited her better than Eden. "I'm Allegra and my sister's Lorelei."

Eden laughed. "You two didn't win the normal-names sweepstakes, either. Yep, as soon as I could, I changed my name."

In the rearview mirror I watched Henry drape himself in a red, white, and blue lei. Eden started singing a cheesy seventies tune about piña coladas. Henry sang along, his voice deep and pleasant. I drove slowly, making the song last, and pulled up to the back door of the Mermaid. "I'll be right back."

"We've got some company, Aunt Gully." I explained the situation to Aunt Gully and Hector, then gathered Lazy Mermaid aprons, T-shirts, and a Gully's Gals hairnet.

I hurried back to the van and handed the clothes through the window. "If you look like you work here, maybe no one will bother you." *Maybe.* Henry and Eden slipped on the clothes, Eden's laugh ringing as she put on the bedazzled hairnet.

Aunt Gully brought out two overflowing lobster rolls. "How awful you can't even eat a meal in peace. You two just relax and enjoy."

Hector set two frosty bottles of lemonade on the picnic table. With his bald head, gold earring, and body-builder muscles, Hector was the last person I'd expect to be tongue-tied around Eden, but he was, instead smiling like a goofy teenager.

"Hector plays your songs all the time." I didn't mention that he played her music for the lobsters. Aunt Gully was convinced that music soothed the lobsters before they met their fate in the steamer. Aunt Gully sang to them, Hector played music.

Eden kissed his cheek. "Hector, thank you. How about a selfie?" Hector held his phone at very muscular arm's length as Eden briefly removed her sunglasses and looped her arm around him.

Henry wolfed down his lobster roll and talked with Aunt Gully about the colorful buoys decorating the side of the lobster shed. "Best lobster roll ever," he said, and gave her a hug. Aunt Gully's cheeks pinked.

One of Gully's Gals came to the door. "We've got a line, Gully!"

Aunt Gully, Hector, and I went back inside the shack. "Do you think people will leave them alone?"

I scrolled to Instagram on my phone and turned it to Aunt Gully. Verity's Vintage was tagged. "Everyone thinks Eden's in a dressing room at Verity's shop."

A few minutes later Hector and I peeked out the back door. Eden and Henry sat, untroubled, at the end of the pier, swinging their legs, looking out at the water.

A Range Rover muscled into the parking lot. To my surprise, Zoe Parker was driving. From director of marketing to chauffeur? Eden and Henry took a selfie with the sparkling river in the backdrop, and then got in the SUV. Hector and I waved as they left.

My phone dinged. A photo of Eden and Henry with

the river behind them was tagged LAZY MERMAID LOB-STER SHACK. Eden'd written, "Best lobster rolls, best views, best friends. Thanks Aunt Gully, Verity, Allie, and Hector!"

"Batten down the hatches," I said. "Code Red. Get ready for a crowd!"

Dozens of Eden fans poured into the shack to find the elusive star. Lorel had caught the mention on social media and drove over. She was distracted, but she was dressed, her hair was combed, and she was smiling.

"Your sister has her spark back," Aunt Gully whispered to me.

Thank you, Eden.

At rehearsal later that evening, the theater buzzed with excitement. The secret about our "German soprano" was out. A storage space was converted into a private dressing room for Eden, complete with security guards. Eden and the actress playing Ondine did a private rehearsal in one of the practice studios. Henry didn't come to the theater.

When rehearsal was over, I ran to the parking lot to see if I could speak with Eden before she left. I was too late. I stood with other cast members, watching the taillights of the Range Rover burn into the darkness.

Chapter 28

Tuesday, July 7

When Lorel, Aunt Gully, and I gathered for breakfast there was an arrangement of yellow roses and carnations on the kitchen table alongside our usual bowl of fruit salad and mugs of tea.

"What's this?" I read the card. *"Dear Miss Larkin, I hope you are feeling better today. If I can be of any assistance, please contact me. Sincerely, Paul Gibson."*

"Paul Gibson?" As soon as the words were out of my mouth, I laughed. My sister had worked her magic on yet another man, the police officer from two days ago. God forbid Lorel be manless for more than a day or two.

"They're very nice flowers." Aunt Gully threw a look at me as she set down a plate of blueberry pancakes.

Lorel shrugged, sipped black coffee, and stared at the television.

Leo Rodriguez's face filled the screen. Over his shoulder, *Model Sailor* bobbed at anchor with a Mystic Bay Police boat tied up alongside.

The camera pulled back. Wind whipped Leo's hair and his knuckles whitened as he held onto the grab rail of a powerboat. The boat rocked and he swallowed hard.

"Water's a bit choppy." I spread butter on my pancakes and dug in.

"Leo does look a little green around the gills." Aunt Gully aimed the zapper at the television.

Lorel held up her hand. "No, wait."

"Not far from where the body of the Girl with the Pitchfork Tattoo was pulled from the dark waters of Mystic Bay, tragedy has struck for a second time." The camera panned from Leo to Stellene Lupo's mansion. "We're less than a mile off Harmony Harbor, the imposing estate owned by modeling mogul Stellene Lupo. Yesterday, the body of a man was discovered in a small boat tied up to Lupo's yacht, *Model Sailor*."

I set down my fork and rubbed Lorel's back.

"The man has been identified as thirty-one-year-old Patrick Yardley of Mystic Bay. Yardley owned the popular restaurant and nightspot New Salt. The entrepreneur was shot several times and died sometime on the night of July fourth or early in the morning on the fifth.

"Police have interviewed the four people who were

aboard the yacht at the time of the death. Police have not yet released their identities."

I hoped they never would.

Tears spattered Lorel's cheeks. Aunt Gully stroked her hair.

"Ms. Lupo declined interviews through her public relations office." Film showed a Range Rover speeding into the tradesmen's entrance of Harmony Harbor.

"Details are still forthcoming. If you have any information to share, contact police at the number at the bottom of the screen." Leo swallowed again and took a deep breath. "Meanwhile, locals are mourning the loss of this successful local businessman."

Film cut to the bar at New Salt. Spar Yardley's face filled the screen. Sorrow carved deep lines in his face, but his chiseled chin was the same as Patrick's. "He was a good boy," Spar said, "a good boy."

Leo continued, "Family and friends are invited to a wake for Yardley at New Salt tonight.

"And in related news, police are still waiting for a break in the case of the young woman discovered by a lobster crew off Cat Island on July second. Officials hope a friend or family member will step forward to identify the body. Will we finally have a name for the Girl with the Pitchfork Tattoo? Reporting live from Mystic Bay, I'm Leo Rodriguez."

"I'm getting dressed." Lorel tightened the belt of her robe and went down the hallway. Aunt Gully watched Lorel go, her lips turned down. She muted the television.

"I wish they'd stop with that name," I huffed. "That girl had other tattoos."

"I wonder if Spar asked Darcie about having a wake at the bar." Aunt Gully took Lorel's untouched plate and poured syrup on her blueberry pancakes.

My tea had gone cold. I put the kettle on and when the water boiled I made tea for myself and Aunt Gully.

I set her cup on the table.

"Thank you, honey."

I put dishes in the dishwasher while Aunt Gully ate. "You're going to the wake tonight?"

Aunt Gully pushed her half-eaten pancakes away. "Of course."

"I've got rehearsal." Maybe the wake would be over by the time I got out.

Aunt Gully read my mind. "If it's a wake run by Spar Yardley, it'll just be getting going after nine. He's the type that likes a real Irish wake."

I wiped down the pink Formica counter. No excuses. But going to the wake would give me a chance to talk with Hayden.

A car horn honked outside. Verity and I planned to run to Harmony Harbor with Eden's dress and Henry's hat.

"Verity and I have a quick delivery to make. I'll see you at the shack."

"You don't have to rush," Aunt Gully said. "I've got some Gals coming this morning."

I grabbed my bag. *Thank you, Gals.*

"What do you mean we can't come in?" I said.

The security guard at Harmony Harbor's main entrance looked up from his clipboard. "You're not on the list."

"But we're supposed to be on the list. Eden put us on the list. Verity Brooks. Allie Larkin."

He shook his head.

"Allegra Larkin?" I tried.

He didn't even look at his clipboard. He shook his head.

Verity and I looked at him. He looked at us. Rather his dark glasses did. His brushy black moustache didn't quiver.

The guard jumped back as Verity scrambled from the Tank and pulled the box holding Eden's Victorian dress from the backseat. She'd tied it with a navy blue organza bow and Verity's Vintage tag. "But I have a delivery for Eden. She's a guest. It's very important. Very, very, very important."

The lens of a security camera above the booth gleamed.

I got out of the Tank, too. I'd have to rein in Verity if she got too pushy. I didn't need any more cops in my life but I did want to talk to Tinsley. This delivery was our only hope of getting into Harmony Harbor.

Verity brandished the box at the guard. The guard threw a look from me to Verity.

I folded my arms and lifted my chin, trying to channel Stellene's air of command.

"Mrs. Lupo says nobody through the gates without special permission. You have to be on the list." The guard's moustache twitched. He moved closer and lowered his voice.

"Listen, I'm not supposed to say anything, but that singer took off anyway. With her boyfriends."

"Eden?" I said. *Boyfriends? He must mean Lars and Henry.*

He nodded.

"Where?" Verity said.

He shrugged.

A car pulled up behind us. The security guard said, "If you please, ladies?"

We got back in the Tank. Verity pulled the car around and we headed back toward Mystic Bay, silent in our disappointment.

"That witch!" Verity fumed. "Eden asked her to put us on the list. I saw her text."

I leaned my head toward the window, letting the air cool my forehead. "It doesn't matter. If Eden and Henry are gone, it's no use leaving their stuff there. But I did want to talk to Tinsley."

"Well, so much for that. No smoking-hot Henry for me," Verity said. "No hanging with a superstar for you."

Suddenly I was bursting to tell Verity Eden's secret. "Remember I told you that *Ondine*'s a showcase for some German opera singer?"

"Yeah?" Verity fiddled with the radio.

"There is no German soprano," I said. "Eden's going to be in *Ondine*."

The Tank swerved. "Are you kidding me? I thought *Ondine* was just going to be some boring opera."

"Gee, thanks."

Verity grinned. "Can I come to rehearsal? And I can give her the dress?"

"She should be there. Opening night's this Thurs-

day." The haunting song from Stellene's party played
in my mind. "She's the Water Witch. She only has one
song, so she hasn't needed to be part of the early blocking and rehearsals." Big stars didn't have to adhere to
the rules everyone else in the theater followed. No
wonder Eden's understudy was so steamed.

"So is she with Henry or not?" Verity said. "Because
if she's not—"

"It's confusing. Maybe they're just old friends. She's
got some guy named Lars, too." I didn't mention that
I also thought Henry was very, very attractive, plus
he'd been so nice . . . and funny . . .

"Did Lorel ever tell Mrs. Yardley that she broke up
with Patrick?" Verity said.

Verity's question brought me back down to earth.
"Nope."

Verity chewed a fingernail. "It would probably
break Mrs. Yardley's heart if she knew Lorel and Patrick broke it off."

"That's what I think." Mrs. Yardley'd always looked
at Lorel as the daughter she never had. The news would
be an additional blow to a woman in a very fragile
emotional state.

As usual, Verity read my mind. "Lorel's going to
have to fake this."

"I hope she does, at least for the wake." I fanned
myself. The air was already muggy and the Tank's air-
conditioning had broken decades earlier. "I could go
for some ice cream." We drove to Scoops, our favorite
ice-cream shop. Even though it was early, a line of
tourists snaked from the order windows.

"It's a tour group," I said. Summer meant we didn't

go to many of our favorite places—the lines were too long, there was no parking, and the workers were too harried to talk. "Let's get some ice cream at the Beach Stop." The Beach Stop was a convenience store that carried pints of Scoops ice cream. Verity drove two blocks down into a strip mall.

Verity pulled into the Beach Stop and we bought a pint of mint chocolate chip ice cream. We put a towel on the trunk of the Tank and ate as quickly as we could as it melted in the July heat.

"I know it was strained with Eden and Stellene but Harmony Harbor's huge. They could have stayed out of each other's way. I wonder why Eden left? Harmony Harbor has security," I mused. "Where would they go?"

"And who wouldn't want all those people to wait on you?" Verity said.

"She probably wants to get as far away from the memory of what happened on that boat as possible. I do." For a second, I saw Patrick in the bottom of the rubber boat. I shuddered and pushed the thought away.

Verity patted my arm. "Death sucks."

"It's funny Stellene would let Eden go. She was all hostess with the mostess at the Fourth of July party, and Stellene arranged for *Ondine* to premiere at Broadway by the Bay." I licked my plastic spoon. I remembered Mac's silent toast to Stellene at the Fourth of July party. His arm around her.

My eyebrow quirked.

Verity said, "I know what that eyebrow means. Spill."

I told her what I'd observed with Stellene and Mac,

how I'd seen Mac's car parked at Harmony Harbor the morning after the party. "Maybe that doesn't mean anything. She must have a billion guest rooms in that house."

"Or they're an item. Well, that's okay. They're the same age and all," Verity said. "They both like theater and music and money."

Talking about Mac had jarred my memory. "Did I tell you that Mac painted a portrait of Margot Kim? It was strange."

"Do you think he's into her?"

"Well, evidently not if he's into Stellene." But there had been another portrait in the studio, the one covered with a sheet. Was that a portrait of Stellene?

"Maybe you'll be next." Verity waved her spoon. "Portrait, I mean. You're much more intriguing than Margot Kim."

"I'm not sure I like Mac's style. He captures the worst in people."

Verity's eyes grew dreamy. "Didn't Henry look adorable in that top hat? Oh, I forgot that at the shop! How did I forget it?"

She scrambled to her feet. I threw the empty pint of ice cream in the trash.

"Let's go get it. And then let's figure out how to get this stuff to them."

I hit my head. "Oh, easy. She's on Instagram."

"Do you think she'll pay attention to that? I'll message her." Verity typed on her phone. "Fingers crossed."

"And if not, just bring it to the theater tonight. And then—" my shoulders sagged—"there's Patrick's wake."

Verity shook her head. "That'll be torture. I guess I'll go. Do you want me to drop you at the Mermaid?"

We got into the Tank.

"No rush this morning. Aunt Gully's got her Gully's Gals. They think it's fun to pick lobster and play restaurant."

Verity laughed. "I could use them to play vintage shop."

"Let's go back to your shop and I'll walk over to the Mermaid. Come with me to rehearsal, then we'll go to the wake together. Um, actually, do you have a black dress I can use?" My wardrobe consisted of workout clothes and a few colorful party pieces.

Verity tapped the steering wheel. "I've got this great maxi. Black with a paisley pattern at the hem. Drawstring waist. It'll look great on you."

We drove to Verity's shop. "All those people in here yesterday chasing Eden made a mess," Verity said as we went inside. She flipped the sign on the door to OPEN. "One of them tore the drape off the dressing room. Then they all whooshed out like a tidal wave."

I helped her rehang the dressing room curtain, then tried on the black loaner dress. It fit, but was a tad short. Story of my life. I dressed and joined Verity. "But I bet a lot of Eden's fans posted what they were doing online. Maybe you'll see more customers today."

"Maybe."

She reached behind the counter and flourished the top hat. "I'd tucked it under here for safekeeping and then forgot it. How could I? It's still warm from Henry's touch." She turned to the mirror, put on the hat, and tilted the brim.

I laughed but remembered Henry's singing in the van, his attentiveness to Aunt Gully at the shack, the way he'd gently draped the robe around Lorel's shoulders. He was more than a hot guy who could play a guitar.

I left Verity rummaging for a box big enough for the top hat. I knew I should get back to the Mermaid, but instead my footsteps turned toward Franque's. When I'd asked him about the jeans, he'd said there was something else about the girl that had struck him. Maybe he'd remembered what it was. Everything that happened with Patrick had taken finding out what happened to the Girl with the Pitchfork Tattoo right off my radar. I felt that familiar stab of guilt.

I stepped inside the green walls of Fashions by Franque. Franque rushed to the front of the boutique.

"Well?" His eyebrows lifted above his heavy frames. "I've been dying for more news!"

"Sorry, nothing new. I thought maybe you'd remembered something," I said.

"Yesterday, a cop came in and asked me about the jeans," Franque said.

His sister walked by with a stack of colorful scarves. "Highlight of Franque's life."

Franque waved her away.

"That's good," I said. "At least they're taking it seriously."

"And I did remember something else," Franque said. "Don't know if it's important."

"What is it?"

"Remember I told you she paid cash." His eyes glowed.

"Yes. Too bad she didn't use a credit card," I said.

He waved it off. "She bought a stack of clothes." He held his hands at his waist and over his head. "And honey, I'm expensive. Get this. This morning, I tried to hypnotize myself to access my memory. I think it worked."

His sister snorted.

Franque cut his eyes at her. "I'm a visual person. It helped that they had the tattoo on television so I could see it again." He closed his eyes and pressed his fingers to his temples. He began to speak with a rolling cadence. "I see her hand with silver rings. I see her hand reaching into her handbag. I mean that's the kind of thing I remember. I see the sexy sundress but an awful cheap bucket bag, pleather, probably bought at one of the marts. And then I see . . ." He paused.

"Yes," I breathed.

"She didn't have a wallet," Franque said. "That cheap bag was stuffed with stacks of cash."

I texted Bronwyn and a few minutes later she knocked at the screen door of the Mermaid's kitchen.

Aunt Gully insisted we eat, so we took lunch, chowder for me, a lobster roll for Bronwyn, chips, and drinks out to the picnic table behind the shack.

Bronwyn wore her beige Mystic Bay Police Intern polo and black biking shorts. "How's Lorel doing?" She had leaned her bike against the lobster shed.

I shrugged. "She's not one to share." Some sisters shared everything, but that wasn't Lorel and me. We were too different. "She doesn't want to talk about it."

Bronwyn bit into her roll. "About the Girl with the Pitchfork Tattoo—"

My heart rose. "Did someone ID her?"

Bronwyn shook her head. "A few people came in, some legit, some nuts. Some disappointed people thinking that she was their family member. I mean, she fit the description for several missing persons, some who've been missing for years. Some of these folks were clutching at straws, since she died so recently. It's sad."

I sipped lemonade. "I've been thinking about it. This girl could've gotten the pitchfork tattoo after she went missing."

"Precisely. All this Girl with the Pitchfork Tattoo stuff is misleading," Bronwyn said.

"So the police are going on—"

"The basics. Missing persons reports. Age, height, weight, hair color. Eye color. Dental records would work. But they can only match those after they have a potential ID."

"What color were her eyes?" I shuddered, thinking of her face.

Bronwyn licked her fingers. "They think brown. The autopsy wasn't as helpful as they thought. The body had deteriorated quite a bit."

I set down my spoon.

Bronwyn smiled. "You'd never want to be a medical examiner. Thing is, I think they've discovered something big."

"What?"

Bronwyn chewed a handful of chips. "Just a feeling I got. Sometimes with identifications, the police'll withhold something, something only a friend or family member would know."

"But you don't know what that something is?"

Bronwyn's round, cheerful face was usually an open book to me, but since she'd begun working with the police department she'd become more reserved. More careful.

She ran a hand through her hair. "The investigators are playing that close to the vest. Hopefully I'll be able to find out soon. There've been some leaks to the press. But it sounds like you found out something from Franque?"

Had Bronwyn Denby changed the subject on me? I told her what Franque said.

"That's cool. Wish I didn't have to run." Bronwyn put on her bicycle helmet. "I'll pass it to the investigative team."

"I have a feeling Franque's probably already called them," I said.

"Thanks for the lobster roll, Aunt Gully," Bronwyn called in through the screen door of the shack. "Talk to you later." She wheeled her bike into the parking lot.

I set my chowder aside. What did Franque's memory mean? The girl had a lot of cash? And what was the "something big" that the police were holding back?

Bit Markey emerged from the lobster shed with a bucket. His nose was sunburned but he was smiling.

"You got some sun." I gathered my trash and tossed it in a bin.

Water sloshed as Bit set down the bucket of live lobsters. "Sammy and I went out in his canoe."

"Cool. Where'd you go?"

"Cat Island and the Harbor Patrol didn't even hassle us this time." He grinned, picked up the bucket, and hurried into the kitchen.

They're probably too busy with all the drama with Patrick and the girl I'd found, I thought with a pang.

Chapter 29

That evening, rehearsal was halted while the director blocked Eden's scene. Henry and I sat in the darkened audience toward the rear of the theater.

Onstage, Eden spoke with the director while crew jockeyed scenery into position. Our director, a New York hotshot in skinny jeans and a polo shirt, was usually peremptory with cast and crew, but now was deferential, almost servile in Eden's presence.

There was a quiet buzz of repressed excitement. Cast and crew hovered in the wings. Several sat in the audience. The secret was out. Everyone in the theater knew that the "German soprano" was the chart-topping pop star. Professionals who'd performed with some of the most famous names in theater lurked in the wings, star-struck. Thank goodness. This took pressure off me. I couldn't stand to talk any more about Patrick or the Girl with the Pitchfork Tattoo.

"So you're a magical mermaid." Henry grinned. "Freaking awesome."

"The technical term is sea sprite." I smiled but was conscious of my sweaty rehearsal clothes. "I'm only in the show for a couple of set pieces, one when Eden sings in her grotto and one at the end, when Ondine and her lover go to mermaid heaven."

"A tragic but beautiful end." Henry gave me a sly, sideways smile.

"That's showbiz."

"And you do it all in the harness," he said.

"Mostly I'm sitting on that boulder." I pointed to a craggy resin boulder stage right. Two crew members draped it in netting and fake seaweed. As Henry turned his head, the scales-of-justice tattoo on the back of his neck peeked above the collar of his snug T-shirt.

"So you're not exactly dancing," Henry said.

"Lots of arms, some harness work. It's perfect since I can't dance full-out on my ankle yet," I said.

"How'd you hurt your ankle?" Henry turned toward me and put his arm on the back of my seat. My heart rate kicked up a notch. I became hyperaware of the heat of his skin, only a millimeter from mine.

I told him the whole story, from the tumble down the stairs back in Boston to my harness training.

"I hope you're healed one hundred percent soon." Henry's voice was soft in the dim light. "It's hard when you can't do what you love. What makes you feel alive."

Violin music swelled from the orchestra pit. Eden's voice soared.

Henry's eyes met mine.

"Not just feel alive, you know? What keeps you alive," Henry said. "Like oxygen."

My mouth went dry. "Like oxygen."

Eden's song ended and the cast burst into applause. Henry took his arm from the back of my seat and clapped. "I hear her sing almost every night and I still can't get enough."

The spell was broken. "I heard you and Eden left Harmony Harbor."

"Yeah." Henry snorted. "Stellene and Eden. Two divas together. Fireworks!" He made an exploding gesture with his hands. "Stellene's pissed because she can't get on her yacht. It's a crime scene but all she talks about is taking Tinsley to Greece. So we're going to stay with Mac Macallen in Mystic Bay."

"Oh, the guest barn," I said.

"The barn's fantastic, but it's probably only a matter of time before people figure out we're there. I mean Eden. Nobody cares about me."

I care. His eyes held mine and I had an overwhelming urge to kiss him.

Verity slid into the row behind us, bumping the back of my head with a box. "Ow!" I rubbed my head.

"Eden's amazing." Verity handed the box to Henry.

"My top hat's in here?" Henry said.

"Oops! I forgot. This is Eden's dress." Verity looked at the ceiling. She was a terrible liar. "I'll get the top hat to you at Harmony Harbor as soon as I can."

"We've moved from Harmony Harbor," Henry said.

"Oh! I bet they're sad you've left," Verity said.

"Well, maybe Tinsley." Henry laughed. "When we were at Harmony Harbor she followed me like a puppy. She's bored to death but can't go out until she heals completely from her kidney transplant."

A shock went through me. "She had a kidney transplant?"

Verity gasped.

Henry nodded. "When she was in Greece, she did some binge drinking, some local stuff that was practically poison. Ended up hospitalized, kidneys shut down. Almost died, plus she lost the sight in one eye." I remembered the way Tinsley tilted her head when she talked to me. "She was on dialysis, then they got a donor. Just like her dad, I guess. Tinsley really wanted us to stay but Eden, when she makes up her mind, there's no changing it."

Suddenly the nurse made sense. The way Tinsley always covered her mouth with a scarf. Like a surgical mask? "That's why she wasn't with the guests at Stellene's Fourth of July party," I said. "Why she had a nurse and stayed away from the crowds." Except when she was talking to me in the conservatory.

"Guess so," Henry said. "Doesn't seem that she's very good at following doctor's orders."

Abruptly the houselights came up.

Verity jutted her chin toward the front row. "Who's that guy?"

I hadn't noticed the man in the front row. His bushy brown hair was pulled back in a man bun. He turned and I recognized the man I'd seen with Eden at Harmony Harbor.

"Lars," Henry said. "Eden's partner."

"Are they a couple?" Verity blurted. "Eden and Lars?"

"Yeah. They've been together for years." He gave me a look. "Did you think Eden and I were—"

"Um, no." I exchanged a look with Verity.

"We traveled together here on the yacht and I think that made some people assume we're a couple. I heard some people at the party talking. We're just old friends," Henry said.

That was what I'd sensed. They acted almost like brother and sister. Eden had known how he liked his tea. The blanket and pillow on the couch of the yacht—he hadn't slept in the stateroom with Eden, he'd slept on the couch.

Henry stood. "Please don't tell anyone where we're staying."

"Don't worry," I said.

"I won't. I don't even know," Verity said.

Henry took the large box, thanked Verity, and joined Lars.

I turned to Verity. "Did you really forget the top hat?"

Verity smiled. "You bet I did."

Chapter 30

After rehearsal, I showered and changed, and Verity drove us to New Salt. A sign on New Salt's door said CLOSED FOR PRIVATE EVENT. Music thumped, but it was Irish folk music. Spar was giving Patrick an Irish wake.

Verity's phone rang. "I have to take this. I'll catch up," she said.

I walked into the bar.

A dozen women, all in their mid-twenties to thirties like me and Lorel, all beautiful, in black dresses too short and heels too high for a wake, crowded one side of the room, flicking mascaraed looks at each other. They made me think of crows trapped in a cage. *A murder of crows.*

There was also a knot of middle-aged men in too tight navy blazers and suits. Cops and Harbor Patrol, many of whom stopped by the Lazy Mermaid for free coffee.

"Hey, when'd you go all *Miami Vice*?" One cop

joked with two men in dark jackets over pastel polos, heavy gold watches, and slicked-back hair. The men laughed too loud then sipped their beers. A couple of the cops shifted their weight and threw shamefaced looks toward the dining room, where Mrs. Yardley sat with friends in a booth.

Kate, the hostess who'd seen me run up to Patrick's room, stepped through a door to a patio. She leaned on the railing overlooking the marina and lit a cigarette.

I joined her. "Can I ask you a question?"

She glanced at the girls at the bar and rolled her eyes. "It's a wonder Patrick got any work done. It's a wonder anyone got any work done. All these beautiful people busy hooking up."

In my mind a little video clip played, Lorel climbing those narrow, steep stairs to Patrick's room, a little drunk, leaning on Patrick's muscular shoulder. I pushed the image away.

Kate pulled a wrap tight across her shoulders. "Nothing lasted with Patrick. It was just sex. You had to understand that."

Light caught on the delicate gold nose ring and deepened the lines that ran from her nose to the corners of her mouth. Kate was older than I'd thought. She was quiet for a moment, a moment that told me that these were Patrick's words to her. "You have to understand that."

Another woman carrying a torch for Patrick Yardley. I swallowed my impatience.

I remembered the night I'd stormed up to Patrick's room, still wondered if the story Margot had told me was even true. What had she said? *I heard he was living with some waitress who moved in with him back in May.* "A young woman worked here recently, who was dating Patrick—"

Kate finished her drink in one long gulp then swirled the ice cubes. "Lots of girls worked here. And dated Patrick."

"Really recently. Um, you know my sister, Lorel, right? Was he living with someone else right before her? Or at the same time?"

"Your sister was a little different for Patrick." Kate blew a long stream of smoke. "Classy. Not that I was keeping track, but they all marched right past my hostess stand. But, yeah, there was one. Just before Lorel. She was different, too."

"Different? In what way?"

"First woman who seemed to call the shots with him," Kate said.

My heart fell. *Lorel didn't call the shots with Patrick.* "What was her name?"

She frowned and rubbed her eyes. "Hayley, I think. She worked here for a while, a month or two ago. Then left. Petite. Cute. Long straight blond hair." She put her hand almost at her waist. "Beautiful," she said begrudgingly. "Lots of girls work here then leave. A regular revolving door, that's New Salt.

"I actually thought to myself, Patrick's finally met his match." Kate snorted. "She stayed even less time than most. He didn't hire them for their work ethic, that's for sure. She was gone fast." She took a long drag on her cigarette.

"Do you know where she lives?" I asked, "or where she moved after she left Patrick?"

She shook her head. "We worked different shifts. Maybe another one of the servers or kitchen staff would know."

So Margot wasn't lying. Poor Lorel.

I hurried through the restaurant, to the stairs to Patrick's room. I wanted to see if there was anything in his bedroom that could tell me about Patrick's last hours, would tell me why he was at Stellene's yacht. Police tape crossed the bottom of the stairway. Just as I was about to slip under the tape, a man came through the door at the top of the stairs and started down.

I stopped short and turned aside, pretending to check my phone. The guy was trying to be quiet but he was heavy. It was one of the men I'd seen earlier, with the too tight jackets and slicked-back hair. He bent awkwardly and hunched under the tape, knocking it away from the wall on one side. He put it back, patted his hair into place, and walked back to the bar.

And what are you looking for, Mr. Miami Vice? I made sure the coast was clear then hurried up the steps. A notice posted on the door was written in all kinds of legalese. I ignored it and turned the handle. There were scratches on the wood by the lock.

Had that guy broken in? Just now?

I slid in and closed the door, dampening the Irish music from downstairs. I flicked on the light and gasped.

Drawers from Patrick's desk and bureau had been pulled out and the contents dumped on the floor.

Clothes had been pulled from their hangers and the pockets turned out. I stepped carefully around clothing and papers and went to the bedroom. The mattress and box spring slumped off the bed frame, as if someone had checked underneath. Bedding ripped from the mattress was piled in a corner.

In the bathroom the cabinet was open, bottles, boxes, and toothpaste jumbled in the sink. Even the top of the toilet tank had been removed.

I kicked through the pile of clothes on the floor, shirts and ties, workout gear, a leather jacket. I bent to pick up a blue striped tie, ran my fingertips over the costly silk. Lorel had bought it for Patrick. I tossed it back into the pile of clothing.

There was Irish music blaring and lots of conversation below, but not loudly enough to hide the sound of someone tossing furniture around like this. Had this been done earlier, before the wake? Had it been like this before the police came? Or had the police done this?

What did Patrick have that someone wanted badly enough to do this? What were they looking for?

Drugs? Money? Maybe a list of Patrick's drug clients?

What had Lorel said? *His backers. Not nice people.*

I eased the door open and hurried downstairs.

Just as my foot touched the bottom step, Mr. Miami Vice turned the corner.

For a moment I froze, then I dipped my head sideways, so my hair would fall forward and hide my face. I giggled and pretended to sway. "Oopsies, ladies' room isn't up here. It's over there." I scurried across the hall to the ladies' room and slammed the door.

Two girls waited in line for stalls.

My pulse raced. I felt unsafe, exposed. Who were these people searching Patrick's room?

I counted to twenty and peeked out the door. The man was gone. I returned to the bar.

Hayden was there, surrounded by a bunch of guys holding bottles of beer.

"Hayden, you have to see something." I tugged his hand and he followed.

Hayden pointed at the police tape. "Allie, you went inside?" Disbelief tinged his voice.

"Yes. Just go in," I muttered. "You have to see it."

Hayden was quiet as he surveyed the first room, then pushed into the bedroom and the bath, taking stock. His breathing quickened. "Allie, go downstairs, okay?"

"But Hayden, the guy who was up here, he's downstairs in the bar," I said.

Hayden took a deep breath and took both my hands in his. His forehead was creased, his warm brown eyes worried. "Okay. Show him to me. Then, I want you to stay away from this, okay? Don't get yourself involved. Please, Allie."

I didn't trust myself to speak. I nodded. My stomach twisted. What had I done? Broken through police tape, gone someplace I wasn't supposed to be. Why was Hayden acting like this? He wasn't a cop. He worked for a marine insurance company.

"Sorry, sorry," I whispered as I followed him down the stairs. I turned my head away. I couldn't face Hayden's disappointed eyes.

We stood in the hall near the bar. "Which guy?"

"Black slicked-back hair, big gold watch, Easter-egg-yellow shirt, navy blazer."

"I have to make a phone call." Hayden hurried toward the kitchen.

Music blared from the bar, along with conversation and too loud laughter. Tears pricked my eyes as I went into the dining room.

Lorel sat at a table with some friends from her high school softball team, an untouched glass of sparkling water in front of her.

At the far end of the dining room, away from the loud music, Mrs. Yardley sat in a booth with her sisters and some friends, including Aunt Gully. They had full glasses of wine in front of them along with a photo album and an arrangement of white roses and daisies. They were enduring this raucous wake. I slid into the banquette seat next to Aunt Gully.

Aunt Gully rummaged in her purse, took out two boxes, set them on the table, and handed me a package of tissues. "Oh! I forgot about these."

Our eyes met.

White jewelry boxes. Tinsley's gifts from our night catering at Harmony Harbor.

Please don't let anyone ask what these are.

"What is it, Gully? A present?" Her friend Mrs. Ruth took a box, opened it, and took out the necklace Tinsley had given to Aunt Gully.

Aunt Gully's mouth made a little red lipsticked *O*. The whole evening at Harmony Harbor washed over me.

Mrs. Ruth held the necklace to the light. "Oh, that's

beautiful!" She tilted the medallion by the flickering candle on the table

Aunt Gully took a deep breath.

"Where did you get it?" Mrs. Ruth asked.

"Oh, it was a gift, from a job." Aunt Gully waved her hand vaguely.

A couple of the women exchanged glances, friends who knew that the only catering job we'd done was at Harmony Harbor. Mrs. Yardley probably knew it, too. A terrible reminder of what had happened to Patrick, not that she needed reminding.

Mrs. Yardley took the necklace but passed it on without looking at it.

The women murmured in appreciation as it went around the table. "What's the design?"

Aunt Gully said, "Not something I'd pick out myself. It's so dramatic."

Mrs. Yardley excused herself and we slid out to let her and two friends out of the banquette. They headed toward the restroom.

Everyone exhaled.

Aunt Gully took the medallion and boxes and shoved them back into her purse. "I forgot I had them."

"Makes sense, though," Mrs. Ruth said.

"What makes sense?" I asked.

Mrs. Ruth taught Classics at the college. "It's a wolf. Stellene's last name, Lupo, means wolf in Latin."

"I didn't know that. Allie, what did you do with your bracelet?" Aunt Gully asked.

"I threw it away." My mind replayed the moment the bracelet sank beneath the water at Kiddie Beach. This was a conversational door I didn't want to go through. "Excuse me." I went to Lorel's table.

Lorel stared down into her drink while her friends talked quietly. I knelt next to her and whispered, "Lorel, can I talk to you a sec?"

"What is it?"

"Those backers, the ones that you said weren't nice guys. Are they here?"

Instead of looking around, Lorel ran a finger around the rim of her drink. "Allie, I have no idea. It's just something Patrick said. About his backers putting the screws to him to pay back his loan. Those were his words. I just thought, you know, people who put the screws to other people are not nice people."

"Come here, I want to show you something. Please." I tugged Lorel's hand and hustled her into a dark corner of the bar, ignoring her friends' raised eyebrows. "See those guys in the bar?" I nodded toward Mr. Miami Vice and his friend.

Lorel rolled her eyes. "I don't know them."

She crossed her arms. Should I tell her? "Lorel. I just saw that guy with the slicked-back hair go into Patrick's room upstairs."

"They can't get into it. It's locked. There's police tape," Lorel said.

"I know it's not locked because I just went in there. The room has been torn apart. It's a total mess."

"What!"

Verity came into the bar. Several people did a double take. She wore a black fifties wiggle dress that fit her like a too tight glove. She'd paired it with dramatically high black stilettos.

"Hi." Verity sipped from a martini glass as she joined us. "Thought I'd need something to fortify myself before I talk to Mrs. Yardley. Oh, hi, Lorel."

Hayden hurried through the bar, his head bent over his phone. My cheeks flamed.

Patrick's whole life was on that phone. Who'd said that?

"Do you remember when you tried to call Patrick the night of the, er, Fourth," I asked.

"Yes." Lorel rubbed her head. "The call went to voice mail." Her voice caught. "He never let my calls go to voice mail."

"Well, yeah, he dropped his phone in the water, right?" Verity sipped her drink.

Lorel stared. "How do you know that?"

Verity choked. We exchanged glances. *Verity knows because I told her I'd seen Patrick drop his phone in the water the night you broke up with him at Kiddie Beach.*

"So what do you do with a wet phone?" I said in a rush.

"I dropped mine in the bathtub once," Verity babbled. "Actually got it to dry out in rice."

"I remember that," I said. "When we found Patrick, in the boat, I didn't see a phone." My thoughts tumbled. Someone had searched Patrick's room. Mr. Miami Vice went up to search, too, but wasn't carrying anything when he left. What would be important to find? I remembered his aunt talking about Patrick's phone. What did she say? *His whole life was on there.* Where was it?

I pulled Lorel by the hand. "They have rice here, right in the kitchen."

"I'm sure you're going to explain this wild-goose chase somehow." Lorel followed.

We hurried into the kitchen. In a pantry to one side, huge bags of rice were stacked on stainless steel shelving.

"You think Patrick left his phone here?" Verity ran her hands over the large bags.

"You ladies need some help?" One of the chefs came over, nodded when he saw Lorel. "Hey, how you doing, honey?"

"Okay, Sean." They hugged. "How 'bout you?"

Sean rubbed his face. "Not good. It's hard."

"This is my sister, Allie, and her friend Verity." Lorel's manners were automatic and beautiful. She always did the right thing at the right time. Thank goodness, because I was ready to explode. I was so sure the *Miami Vice* guys were bad guys and that we had to find Patrick's phone *now,* before they did.

So I could show Hayden I wasn't a screwup.

"Did Patrick ask you for rice, recently, by any chance? For a wet cell phone?" I waved at the rice bags.

"Yeah," Sean said. "As a matter of fact we were joking about it. I gave him a smaller bag and he took it with him."

"With him?"

"Yeah, I was closing up the kitchen on the night of the third. Really late. Next day was the Fourth"—Sean winced—"so easy to remember."

"Did he stay here that night?" I pressed.

He shrugged. "Not sure. I remember he went out the back door with the bag. Said he was going to check on his boat. That's the last time I saw him."

His boat. Miranda. Maybe he wouldn't have left his phone here. Maybe he knew that bad guys were waiting to search his room.

"Thanks. Nice to meet you, Sean," I said.

"Good night, Sean." Lorel went back into the bar and Sean returned to his work.

I tugged Verity's hand and we exited through the door into the rear parking lot. The door thudded shut, muffling the music and kitchen noise.

The parking lot wasn't the most attractive spot at night. Cars and empty crates jammed the gravel near the Dumpster. Verity and I walked around the building, Verity holding my arm as she tottered on her stilettos in the gravel.

The marina wrapped around one side and behind New Salt. Docks with dozens of boats ran the length of the parking lot.

We hurried down the uneven planks that led to the marina. *Miranda,* my dad's old lobstering boat, was in a slip at the very end of the dock. The music and light of New Salt faded and the gentle creaking sound of boats on the water grew louder as Verity's shoes tapped on the uneven wood.

Verity and I stepped onto *Miranda*. Usually, seeing the boat was like visiting an old friend. Lorel and I loved her almost like a pet. In the darkness, I picked my way across the floorboards, threading through stacked lobster pots and coils of rope.

"Why're we here?" Verity whispered.

"Because." I shined my cell phone flashlight on the lobster pots. "Patrick left with rice. Out the back door."

"Maybe he was going home." Verity sat in the wheelhouse. "He probably parks in the back lot."

Where was home for Patrick Yardley? That apartment over the bar? His old room at his parents' house? Somewhere else?

"Maybe." I wondered if the police had taken his car. As I searched, I told Verity about the tossed room and the man I'd seen coming downstairs.

"So you think these guys want Patrick's phone?"

"Maybe?" Could they be looking for something else? "Maybe there's something incriminating on it."

"Maybe the police took it already," Verity said.

"Probably." I sighed. "Maybe if we could find it we'd figure out what was up with Patrick. Why he came out to Stellene's yacht." I shined the light under some flotation devices. "I know he needed money. But he didn't sell *Miranda*."

"Well, that's sweet, right?" Verity said. "He knew selling *Miranda* would upset Lorel."

Sweet wasn't how I'd describe Patrick Yardley.

I shined the light around the boat, spotlighting wooden planks, coiled rope, and stacks of lobster traps.

"I remember my dad and his friends talking about smugglers who used lobster traps to transport drugs," I said. "I wonder if that's why Patrick kept *Miranda*."

"Smuggling drugs in lobster pots?" Verity asked. "Oh. I guess you could. One boat drops off in the pot and another pulls the stuff in."

"And nobody's out there watching," I said.

The boat swayed gently underneath us.

"What are you sitting on, Verity?"

She stood and I shined my light on a large cooler.

"Open it!" I said.

Inside, my cell phone spotlighted a bag of rice. "No way," Verity whispered. She aimed her cell phone light at the rice as I dug inside the grains. "Oh my God, that's a cell phone!"

"Oh! Fingerprints."

I dropped the phone back into the rice.

"Hang on." Verity reached into her clutch. "I have this great silk scarf." She handed it to me.

"Wait! I should keep it in the rice, right?" I wrapped the scarf around the entire bag with the phone in it and put it in my purse. My bag bulged.

"Now what? Isn't that evidence?" Verity said.

A blast of Irish music made me look up. Two shadows moved from New Salt's kitchen door. Large shadows. They passed under a security light by the fence. Mr. Miami Vice and a friend headed toward the dock.

"Verity," I whispered. "Shh! Don't say a word. I bet they're coming here." I dialed my phone.

"You mean the bad guys? Oh, God," Verity grabbed my arm. "We're at the end of the dock. We're trapped."

"Mystic Bay Police," said a staticky voice on the phone.

"Two men are trespassing on *Miranda* at the Mystic Bay Marina," I whispered. "Behind New Salt restaurant. End of the dock."

"Name, please."

I hung up and smacked my head. "That was dumb. I just called with my own phone, and then didn't give them my name."

"What do we do? I don't want to jump overboard. I'll ruin my dress," Verity said.

"And the phone, we can't get it wet again." I weighed our options. These guys were bad, no doubt about it. I could feel it. But would they hurt us? Were they looking for the same thing we'd just found? The rice and phone were so heavy—I shifted my bag under my arm like a football. The handbag felt radioactive, as if there was a sign blinking above it: WHAT YOU ARE LOOKING FOR IS IN HERE.

"Too late for us to run." I kept my phone in my hand, ready to redial the police. "Let's just play it cool. Come on."

Verity and I walked back toward New Salt. "Play it cool," she muttered, "play it cool."

"Casual, right? Walk slow, right past them, then we'll run." Verity's shoes clacked on the boards. "If we have to run, kick off your shoes."

Mr. Miami Vice spread his arms, blocking our way. "Ladies."

Verity looked at me. I swallowed hard but lifted my chin.

"What brings you out here?" he said.

Verity put her hands on her hips. "None of your business."

"We're just taking a walk." I shined my cell phone light at his face. He flinched and raised his hand.

Verity fumbled hers out of her clutch and aimed it at Miami Vice's pal.

"Hey! Cut it out!" he said.

He looked familiar. "Have I seen you before?" I lowered my phone.

Blue lights strobed from the parking lot. The police. Miami Vice's friend rubbed his eyes then looked at me. His expression relaxed. "Oh, yeah, you're one of the girls from Aunt Gully's lobster shack. How you doin'?"

The men's posture relaxed. Everyone laughed nervously. Miami Vice's head swiveled to the police car in the parking lot. "Well, you young ladies have a good night." He stepped aside.

Verity and I hustled past them.

Two police officers stepped onto the dock. "Are you the ones who called about trespassers on a boat?"

I hurried toward them, dragging Verity with me.

Farther down the dock near *Miranda,* a match flared. The cop shined a flashlight on the two men.

"Hey, that you, Alex?" the cop shouted.

Miami Vice's friend shouted, "Yeah, just getting some air. We were at the wake."

The cop was one I knew from the shack. He lowered his voice. "Allie, is everything all right?"

"Do you know those guys?" I said.

"Yeah, they work Harbor Patrol."

Harbor Patrol?

"Sorry to bother you. There's no one there now." I knew those guys would wait until we all left and board *Miranda* the second we were gone.

The cop walked back toward the restaurant with Verity and me. "Sorry to bother you. I thought I saw someone on *Miranda,*" I said.

"So you're sure everything's all right?" he said.

I nodded.

"Okay, well, this gives me a chance to pay my respects to Patrick's parents, then I'll take a walk down along the dock and make sure everything's okay."

We said good night, then Verity and I got in the Tank. She locked the doors.

The red ends of Miami Vice's and his friend's cigarettes burned like devils' eyes as they stood in the dark near *Miranda*.

"Should we film them?" Verity held up her cell phone.

"I don't know what to do, Verity. Every time I do something it's wrong. Those guys are Harbor Patrol. Maybe they're investigating Patrick's murder."

But that didn't seem right. Harbor Patrol managed the harbor, making sure people got the right boat slips, stuff like that. If there was a problem they helped boaters. If it was a true emergency they called the Coast Guard or the Mystic Bay Police.

"You know, it's funny, Verity, I remember seeing Harbor Patrol guys at the shack, the Harbor Patrol SUV rolling past our house, always when Lorel and Patrick were there. I think they were following Patrick." I shivered. "And Lorel."

Plus, tonight Mr. Miami Vice's body language had been so threatening. "We're going to have to be very careful, Verity."

"We have Patrick's phone," Verity said. "Now what do we do with it?"

A voice in my head said, *Take it directly to Detectives Rosato and Budwitz.* "We need gloves."

Verity reached into her glove box. "I have gloves we can use. Winter ones with the touch-sensor thingies."

"You actually keep gloves in your glove box?"

"That's why they call it a glove box."

I put on the gloves and pulled the phone from the rice bag, trying not to spill rice all over the front seat. The screen lit up.

"Yes!" Verity said. "It works!"

"Oh, great," I said. "He has it set so his password is his thumbprint."

"You can still override with a password," Verity said. "What would Patrick use? An important word. His girlfriend."

I tried *L-O-R-E-L.* Verity watched as I spelled. It didn't work.

"I just remembered something." I sighed. "When Aunt Gully got her phone and she couldn't figure out how to use it, she always used to get locked out. I don't want this locked."

"Or have the battery die." Verity opened the glove box. "I have an emergency battery-charger." I attached the phone to the charger.

"I just thought of something when you were typing Lorel's name," Verity said.

"What?"

"What if there are, um, photos of Lorel on there? You know. Girlfriend photos."

"Oh, God." Would my straight-arrow sister let her boyfriend take nude photos of her? I wrapped the rice bag and phone in the scarf and stuffed it into Verity's glove box. "I can't let the cops look."

"So what do we do?"

I texted Lorel and Aunt Gully that I was leaving. My stomach churned. "The phone is evidence, right? It has to go to the police. I guess it's more important to catch

Patrick's killer than worry about some random cops looking at naked photos of Lorel. Besides, Lorel just wouldn't." *Would she?*

I ran my hands through my hair. "I can't just walk in to the police station. Detective Rosato makes me nervous. What if they want to question me? I have to dance in *Ondine*. I can't get arrested."

"Or Lorel," Verity said. "She makes a lot more sense as a suspect than you."

"True."

We watched the red dots at the end of the dock. The two men were still there, talking.

"What if the police ask where we got the phone?" Verity said.

"I need advice. I'm going to call Bronwyn." I dialed. Bronwyn picked up.

"Hi Bronwyn, are you at work?"

"Nope. At home relaxing with a forensics textbook. How about you?"

"Verity and I aren't far from your house. Can we stop by?"

"Sure. I'll be on the porch."

Chapter 31

Verity pulled up to the curb in front of the Denbys' sprawling red Cape. Bronwyn's dad was a carpenter who'd added on to the house with the arrival of each new child. The driveway was jammed with beaters that belonged to Bronwyn's four teenage brothers.

We climbed the stairs to the porch, where Bronwyn sat holding a mug. Video game explosions blasted from a screened window.

"Hi, want a drink?" Bronwyn still wore her Mystic Bay Police outfit.

"No, thanks," Verity said.

I shook my head no. We settled on sagging wicker chairs ringed around a table cluttered with citronella candles, books, and newspapers. A floor lamp spilled a circle of light onto Bronwyn's chair, the cord looped over the windowsill from inside.

"Did you just get off work?" I asked.

"Not too long ago. Stuff's happening." She straightened a stack of paperbacks on the cup-ringed coffee table.

Verity looked from me to Bronwyn. "Patrick Yardley stuff?"

Bronwyn frowned and shook her head.

"Stuff about the girl I found?"

Bronwyn's shoulders relaxed. The Patrick stuff made her nervous. Obviously, I didn't want to ask her to do anything against her vows or whatever it was with the police. But I had nowhere else to turn for help.

"Sounds like someone has stepped forward to ID the body of the girl you found." Bronwyn smiled. "She's coming to the station tomorrow."

"Oh, that's great," I said.

"Won't it be awful to view the body?" Verity said.

Bronwyn exhaled. "Well, the body's at the medical examiner's office. Anyway, viewing the body would be problematic. When they've been in the water they deteriorate pretty quickly."

Verity clutched her throat.

"Viewing of the body is often done with photos now, not the actual body. They got photos before she got, er, too unrecognizable. And we were able to get photos of the tattoos. Hopefully they can get an ID, then they can verify with dental records."

The way Bronwyn said "we" when she talked about the police made me hesitate. How on earth would I bring up the phone? Still, my heart rose. "That's the best news I've heard in ages."

Bronwyn smiled. "There's something else. Remember I told you how the investigators withhold information, so they have a detail that only a legitimate friend or family member would know?"

I nodded.

"Well, the investigators have been playing it very close to the vest, but I found out. The girl had another tattoo. A semicolon."

"A semicolon?" Verity said.

"People who struggle with addiction get it. Or people who tried suicide."

"What does a semicolon have to do with suicide?" I said.

"A semicolon's not a period," Bronwyn said. "A period's a full stop. A semicolon means you continue."

The video game battled with the sound of crickets chirping. The microwave beeped and footsteps thudded upstairs.

"That's so sad," Verity said.

Bronwyn again adjusted the stack of paperbacks. I'd never felt uncomfortable around her, but now I felt like she was on one side of a wall and I on the other.

"It's Lorel, isn't it?" I said. "You heard something about Lorel."

Bronwyn shook her head. "I shouldn't even shake my head, Allie. It's hard because I shouldn't be telling you anything."

I leaned toward her. "But what if we could help?"

"How?" Bronwyn crossed her arms.

"What if we found Patrick Yardley's phone? Huh?" Verity said.

Bronwyn bit her lip. "Oh, boy. Okay. I'm not even going to ask. If you guys have anything that could help with the investigation, bring it to the police right away.

Not me. The police. Actually, call and don't touch anything." She gave me a level look. "Or is it too late?"

"We—" Verity began.

Bronwyn winced and held up a hand. "Don't tell me. There's something called the chain of evidence." Her voice was urgent. "Please tell me you didn't take anything from the crime scene."

"Crime scene?" I was thinking fast. No. Not from Stellene's yacht. From *Miranda*. Was that a crime scene?

I shot another warning look at Verity.

"The boat where Patrick died, right?" I kept my voice neutral. "Or Stellene's yacht?"

"They're treating the boat and the yacht as the crime scene. We don't know enough about what happened that night," Bronwyn said.

"I told the guy, Budwitz." I tried to act relaxed. "Nothing happened. We were all drunk on Stellene's champagne."

"Just as long as you didn't take anything from the rubber boat or the yacht." Bronwyn held my eye.

I was starting to think that Bronwyn knew a lot more about what was going on than she was telling.

"What's this 'chain of evidence' thing that's so important?" I said.

"It means that it must be very clear that evidence was not tampered with or moved from its original discovery point without meticulous recordkeeping." Bronwyn sounded like she was quoting from her textbook. "Otherwise it could get evidence thrown out of court." Her eyes bored into mine.

"Okay." The phone was evidence, I was sure of it.

Had I just messed up evidence that could identify Patrick's killer? And prove Lorel's innocence? My mouth went dry.

"So was that why you stopped by? To talk cop shop?" Bronwyn said.

With a pang I realized the only times I'd called Bronwyn this summer were when I had a crime question.

I thought fast. "Actually, no. You know how I told you there's a German soprano singing in *Ondine*? There's no German soprano. It's really—"

"Get ready." Verity bounced in her seat.

"Eden!"

"No way!" Bronwyn beamed. "Are you kidding? I love her music."

"I had to tell you," I said. "I'll make sure you get a comp ticket at the door for the premiere Thursday night, okay?"

Bronwyn was still smiling as we said good night. Her smile made me hate my lying self.

Crickets kicked up a hellish chorus as Verity and I returned to the Tank.

"Allie, does this mean we have to return the phone to *Miranda*?" Verity turned the key.

I nodded. "But for now, let's keep it in the glove box until I figure out a plan to put it back."

"Without those creepy mob guys seeing us," Verity added.

I ran my fingers through my hair. "And get the detectives to *Miranda*."

"Without getting caught."

I slumped against the door. "Without getting caught."

Chapter 32

Wednesday, July 8

The next morning, Lorel curled up on the couch as I stretched on Aunt Gully's braided living room rug. She was dressed but had wrapped her old comforter around her shoulders.

I realized that with everything that had happened, Lorel and I still hadn't talked about that night on *Model Sailor*. It took a few minutes for me to figure out how to begin. Talking with Lorel was like using muscles that had stiffened from disuse.

"Lorel, do you remember the popping noises? After we went to bed on Stellene's yacht?"

Lorel shook her head. "I didn't hear anything. I slept like a rock, got up, walked to the back of the yacht, saw Patrick lying in the RHI. I don't remember much after that except for Chief Brooks. How disappointed he looked when he asked about partying with Patrick Yardley."

I didn't know what to say. I sat next to her and rubbed her arm.

"I've got to get back to Boston. I know Dr. Strange and Aunt Gully wanted me to stay and rest, but I'm fine." Lorel didn't say it, but I knew "get back to Boston" meant "get away from here."

"Will you come to my opening night tomorrow?" I asked.

Her surprised expression told me she'd forgotten it.

I lowered my eyes. It was too early in the morning to feel this disappointed.

"Did you see the gun in the boat with Patrick?" I couldn't remember seeing it. "Was it the same gun you all had touched?

Lorel winced. "Yes. I don't know if it was the exact same gun, but it looked just like it. I didn't pick it up."

"That's weird." I stood and paced. "If you were the killer, wouldn't you drop the gun overboard? Nobody would find it. Actually, why not untie Patrick's RHI altogether? The boat would drift away."

Lorel threw the comforter off. "I don't want to talk about this anymore." She stalked down the hallway. "I've got to prep for phone meetings."

The killer had left the murder weapon behind. The killer shot Patrick and left—or went back to their bed on *Model Sailor* and pretended to be surprised in the morning.

Through Aunt Gully's big picture window I saw a Mystic Bay Police cruiser. I darted to the window. It parked in front of Fast Times, the house next to the breakwater.

Oh, no. Were they going to report Lorel's fight with Patrick Yardley on the breakwater at Kiddie Beach?

"Let's roll, Allie!" Aunt Gully called from the kitchen.

We gathered our things and left the house. Aunt Gully cast a quick look at the police car as we got in the van and headed to the Mermaid, but said nothing.

The more I thought about it, the more I thought that the answer to Patrick's murder was on his phone. The answer to the question that churned in my mind.

Why did Patrick come out to Model Sailor *that night?*

Car horns blared on Pearl Street as a giant news truck with a satellite dish tried to squeeze down the narrow street. Now what?

"Early for a traffic jam," Aunt Gully said as we went into the Mermaid's kitchen.

Hector turned from the steamer. "Have you heard? Eden's been brought in for questioning about the death of Patrick Yardley!"

"News trucks, tourists, Eden fans. It's a perfect storm of traffic," Hilda said.

"I'm going to get some lobsters from the shed," Hector said as he stepped out the door.

"Don't even think of going up there!" Hilda called after him. Aunt Gully went back outside to hang up her American flag.

My phone buzzed with a text from Bronwyn. *Eden's at Plex. Stellene told cops that Eden was spooked and may have mistaken Patrick for a stalker.*

I read the text out loud.

Hilda scoffed. "Since when does Stellene tell the cops what to do? And how does Stellene know what happened on the yacht?"

I picked up a knife and helped Hilda chop cabbage for cole slaw.

"I wonder about Stellene," I said. "I heard she was buying drugs from Patrick."

Hilda shook her head. "Forget drugs. It was probably an affair. It's Patrick Yardley we're talking about."

And Ken Jackson had told me he'd seen an RHI like Patrick's visiting *Model Sailor.*

Hilda's voice faded as I considered. *Maybe Stellene had an affair with Patrick, but wouldn't it be more likely that Tinsley would? They were closer in age. But Tinsley's been ill and she's recovering from a kidney transplant. She could still fall for him. What had Henry said?* She followed me like a puppy . . . Maybe she'd followed Patrick. . . .

Hilda's knife hit the wooden cutting board with an especially hard *thwack.* "Well, she has people to do everything for her. What was her assistant's name? Zoe? Maybe she did the drug buying for Stellene."

Hilda was back to the drugs. "Zoe Parker?" I couldn't imagine her doing something as sordid as buying drugs. "Doesn't seem the type." But she had, despite her fancy title, done lots of errands for Stellene. Buying vintage clothes for a photo shoot. Chauffeuring Eden and Henry.

As I worked, I ran the scenario concocted by Stellene over and over in my mind: Eden thought Patrick was a stalker and shot him. But no matter how many times I visualized this scenario, it didn't hold water. Eden had been drunker than any of us.

I pictured the blanket and pillow in the saloon. Henry had slept there. If Eden went to the saloon to get the gun, she would've seen Henry. Wouldn't it make more sense to wake him for protection, instead of silently taking the gun and shooting Patrick on her own?

I froze, knife in midair. What if Eden went to the saloon and woke Henry? Would he have shot Patrick for her?

A guy who had criminal-justice training probably wouldn't grab a gun and shoot a complete stranger. Or would he?

The blur I'd seen pass my window on the yacht. Eden was blond. Henry was blond.

I shook my head. It still didn't make sense that Henry or Eden would shoot Patrick. If they'd confronted him—especially with a gun—Patrick probably would've left.

Probably.

I was itching to find some answers. With a shock I remembered *Ondine*. Would Eden be freed in time for rehearsal? Opening night was tomorrow.

Verity slipped in through the screen door. "Allie, I've got actual adult supervision at the shop. Let's make that delivery."

"Delivery?" Hilda said.

"For Henry Small. The top hat? Remember? The one I forgot?" Verity said.

Aunt Gully bustled back in.

"Is it okay if I take a break?" I said.

Aunt Gully looked at the clipboard with the schedule. "Looks like Aggie's coming in. Go on, you two."

I stripped off my plastic gloves and hung up my apron.

"If you see Eden, you'd better let Hector know," Hilda said.

"Will do."

Verity and I got in the Tank. "I've still got to figure out how to get the phone to the police," I said.

"Well, while you plan, I've got to give this top hat to Henry," Verity said. "Now, where did you say he was staying?"

After ten minutes of excruciatingly tangled traffic, Verity and I pulled up to Mac's house. She nodded at the red barn, freshly renovated from the tip of the rooster weathervane to the double garage doors and swaths of golden lilies at the foundation.

"So that's where he's hiding out." She sighed. "All rustic and romantic."

"I wonder if Henry's at the Plex waiting for Eden." I tapped my feet.

"You're so jumpy," Verity said. "The cops aren't interested in you."

"I'll believe it when they catch Patrick's killer."

"Well, they're doing their jobs." She patted my knee. "And they aren't going for Lorel. That's good news."

"It's only a matter of time. There was a cop at Fast Times this morning," I said.

"Sheesh. Well, for now let's just focus on handsome Henry."

"You're relentless."

"I want to make sure he gets his hat. From me. Personally." She smoothed gloss over her full lips. "Something to remember me by."

"I hate to tell you this, Verity, but I don't think he'll have any trouble remembering Mystic Bay." We got out of the car.

Mac's red Mini was in the driveway. "I'm going to let Mac know we're here." I knocked at the front door, but there was no answer.

We tried the bell at the side door of the red barn/ guesthouse, but no one answered there, either. In the backyard, a powerboat bobbed at Mac's dock. The garden was lush with color, the scent of roses intensified by the heat.

"Guess he's not here. Should we just leave it?" I said.

"Are you out of your mind!" Verity hugged the box close.

"Hello?" Mac took off headphones as he stepped through the French doors onto the patio. He wore a painter's smock that was buttoned wrong and splattered by light blue paint. "Oh, hello, Allie." He pulled the doors shut behind him.

Verity and I crossed the lawn. "Hi, Mac. You remember my friend Verity?"

"Of course. Hello, Verity." He looked at the paintbrush in his hand as if seeing it for the first time. "Well, you've probably heard about Eden being questioned by the police. What a disaster! Even if they let her go, I don't know if she'll be in the best frame of mind for the performance tomorrow."

"Mac, I'm sure it'll be fine." Verity and I climbed

the steps. I squeezed his arm. "Her role doesn't require a lot of movement onstage." *Oh my God, what a mess. Eden's understudy is good, but she's no Eden.* I smiled and spoke with conviction. "Eden's a pro."

"Maybe you're right," Mac said.

"Sorry to interrupt your painting." I angled to his side, looking through the French doors.

"Usually it's so calming but not today." He stepped toward the next set of French doors. "Can I get you something from the kitchen? A beverage?"

"No, thanks," Verity said. "So, is Henry here?"

"He stepped into the studio a few minutes ago when I was painting." Mac's forehead wrinkled. "Suddenly he said he wasn't feeling well. Said he needed to go for a run. Do something physical. Probably all the stress."

"Oh, too bad." Verity pulled me away. "We'll come back."

As we crossed the lawn and went back to the car, I threw a glance back at Mac. He waved and I waved back. I got the feeling he wanted to be sure we left.

Verity and I got in the car. "We'll try later. Now what?" Verity pulled from the curb and I turned the radio to the all news-station.

A voice with a New York accent said, "Sources confirm that police expect a break in the case of a body discovered by a lobster crew in Mystic Bay, Connecticut. They report that an identification will be made shortly. The young woman has become known as the Girl with the Pitchfork Tattoo because of her distinctive tattoo. And now to the sports desk—"

I turned the radio off.

"A break!" I breathed. "Finally! She does have someone who cares."

"Fantastic," Verity said.

We discussed who the girl might be as we headed back to the Mermaid. Just as we were about to turn onto Pearl Street, Verity spun the wheel toward the Plex. "I had a brainstorm. Maybe Henry ran over to the Plex to keep Eden company."

I slouched in my seat. "No, Verity! No police!"

"I'll just be a sec." Verity cruised slowly past crowds clogging the sidewalk. "Please, I'm besotted. I may never get to see him again." A truck pulled out from a space right in front of the Plex. Verity swooped in. "Henry may need a happy moment."

"Verity!" I groaned.

Verity ran up the steps as a woman exited. Despite the humidity, the woman was dressed in a pair of baggy jeans and a shapeless long-sleeved tunic with embroidered red, white, and blue dolphins. A brown pageboy haircut swung in front of her face, which was already almost hidden behind big, round glasses. A plastic shopping bag swung from her arm. She strutted, stiletto heels ringing on the cement sidewalk, toward a Range Rover. The red soles of her designer shoes flashed with each step.

That strut. Those gorgeous shoes. That had to be Zoe Parker. But why had she disguised herself like this? I got out of the car and hurried after her. The designer shoes certainly were hers, but the rest of her outfit looked like she bought it at a rummage sale. What was up with her hair? Was that a wig?

"Zoe?" I called.

The woman hunched her shoulders and threw herself into the Range Rover. She ignored me as I waved from the sidewalk. The Range Rover screeched from the curb.

I got back in Verity's car. Moments later, she returned.

"No Henry." She slid the box into the backseat.

"Did you see that woman with the brown hair and dolphin tunic?" I said. "Going out when you were going in?"

Verity snorted. "Hard to miss that dolphin tunic."

"That was Zoe Parker."

"Zoe Parker? In that outfit?" Her eyes widened. "The guys at the desk were talking about her, well, about the lady with the dolphin tunic. Said she wanted to identify the body of the Pitchfork Tattoo girl. Then she got a text and suddenly she said she was mistaken. She ran out."

"Why would Zoe know the Girl with the Pitchfork Tattoo?"

"*If* it was Zoe," Verity said. "Are you sure? 'Cause when she was in my shop she looked like something out of *Vogue* or *Ebony*."

"Maybe I'm mistaken." But my gut told me otherwise. That strut was Zoe Parker.

"Now what?" Verity started the car.

"I have to figure out how to get that phone back on *Miranda*."

Verity said, "I wish Bronwyn wasn't so ethical."

"The cops might think we tampered with the phone since we moved it." I wrapped my hair around my finger.

"Do you think the mobby-looking guys're still watching *Miranda*?"

Harbor Patrol had an office in the marina. "We have to assume they are. We've got to go right into their lair."

"How do you think they fit into all this?" Verity asked.

"Remember Patrick had backers for New Salt, right? Lorel said they weren't nice guys."

"But these guys are Harbor Patrol," Verity said.

I thought aloud. "Harbor Patrol manages the harbor and marina, but they aren't cops. There's an actual Mystic Bay Police boat for law enforcement. And of course, there's the Coast Guard. But they're for big stuff. I think Patrick was smuggling in his drugs and the Harbor Patrol guys were helping. Nobody would suspect a thing if they were going all over the bay in their boats."

"Why were those guys following Patrick?"

"Lorel said Patrick owed lots of money. I bet he had something they still want. Drugs. Information, on his phone, I bet. Money." *Money. Who had said something to me about stacks of money?* "We have to get the phone back onto *Miranda*. Then make sure the real police get there to find it right away, before the bad guys can."

"Right. And now the bad guys know what we look like. We can't just waltz back in there. I don't suppose Lorel would help us out and put the phone back for us?" Verity asked.

I looked at her.

"Okay. No Lorel."

Bit Markey and his friend Sammy clacked down the sidewalk on skateboards, slaloming through tourists, oblivious to surprised looks and angry gestures.

"Verity, I've got an idea. Stop here. I need to talk to Bit. And get a newspaper."

Chapter 33

"Are you guys ready?" I said.

In the backseat of the Tank, Bit and his friend Sammy nodded.

"This sounds like secret-agent stuff," Bit said. Sammy and Bit did a hand-slapping, fist-bump thing.

"We're just putting something back where it belongs," I said.

"Decoy ready." Verity'd changed back into the hot black wiggle dress from the day before. She'd added a black straw hat and sunglasses. She'd stand out like a sore thumb at the marina.

Perfect.

I took the phone in the bag of rice from the glove box and rewrapped it in a sheet of newspaper.

"Operation Put the"—I glanced at the boys in the backseat—"Stuff Back Where It Belongs is about to start."

We rolled into the lot behind New Salt. "I'm pretty

sure I saw a wall phone in the kitchen." I didn't want to use my own cell for the call I was about to make. I didn't need to get caught making another phone call to the police in twenty-four hours. "When I'm sure I can use the phone, I'll wave out the door and you guys go into action."

"Got it!" Sammy and Bit fist-bumped again.

Everyone got out of the car. My stomach twisted. This plan had to work.

The marina bustled. Crowds of tourists, not just boaters, strolled along the dock. Verity and the boys looked at me expectantly.

"Remember what I said. Act casual. Walk slowly. We don't want to call attention to ourselves. Except for you," I said to Verity.

I handed the newspaper-wrapped phone to Bit. "*Miranda*'s the last boat on the right." I pointed. The boys nodded. "Wait for my signal."

I knocked on the kitchen door. Chef Sean opened it. "Hey, how are you? Allie, right?"

"Yes, hi, Sean. I need to make a phone call and my phone's dead." I pointed to the wall phone next to a broad screened window overlooking the parking lot and marina dock. Verity and the two boys waved. "Could I use that?"

"Sure, sure." He went back to his worktable. His knife flashed as he chopped a mound of onions.

The phone was one of the old-fashioned wall ones like Aunt Gully's. I waved out the window then dialed Detective Budwitz.

Heads swiveled as Verity minced toward the Harbor

Patrol office. Sammy and Bit dashed the opposite way down the dock toward *Miranda*. They took off like sprinters bursting from their blocks. *No!*

Almost immediately, two older men in khaki shorts and golf caps collared the boys and started lecturing them loudly. One of the men actually waved his cane.

Uh-oh.

Budwitz's phone rang and rang.

"You guys are staying open?" I said to Sean but I kept my eyes on the boys.

"The owners thought it best to keep going," Sean said.

"How many owners are there?" I tried to keep my voice neutral. *Let those kids go, you meddling old men!*

Bit and Sammy hung their heads as the men on the dock wagged their fingers and lectured. The boys glanced at each other and slowly backed away from the men. Bit held the newspaper-wrapped package close to his chest.

Sean's knife was a blur. "Patrick had quite a few backers, some local, some from Boston. We'll close when we all meet to scatter his ashes. We're working on that with the Yardleys."

Budwitz, pick up! Just when I was sure it would go to voice mail, he answered.

"Budwitz."

"Um." I lowered my voice, turned my back on Sean, and hunched over the phone. "Could you please come to the Mystic Bay Marina? Behind New Salt. You'll find something you need to see on a boat called *Miranda*."

"Who's this?" Budwitz barked.

"Please hurry. *Miranda,* it's a boat at the end of the dock, behind the New Salt restaurant." I hung up.

Now the two old Golf Cap Guys followed behind Bit and Sammy. One still held Sammy by the shoulder of his T-shirt but Sammy squirmed sideways and broke free. He and Bit sprinted away from their captors, knees high. The men shouted and followed.

Verity turned at the noise and headed back, wiggling and tripping in her tight dress.

Sean came closer, the knife held in midair. "What's all the yelling about?"

"Not sure. Thanks." I hurried out to the parking lot.

People on the dock turned to stare as the boys dashed to the boat, their footsteps thudding on the wooden planks. To my horror, Mr. Miami Vice stood at the end of the pier, talking on a cell phone. How had I missed him? He was still watching *Miranda*?

Watching for me?

The boys jumped aboard and dove into the wheelhouse. The two old men shambled after them. "You hooligans can't play here!" they hollered.

I ran past Verity as she huffed toward the boat.

The Golf Cap Guys stood on the dock and shouted toward *Miranda.* "You boys better have a good story! Where are your parents?"

Mr. Miami Vice saw me and smirked. I passed the two old men and leaped on aboard. Sammy and Bit, chests heaving, sat on the cooler, just as Verity had the night before.

The two older men stopped short of boarding. "Do you know these boys, young lady?"

"They're with me." I caught my breath. "We all knew *Miranda*'s owner, right, boys?"

"The dead guy," Bit said to Sammy.

"Oh, yeah, on the boat." Sammy nodded.

"This is Allie's boat, anyways." Bit folded his arms. Sammy mirrored the action.

Not anymore.

Verity panted up behind the two men, hand pressed to her side. She took off her hat and fanned herself. For a long moment, all the men looked from her to me to the boys.

Sammy stood and straightened his Red Sox T-shirt. "We should pay our respects to the dead guy." He bowed his head. Bit stood and did the same.

I blinked. The Golf Cap Guys looked at each other. One took off his cap and the other followed suit. They bent their heads. Verity bowed her head. I dipped my chin but kept an eye on Mr. Vice. His eyes were hidden behind his sunglasses, but his hands were balled into fists, his stubbled jaw hard with repressed energy.

Sammy cleared his throat. "Dearly beloved, we are gathered here to remember our brother, ah—" Sammy looked up at me.

"Patrick." My throat closed up.

"And are sad that he died," Sammy continued. "We hope that he's in heaven."

Fat chance.

"With you, our Lord. Amen."

"Amen," I said.

Verity burst into tears.

The Golf Cap Guys looked at each other. "Amen." They put their caps back on. "Very sorry for your loss," one said. The other nodded to me then the two men walked back up the pier.

I wanted to wipe the smirk off Mr. Vice's round face. "So, were you a friend of Patrick's, Mr.—"

"We're all friends of Patrick's." He spat on the dock. "Well, nice service, kids." He made a right-this-way gesture.

"We're not leaving. I wish to commune with Patrick's spirit for a bit." Verity stalked in front of him onto the boat.

"That was a beautiful service." I threw a glance toward the parking lot. No police car. *Hurry.* "How did you know how to do that, Sammy?"

"My dad's a chaplain in the navy," Sammy said. He and Bit clambered over coiled rope to the rectangular metal lobster pots in the back of the boat. Mr. Vice shifted from foot to foot. My pulse quickened. Had he seen the boys put the phone back in the cooler?

A gray car swooped into the parking lot. "Look," Verity said. "That looks like an undercover cop car."

Mr. Vice gave me a long look then sauntered away down the pier.

"Verity, take the boys and go," I said when Mr. Vice was out of earshot.

Bit tugged my hand. "Just run with us, Allie!"

"This isn't the way we planned it," Verity said.

"Half what we planned. You guys did great." The boys beamed and fist-bumped again. "Go with Verity. Wait for me in the Tank. I'll be right with you. I want to talk to the police for a minute but I don't want you involved. There's a chance they'll let me go." *A snowball's chance.*

Budwitz and a woman in a dark suit and sunglasses strode toward us. Verity glanced back at me, and then tugged the boys' hands. The woman was Detective Rosato. I groaned. The two detectives stopped short of coming on the boat.

"Miss Larkin." Budwitz put his hands on his hips. "Was that you who called? I thought I recognized your voice. I hope this is important. We take false police reports very seriously."

Verity and the boys reached the parking lot, throwing looks over their shoulders.

"Yes. Hi, Detective Budwitz. Detective Rosato."

Detective Rosato's face betrayed no emotion.

I thought quickly. "I was here last night for Patrick Yardley's wake. And I thought, maybe the police don't know that this was Patrick's boat. It might be important to the investigation. I wanted to be sure you knew that this boat was his."

Budwitz and Rosato shared a glance. Maybe they didn't know.

"Thank you, Miss Larkin. You may go," Budwitz said.

Relief and confusion flooded me. "I can? Are you sure?"

"Yes." Detective Rosato pulled her phone from her jacket pocket.

I stepped onto the dock. *Dismissed.* "Also, you should know that some of the Harbor Patrol guys have been very, very interested in this boat."

They looked at each other. Such good poker faces.

"Thanks," Budwitz said.

That's it? Thanks? "Okay."

I moved as quickly as I could back to the Tank without actually running. I threw a glance back at them. After I helped her with the last murder investigation in Mystic Bay, I thought Detective Rosato and I had an understanding. Evidently not. I was a little hurt.

I got in the Tank and slammed the door. "Drive! Before they change their minds."

Chapter 34

At rehearsal that evening, the magic of the previous day evaporated. Cast and crew were devastated, going through the motions. What if the police arrested Eden? What would happen to the show? Mac Macallen sat in the last row, his tie askew, his shoulders slumped. I sighed and adjusted my mermaid tail.

"Places."

Halfway through Act One, just as Eden's understudy finished her song, the theater door banged open. Heads turned toward the sound.

Eden strode into the theater. "Well, chickens, we've got a show to put on!"

"Eden!" Everyone burst into applause.

Eden's understudy muttered, "Great, just great."

After rehearsal, Eden and Mac swept through the dressing room. She wrapped me in a hug. "Being interrogated wasn't totally awful. Now I'm dying to do a legal drama. Maybe I can get Lars to write another show for me."

"I'm so glad you're back," I said.

Her eyes glowed. "The show's going to be wonderful, Allie." Mac Macallen beamed at her side as they left the theater.

Relief coursed through me. I dressed and shouldered my dance bag. I couldn't wait for opening night.

As I headed for the door, I became aware of sobbing. Who was crying? An old television in a corner blared a news show theme. Voices stilled as a sudden quiet spread through the chatter of the dressing room. People crowded around the television. I joined the group, craning to see.

Onscreen, Leo Rodriguez stood in the marina behind New Salt. With a shock I recognized the woman with him—Kate, the hostess I'd spoken to last night at the wake. Leo Rodriguez held a microphone toward her, as curious tourists crowded behind them.

A voiceover said: "The Girl with the Pitchfork Tattoo finally has a name."

The words hit me like a rogue wave. My bag slid from my shoulder to the floor. Cody put his arm around me.

"Police have announced a break in their search for the identity of the young woman whose body was discovered in Mystic Bay last week. The young woman's been identified as Hayley Castle, an actress who recently appeared at Broadway by the Bay."

Several cast members murmured the name.

The camera cut to the hostess. After I spoke to her, Kate must've asked her coworkers about the girl. Someone there must've called the police.

My head pounded. Leo spoke but I could barely make sense of his words.

A photo of a young woman flashed onscreen. A straight cascade of blond hair flowed over her shoulders from a middle part. A strong jaw, wide-set dark brown eyes, heavily lined with mascara and eyeliner. Silver ear cuffs. Small pert nose. A stubborn face.

Behind me, a girl gasped. "No!"

Long blond hair, Kate had said. *She called the shots. Patrick had finally met his match.*

"Did you know her?" Cody whispered.

"No. Just glad she has a name now. Thank God. What a relief."

The girl who had gasped melted back from the group to a corner, her face stricken. I followed her.

"Did you know Hayley?" I asked.

"She'd just finished a road show of *Hair* when she had that photo taken," the girl whispered, her voice hoarse. "She was in *Mame* with me here. In the chorus." She shuddered and rubbed her arms. "I didn't pay attention to all that stuff on the news. That artist's sketch didn't look like her. They said the girl had short black hair. Hayley had such beautiful long blond hair. They made such a big deal about the tattoo, but I never even noticed that tattoo. Sometimes she wore a flesh-tone wrap on her wrist. I thought she sprained it."

We sat on a couple of folding chairs. "You okay?" I said. "Can I get you some water?"

"No, thanks." Tears spattered her cheeks. "To be honest, I didn't even like her that much. That's awful to say, isn't it? But she was pushy. Well, maybe we're all pushy. Right? To make it in this business?"

"What happened to her? After *Mame*?" *Why did no one realize she was missing?* A thought made me pause. *Did Patrick know she was missing?*

"After *Mame*?" She shook her head. "She never made it to opening night. She quit halfway through rehearsals in May. They'd already printed the programs, so her photo and bio were in it." She jutted her chin at the television. "That's the photo they just showed now on the news. She missed a couple of rehearsals and then pouf!"

The girl sniffed. "Most members of the cast left after *Mame* and joined a touring show, so everyone who knew her left town weeks ago. I stuck around here because I wanted to be in *Ondine*." She inhaled shakily. "Hayley wanted to go to acting school. She talked a lot with Mac about it."

"Where was she from?"

"Midwest, maybe? Hayley didn't talk much about her personal life though she did mail a copy of the program back home."

"To her family?"

She shrugged. "She just said she wanted her friends to be proud of her."

"What was she planning to do next?" I asked.

"Said she had a gig that would pay enough for acting school." The girl wiped her eyes with the back of her hand. "She laughed when she said 'gig.' I asked her why she laughed and she said it was overseas. A once-in-a-lifetime role."

Huh. I wondered what that meant. I thanked the girl, gathered my dance bag, and ran to the van. My hands shook so badly I could barely fit the key in the ignition.

That long blond hair. The stubborn chin. I'd seen her before in the portrait at Mac's. Why didn't he say anything to the police about this?

Questions buzzed through me like an electric charge as I sped through the quiet streets of Mystic Bay, humid air streaming in my open window, my hair whipping around my face. If Mac knew her he must have noticed the tattoo, right? I slowed. This girl just told me Hayley wore a flesh-tone wrist brace. Maybe Mac didn't notice.

The van's brakes squealed as I pulled in front of Mac's house and walked toward his front door. My steps slowed. Every dumb slasher movie I've ever seen went through my mind.

Mac. I'd known him for years. His tweedy jackets and horn-rimmed glasses, his gorgeous silk ties. The caring way he listened made you feel like you were the only person in the room.

Afraid of Mac? You're being ridiculous, Allie.

Before I could think, I pounded the door knocker, the noise shockingly loud in the quiet street.

Mac opened the door holding a tumbler of amber liquor. His eyebrows flew up over the rims of his glasses. "Allie! Is everything okay?"

I felt like a fool. "Can I talk to you for a second?"

"Of course. Drink?" He held up his glass. I shook my head and stepped into the hallway. The click of the door closing was loud in hallway, carpeted with antique oriental rugs.

"You heard the news? About Hayley Castle?" I said.

Mac bent his head. "I heard the news when I got

home. I drove Eden back here, said good night to her, came in the house, and there it was on television."

"You knew her." My voice sounded too loud, strained.

Mac started down the hall. "Allie, come with me."

I hesitated, my feet refused to move.

You don't owe this girl Hayley anything. She ended up dead.

Come on, Allie, it's Mac.

Still, I slid my cell phone out of my bag. I followed slowly into his studio.

His easel reflected in the black shine of the French doors. A jumble of paints, brushes, and a palette smeared with paints covered a worktable. A half-empty bottle of Scotch was on the floor next to a straight-backed chair by the easel.

I texted Verity. *I'm at Macs.*

"I've been going for something different." Mac waved his glass at the portraits I'd seen from the patio.

"Mac, these are . . ." I groped for a word. They looked different now that I was better able to see them, instead of peering in through the French doors. "Striking."

"I've been taking portraiture lessons." Mac sat heavily in the chair by the easel. "Painting people from the theater."

I stopped by the portrait with a haughty sculpted face and an exaggerated black ponytail. "Margot. You captured her."

He smiled ruefully. "Sometimes, something comes

out in the portrait that makes it, I don't know. Maybe too honest, too close to the truth."

That sound, like Mac. But still, I stayed near the wall, close to the French doors. "Isn't that what art does?"

"A comment right after my own heart, Allie." He tilted his head at Margot's painting. "I'm going to have to soften that somehow. She wants it."

Another huge canvas was propped against the wall. I turned it around.

"That one turned out particularly well. Not to brag." Mac loosened his tie.

Cold colors, gray-white, silver, and light green slashes formed the face but from them came strength, energy, and elegance. A chain of medallions around the neck. The white silver hair swept up into a loose bun.

"Stellene Lupo," I whispered. My heart hammered. Mac. Stellene. Hayley. Was there a connection? I couldn't see one.

Mac's smile was pained. "I just put the finishing touches on it. I can't wait for her to see it. I put it aside when I was, well . . ." His voice faltered.

"What did you want to show me?" I kept my distance from him, my back to the wall.

"Allie, when I heard about that girl. The one you found." He put his glass on the floor, then straightened as if he'd come to a conclusion. "Hayley Castle was a girl in the chorus of *Mame*. She was something special. It wasn't exactly charisma in her case, but a life force. I fell under her spell. I was bewitched," he said in a quiet voice. "If I'm honest, I was a little afraid of her. Have you ever felt that way?"

He didn't wait for an answer.

"I let her stay here for a bit. Then she left." Mac's eyes, warm brown, turned to me. "I'm not sure where she went."

My eyes must have asked a question.

"It wasn't romantic between us at all—not like that at all!" He held up his hands. "Allie. I was a fool. You're familiar with the term 'she played him like a violin'? Well, I was the violin. The first time she came here was during rehearsals for *Mame*. I'd had a root canal. We'd never talked much, so her visit was a surprise. She brought me a chocolate milkshake, and then told me she needed a place to crash for a few days. Well, I have this big house, and the guest apartment over the barn. She'd probably heard me talking about that. And she saw my studio and said I could paint her portrait."

My heart was beating so hard I could barely hear him.

He went to a portrait on the easel and turned it so I could see. "This is Hayley Castle."

It was the portrait I'd seen through the window, with the long blond hair, flames, and cuffs. For a moment water and seaweed cascaded from the easel. I took a deep breath to steady myself.

The girl in the portrait was not traditionally beautiful, and that probably wasn't just because of Mac's technique. Her jaw was strong and square, her eyes wide and circled with black. Long white-blond hair flowed over her naked shoulders. Mac had captured an energy that went beyond mere physical resemblance. Her chin tilted up, defiant. She wouldn't blink first.

But now, instead of the black and pink slashes I'd seen before, her neck and the bottom of the painting were covered with blue gauze, like a scarf. Or water.

"Where are her tattoos?" I said.

Mac closed his eyes. "Hellion. In block letters. With the pitchfork." He shook his head. "I got the impression that she probably was one, especially when she was a teen."

I visualized the tattoo. "When I saw it, I couldn't make it out at first."

Mac nodded. "She insisted that I add it to the painting. I didn't want to. It's so badly done, not centered on the wrist, the letters are blurry. I'm not proud, but I painted it out when I heard the news . . ."

Mac's voice was pleading. "She often kept it covered with a wrap, like a bandage. Wore lots of bracelets. A tattoo was wrong for *Mame*. And then today I covered it all with blue. I'm not sure why."

Hayley looked like a fighter who'd punch above her weight. Unlike Mac, who was hiding behind a thin layer of blue paint.

My fear dissolved, replaced by disappointment and disbelief. I folded my arms.

Mac stared at the portrait. "I felt used. She'd stolen from me."

"Stolen?"

"Not money." Sweat gleamed on Mac's forehead despite the air-conditioning. He wiped his brow with a silk handkerchief. "That first visit. With the milkshake. She'd excused herself to, you know." He waved.

"Powder her nose."

He nodded. "Later, when I went to get some of my pain pills from my prescription, I noticed that, well, they were almost all gone. It was a brand-new prescription. I hadn't taken any of the pills, so I knew how many were supposed to be in the bottle. And there were only two left."

He sipped his drink. "I remember thinking, this girl's not going to come to a good end."

"Mac, you have to tell this to the police," I said.

Again, he didn't seem to hear me. Mac cradled his glass, staring at his reflection that looked back from the French doors. "I'm not proud, Allie, that I didn't step forward when I heard about the tattoos. You, the news, they all said she had black hair, I just thought, it can't be her. I didn't want it to be her. And she'd told me she had no family, so . . ."

I could tell there was so much he wasn't telling me. Did Hayley have something on Mac? Had he silenced her? What did I really know about Mac Macallen?

"Yes," Mac said. "You're right. I'll go to the police. That's the least I can do for her."

I needed to get away from Mac, away from the portrait. "I'm going home. Good night, Mac." Mac stayed seated, staring at the girl in the portrait, as I hurried from the room.

Mac's front screen door banged shut behind me as I ran to the van and started the engine. Mac didn't follow. I didn't think he'd killed Hayley Castle, but the Mac I'd known was gone.

Lights glowed in the apartment above the barn. How

long would Eden and Henry and Lars be able to hide out from their fans?

I turned toward home.

Hayley Castle. My overriding emotion for her had been pity. She hadn't looked like the kind of person who'd steal drugs from someone who was trying to help her, a guy who seemed to be a teeny bit obsessed with her. The word echoed. *Bewitched*.

At home, Aunt Gully crocheted in Uncle Rocco's big old recliner. I sat down on the arm of the chair and she set down her yarn. We put our arms around each other.

"You saw the news?" I said.

Aunt Gully sighed. "Now that girl can go home, Allie."

We were quiet for a moment.

"Where's Lorel?" I said.

"Bed." Aunt Gully inclined her head toward two jewelry boxes on the coffee table. "Those gifts from Tinsley are beautiful, but I can't keep them. I'm going to donate them to the women's shelter fund raiser."

"That's a good idea." I opened the square box, took out the bracelet, and held it to the light. The tiny medallions were etched with tiny wolves. A memory struggled to surface. "I'll be back in a few minutes, Aunt Gully. I need a walk."

Down on the beach, a bonfire flickered. Someone strummed a guitar. I walked toward the breakwater but turned away when I realized a couple was sitting there. I couldn't wait for the summer people to leave, when the beach stretched out uninterrupted and peaceful for me and the other locals.

My toes slid into the sand. The murmuring ocean, soft music from the bonfire. My heart rate slowed. Sadness filled me.

With all that was happening, the fact that my sister wasn't staying to see me dance pierced my heart most. I sank to the sand and let the tears flow.

The whoosh of the waves on the sand calmed me. *Stop being a drama queen.* I was being stupid about Lorel. There were bigger problems in the world. I threw a pebble into the water.

Hayley and Mac, Hayley and Patrick. Were they all connected? Did Mac know of Hayley's relationship with Patrick? Was he jealous? The idea of Patrick being jealous of Mac was laughable.

I thought back to what Franque said about when he'd met Hayley. He said that she'd had a bag full of cash. The theater certainly didn't pay well. Why did Hayley have so much cash?

I cast my mind back to the day I found Hayley, forced my mind to concentrate on the memory instead of pushing it away. The tattoo. Hellion. Why did it disturb me now even more than when I found her?

The pink bracelet that anchored Hayley to Bertha's lobster pot. My heart thudded. The medallion on it was a wolf's head, just like the ones on the gift bracelets from Tinsley. Hadn't Stellene said that Tinsley's jewelry line would be released in the fall? Hayley was dead long before the party. When had Hayley gotten her bracelet? *Why* had she gotten a bracelet?

I flashed back to Zoe Parker in the kitchen of Harmony Harbor as she handed me the beautifully wrapped gift box holding my bracelet. *Tinsley wanted to thank you*.

A snippet of conversation replayed in my mind. Kurt Lupo almost died because he let a gravely ill teen get the kidney that had been meant for him. Stellene was president of his foundation.

Tinsley had been ill. She'd had a transplant. She had a nurse.

Horror washed over me. I knew.

I knew why Zoe was at the police station dressed in an awful tunic top.

The bracelet was the key.

What role did Patrick play? That made me pause. Because it was so terrible.

Chapter 35

**Opening Night of *Ondine*
Thursday, July 9**

The next morning, I woke before my alarm. For the first time in days I felt my thoughts clear.

I had to talk to Tinsley Lupo.

I hurried downstairs to Lorel's room and burst in. Lorel lay on her back, pink gingham sheet smooth and tucked under her chin. She even slept in an orderly and mature way. "Lorel, do you have Tinsley's number? Or Stellene's?"

"Would it kill you to knock?" Lorel groaned. She rubbed her eyes and mumbled, "Nobody has Tinsley's or Stellene's number."

"Do you have Zoe Parker's, then?"

She waved at her phone on the bedside table. I found Zoe's number and dialed.

"Allie!" Lorel sat up and grabbed her bedside alarm clock. "It's seven A.M.!"

Zoe didn't pick up. No surprise. I considered what message I'd leave. Best not to. Not yet. I put the phone back. "Stellene's check cleared, right?"

Lorel pulled the covers over her head. "Yes."

Aunt Gully was in the kitchen doing the crossword puzzle. "Good morning! I'm so excited about opening night!"

"Tonight? Oh, yes." I gave her a hug, trying to pull my whirling thoughts to the present. Aunt Gully had made a breakfast bake, a casserole stuffed with sausage, eggs, heirloom tomatoes from the garden, and cheese. "Mmm." I helped myself and dug in.

Lorel came into the kitchen adjusting the belt on a beige sheath dress.

"Aren't you a little overdressed for a shift at the Mermaid?" I said.

Lorel poured herself a cup of coffee. "It was only a matter of time."

"What was?"

"I got a call last night asking me to meet Detective Rosato at the Plex," she said.

"You didn't mention that!" Aunt Gully exclaimed. I struggled to swallow my mouthful of eggs.

"I didn't want to upset anyone."

"I'm more upset that you didn't say anything!" I said.

My mind flashed back to the police car I'd seen yesterday in front of Fast Times. The renters there must have reported the fight Lorel had with Patrick.

And maybe the police had gotten access to Patrick's phone. I squeezed my eyes shut. God, I hoped there weren't any photos of Lorel on it.

"Are you okay, Allie?" Aunt Gully said. I took a deep breath and nodded.

"It's just a formality, Aunt Gully." Lorel's voice was flat. "I'll park at the Mermaid, walk up to the Plex, do my interview, and walk back for lunch shift. Then I'll take off for Boston."

"I'll walk up with you," I said.

Lorel and I threaded through tourists snapping photos of the boats on the river as we walked from the Mermaid to the Plex. Lorel didn't say a word all the way over from Gull's Nest. She twisted her hands.

"Lorel, honestly, you have nothing to worry about."

"Easy for you to say, Allie."

"Actually, I'm getting a complex about why they haven't interviewed me again. I feel like chopped liver."

Lorel laughed. Even in the humid air her hair was smooth. Mine stuck to the nape of my neck. I twisted it into a bun.

"Let's not fight." Though I was still steamed that she was blowing off my opening night.

"It's okay, Allie." Lorel smoothed her already smooth hair. "I'm a big girl. Go back to the Mermaid and keep an eye on Aunt Gully. You can't do anything here anyway."

She was right. I swallowed. "Lorel, it's going to be fine."

"Right. It's going to be fine."

I gave her a quick hug, and then Lorel walked up the rest of the steps to the Plex, head held high. A cop held the door for her. I watched as the door closed, with what felt like a sickening finality.

* * *

I turned back to Pearl Street, my mind churning. Last night, I'd been so sure about who killed Patrick, but Mac Macallen haunted my thoughts. Perhaps he'd been obsessed with Hayley.

Mac had stayed overnight at Harmony Harbor on the Fourth of July. Ken Jackson said there'd been a kayak on the beach when we returned that awful next morning. Could Mac have taken the kayak out to *Model Sailor*? It was definitely doable. Nobody would have seen him. But why? He seemed to have a thing going with Stellene. But maybe that was a ruse. Maybe he was jealous of Patrick's affair with Hayley? But how would Mac know Patrick would go to *Model Sailor*? Could Mac have arranged the rendezvous?

I texted Bronwyn. I wanted to tell her about Mac Macallen and his obsession with Hayley.

Meet me at the town dock, she texted back.

I picked up a coffee for Bronwyn and tea for me at the Tick Tock Coffee Shop. We met at the dock.

"Your sister had every cop at the Plex checking her out." Bronwyn took the coffee. "Thanks."

"They can get in line behind Officer Paul Gibson," I said.

Bronwyn laughed. "Seriously?" She sipped her coffee.

"He sent her flowers."

Bronwyn choked.

I shrugged. "She has that effect on guys."

Quickly I told Bronwyn of the events of the last couple of days, fudging slightly about Patrick's phone.

"We discovered it on *Miranda* and called Detectives Rosato and Budwitz." *After you warned me about the chain of evidence.*

Bronwyn nodded. "Listen, Allie, I don't know about those Harbor Patrol guys. They sound creepy, that's for sure. But maybe they're just keeping an eye on things. That's their job at the marina."

I gave her a level look. "This is the most important thing, Bronwyn. I remember you told me that the investigators hold some things back."

"Yes," Bronwyn said. "I told you. The semicolon tattoo." I've known Bronwyn since we were in preschool. She wasn't lying. She didn't know. I tossed my half-finished tea in the trash.

"Do the police know that Tinsley Lupo recently got a kidney donation?"

Bronwyn blinked. "I don't know. What's that got to do with Hayley Castle? Or does it have to do with Patrick's death?"

"Maybe both?"

"Listen, I've got to go." Bronwyn's gray eyes were troubled. "I know you've got a lot of skin in this game, what with Lorel and Patrick, and you being a friend of Hayden's, not to mention that you were the one who found Hayley Castle. Just be careful, okay? Let the police do their jobs."

"You'll keep an eye on Lorel, right?" I said.

"Her interview's just a formality." Bronwyn looked away. Now I was sure she was lying.

She jogged back to the Plex.

Suddenly, I was dying to see Hayden. We'd left on

such bad terms. I called him but he didn't pick up so I left a message.

"Hi, Hayden. I just wanted to say hello. I'm sorry about the other night. I guess I'll see you, um . . ." When would I see Hayden next? It struck me that no one had said anything about a funeral for Patrick. "I'll try you later."

Back at the Mermaid, I looped a pink apron over my head and joined Aunt Gully at the counter. "Aunt Gully, is Mrs. Yardley having a funeral for Patrick? His friend at New Salt said something about scattering his ashes?"

Aunt Gully took a plate from the pass-through window. "Patrick wasn't religious. Ages ago he told his mother he didn't want a church service."

Mrs. Yardley was the president of the St. Peter's Church Ladies' Guild. This probably didn't make her happy. Poor woman.

Bertha banged through the screen door. "Lemonade all around!" she crowed. "And my usual."

"Bertha's usual," I called into the kitchen. "Good news, Bertha?"

Bertha took the last seat at the counter. "Remember I told you I did some cleaning for Mrs. Lupo? Her assistant just called me."

"Zoe Parker?" I handed Bertha a lemonade.

"Thanks." Bertha took a swig. "She said Mrs. Lupo needed the Cat Island guesthouse cleaned and would I mind doing it as soon as possible? And she's paying me a pretty penny to do so."

I wondered if there was a phone on Cat Island that

might be programmed with a number for Harmony Harbor. My pulse quickened. Maybe I would be able to reach Tinsley.

"Bertha, could you use a hand with the job?" I set her lobster roll in front of her.

"Thank you. Sure." Bertha bit into her roll.

"When are you going?"

Bertha swallowed. "Leaving on *Queenie* soon as I finish this roll."

"We'll be back by four, right? I have opening night tonight."

"No problem. It's never dirty there. I just put a shine on it."

I turned to Aunt Gully.

"Go." She laughed. "Shoo! I'd already scheduled Aggie—I thought you'd like the day off with it being opening night tonight. You've been nervous as a cat. Time on the water will calm you down."

Verity came through the screen door. "Hi, everyone. I got a free moment, Allie. This top hat isn't going to deliver itself."

I pulled off my apron. Bertha licked her fingers and rose from her seat. "We're off to Stellene's cottage on Cat Island."

"Seriously?" Verity's eyes glowed. She pulled out her phone. "I'm coming with you. I didn't go to Harmony Harbor with you on the Fourth of July and look what happened."

Chapter 36

At Cat Island, I stepped from *Queenie* onto the pier and looped a line around a rusty cleat. Verity and I followed Bertha up worn granite steps mossy with lichen to the cedar-shingled cottage.

From the northern approach to Cat Island, Stellene's guest cottage looked like a snug artist's getaway, small shuttered windows winking behind trees and bushes, faded lobster buoys covering the one wall.

But as we rounded the house we could see a sprawling addition and another, newer pier on the south side of the island. A wide emerald lawn with a cement circle was hidden by brush and rocks.

"Wow, that's a helicopter pad!" Verity said.

We *oohed* as we walked across a broad slate patio topped with a pergola spilling over with grapevine and wisteria. Blue-striped awnings shaded the windows on this side of the house. Pots of red geraniums stood by the door.

"Didn't I tell you? Like a magazine picture." Bertha grinned.

A gust of wind tossed my hair around my face and stirred the wind chimes on the deck. The jangling quickened my heart rate. I felt watched, no, more than that, I felt as if I was onstage and a restless audience was waiting for the show to start.

Bertha pressed buttons on a security keypad. The door clicked open.

We stepped through a mudroom lined with slickers and sunhats into a kitchen that was easily thirty feet long. A granite island ran the length of the room. There were two sets of double ovens. Two refrigerators. I scanned the walls and counters. No phone here.

"This is the most beautiful kitchen I've ever seen." Verity ran her fingers along gleaming copper pots hanging from the ceiling.

I opened the tap. The water flowed easily. "Stellene said there was a plumbing problem." Stellene lied. I guess she didn't want Eden and Henry staying with her anymore.

Bertha opened a closet and pulled out buckets, cloths, and a vacuum cleaner. "She must've gotten the plumbing fixed."

Maybe she was readying the cottage for other guests. I opened another cabinet and a trash can slid out. "Ew, that stinks." Banana peels, takeout boxes, two bottles of champagne with the same gold label as the bottles she'd given us that night on *Model Sailor*. Stellene must have a thousand bottles of champagne.

"We'll get the trash on the way out. Zoe said all the

trash had to go. She repeated it twice and said don't miss anything in the bathrooms," Bertha said. "And we have to pack up everything left in the blue bedroom."

I took the vacuum cleaner and Verity and Bertha carried buckets of cleaning supplies upstairs.

We climbed to a gallery running the length of a light-filled, two-story great room. A wall of windows with French doors looked south toward Fishers Island. Below, a white rug lay on the shining mahogany floor topped with a navy-blue-striped accent rug and pristine white leather couches. Fishing nets hung on the wall of the gallery, spread out like modern art. It was so tasteful my teeth hurt.

I set down the vacuum cleaner in a spacious, all-white bedroom. "Master bedroom," Bertha said. There was no phone on the bedside table, just a stack of art books. Over the bed hung a huge abstract painting, gray, silver, and white splatters on a rich blue background. In the corner the artist had signed, MM.

Was that Mac Macallen's signature?

"Allie! Look at this gorgeousness!" Verity spun around on the deep carpet like Julie Andrews in *The Sound of Music*. "It's a dream." She opened the doors of a walk-in closet. "Robes. Ah, cashmere. And terry cloth, practical—"

Bertha plugged the vacuum into the wall. "Girls, stop gawking. One of us is getting to work." Bertha tossed me a box. "You can start packing up that blue guest bedroom." She jutted her chin at Verity. "I'm not paying her."

I carried the box and a bucket of cleaning supplies into the smaller guest bedroom across the hall. French doors opened onto a balcony that framed Harmony Harbor in the distance. Sea-blue walls with large mirrors matched a sumptuous silk duvet.

No phone here, either. How would I get in touch with Tinsley Lupo? I kicked the box. What a bust, and now I was stuck doing housework.

I opened the closet door. Dozens of items hung on the rail over a pair of pink running shoes, flip-flops, and several pairs of strappy sandals. I pulled a terry-cloth robe from a hanger, folded it, and put it in the box. Next I reached for a sundress, and then jerked my hand back. Several tops and dresses still had tags. My breath caught. Green tags. I turned one over. Fashion by Franque.

What had Franque said? *She wore a sundress and a big black sun hat. She bought a stack of clothes and I'm not cheap.* I was certain I'd seen a black sun hat in the mudroom downstairs.

It felt like I was in a dream, watching myself from the outside. In the mirror I saw myself walk to the bureau and open the top drawer.

My hands trembled. The top drawer held makeup, sunglasses, sunscreen, and a dozen pill bottles with names I couldn't even begin to pronounce. Some I could. Percocet. Valium. Oxycodone. I reached to pick one up, and then remembered the plastic cleaning gloves. I pulled them on and turned the bottle so I could read the label: *Hayley Castle.*

Why had Hayley Castle been out here on Cat Island?

I hurried into the spacious bathroom off the bedroom, opened the medicine cabinet. More pill bottles, many with the labels peeled off. I opened the lids and compared them to the pills in the drawer. They were duplicates. Some bottles were completely empty.

Why two sets of all the pills? That was a lot of drugs.

What had Bronwyn said? Hayley had another tattoo, a semicolon. People who struggle with addiction or have tried suicide get them because a semicolon's not a full stop.

The toxicology report said Hayley Castle died of a drug overdose.

Full stop.

Across the hall, the vacuum hummed.

Thoughts tumbling, I ran back to the bathroom.

A cabinet under the sink held a few cleaning supplies. A box of hair dye. Black. I went back to the bureau. The drug labels reflected back at me from the mirror.

Hayley's tattoo was badly done, probably in some disreputable tattoo parlor.

My hands shook as I tore off my gloves and took a pen from the drawer. In the bedside table I scrabbled and found a notepad.

What had Henry said? *We had a band, 3H.*

I wrote "3H" on the pad. Turned it to the mirror. I stared at the reflection as I realized what it meant.

HE. The *E* of Hayley's tattoo had the rounded shape of a 3. Hayley had had her tattoo of the name of the band she was in with Henry and Eden turned into the word "HELLION." Why?

Henry and Eden laughing in Aunt Gully's van. "I was born Hilda, just like an old farm wife."

Henry.

Hilda.

Hayley.

The girl at the theater had said Hayley sent a program to friends back home, so they'd be proud of her.

I remembered what Eden told me in Verity's shop. Henry was glad to come to Harmony Harbor because he wanted to look up an old friend in Mystic Bay.

I remembered the blurry old photo of Eden singing in the Boston bar, with Henry and a backup singer behind her. What had Rafael said? Something about Henry being left at the altar. Or was it the other way round? Had Henry left someone else at the altar? Hayley?

And Hayley had turned "3H" into "HELLION."

A flash of movement made me turn. I hurried to the window, just in time to see one of Stellene's motor launches pull into the southside dock. Two figures stepped out of the boat. Henry and Tinsley.

I ran downstairs.

Through the living room's French doors I watched Henry and Tinsley walk across the patio. They were holding hands. Tinsley wore a flirty pink skirt, delicate gold sandals, and a distressed jean jacket over a slim T-shirt. She was dressed for a date.

But the body language was wrong. Henry dragged her forward and Tinsley lunged toward the boat. Henry jerked her back, then slapped her face. I gasped. Tinsley collapsed and fell to her knees. Henry slung her small form over his shoulder.

"Verity! Bertha!" I screamed. The vacuum whined above. Before I could decide what to do, Henry opened the French doors.

He stopped short. "Allie!" He laid Tinsley on the couch, her body limp, his handprint livid on her cheek.

"What're you doing?" I stepped toward the stairs.

Henry took a gun from his jacket pocket, gestured at a leather chair in front of a mirror. "Sit there, Allie." he spoke in a monotone. "You know, the Lupos have way too many guns lying around that house."

I lowered myself into the chair, my eyes on the gun.

Henry sat on the arm of the couch. He rubbed the stubble on his chin and his expression softened. "I'm sorry, Allie. I wish you weren't here to see this. I think we understood each other, maybe even could've had something."

I raised my eyes to his. "Why are you doing this?" I whispered.

"I guess I owe you that." Henry inhaled. "When I heard the news reports about the Girl with the Pitchfork Tattoo, I dismissed it. Hayley didn't have that tat when I knew her. That police sketch looked nothing like Hayley. And the short black hair?" Henry shook his head. "Why did she change her hair?"

Hayley was disappearing. I remembered the hair dye upstairs. That was probably part of the deal she struck with Stellene.

"When Hayley sent me that program of her in *Mame,* she told me a friend helped her get a gig that paid enough money for acting school." Henry pushed back his hair. "She didn't tell me it meant selling her kidney to Tinsley Lupo."

"The friend was Patrick." So it was true. My crazy idea was true. "Did Tinsley tell you this?"

Tinsley moaned softly and her eyes fluttered open.

"Tinsley told me all about her friend Hayley who gave her a kidney." Sarcasm made his words bitter. "Her friend Patrick Yardley introduced them. Hayley was a match! All part of her little fairy tale of good-hearted people who wanted to help little old her." Henry chuckled. "Hayley was a lot of things, but good-hearted wasn't one of them."

The vacuum droned overhead.

Henry followed my glance upstairs. His knuckles whitened around the gun.

"I saw your face at Verity's shop," he said. "When I reached up to get that stupid hat, you looked like you saw a ghost. I understood after I saw the portrait at Mac's; '3H' became 'HE.'" A vein throbbed in his temple. "Hayley turned her tattoo into HELLION. I drove her to that."

He swore. "Sometimes, you're just too late, you know? When I got to Mystic Bay for Stellene's party, I called Hayley, but her phone was disconnected. Then all that stuff happened on the boat." Henry took a deep breath. "When we moved into Mac's guesthouse Eden told me he ran Broadway by the Bay so I went to talk to him. When I walked in and saw Hayley's portrait in his studio, saw the pitchfork tattoo on her arm." He inhaled. "It all came together—the dead girl on the news was Hayley. I lost it. And then I remembered how Tinsley told me about her friend Hayley and her cool tattoo that said 'Hellion.' So I asked Tinsley, to make sure. She told me straight out. Her friend's name was Hayley Castle. My Hayley."

"Hayley, Henry, Hilda, before she was Eden," I whispered.

"You know where Hil got that name? We were hitchhiking past a town called Eden. Right then and there, she changed her name." He laughed but the gun remained steady.

Tinsley curled onto her side and rubbed her cheek, crying. Henry shifted, now watching Tinsley. "Hayley and I almost got married. But Hayley didn't fit into Eden's new band. When Hil and I dropped her she got into drugs, tried to kill herself. I felt responsible." His face reddened. "No, I was responsible. It's a debt I have to pay. It's not right that you should live with a part of Hayley in you when she's dead."

Tinsley's voice was ragged. "My mother was wonderful to Hayley. Hayley was my friend!"

"Keep telling yourself that, princess. If your mother was so awesome to her, why did Hayley end up dumped like trash on the bottom of the ocean?"

Tinsley's voice was small. "I don't know."

"You do know, Tinsley," I said. Keep her talking. She had to have heard something—there were so many places to eavesdrop in Harmony Harbor. Bertha had to stop vacuuming soon and would see Henry with the gun. She or Verity'd call for help. I hoped.

"Patrick was to blame for all of it," Tinsley pleaded. "My mom paid for all Hayley's expenses, plus she gave her fifty thousand dollars so she could go to acting school. But Patrick only gave Hayley twenty thousand. He used his portion to pay off some investors. So

Hayley asked Mom for more money. It was hers! Patrick was a thief!"

Patrick and Hayley would keep asking for money. Tinsley's kidney donation fairy tale would crumble when it became known that all that money changed hands with her mother's old drug connection to make it happen. Kurt Lupo's own daughter, and his wife, the president of his foundation, betrayed his principles with a drug dealer.

Henry sighted along the gun, pointing it at Tinsley.

"Henry!" My voice shook. "There are security cameras everywhere." I shifted so my weight was forward, on my feet. Maybe I could spring at him and wrestle the gun away.

"Henry, did you kill Patrick?" I asked, but I knew who did. On the night of Stellene's magical Fourth of July party, Henry didn't know Hayley was dead. But Patrick did. And so did someone else.

Henry lowered the gun. "No, but I'd sure like to shake the hand of whoever did. I have my suspicions. Oh, come on, Allie, you must have some suspicions." He grinned at me. "You'll figure it out, you're a smart girl. The police are fools for thinking that Eden killed Patrick because she was panicked by fans. Eden was unconscious from the stuff in the champagne."

It dawned on me—that's how we were all so intoxicated after sharing only two bottles of champagne. "Stellene drugged us." I thought of the champagne bottles I'd just seen in the trash. Had Stellene done the same to Hayley?

"There were sleeping pills in the champagne,"

Henry said. "When I woke up the next morning, I knew something was up. She had to get us out of the way because she had plans on the yacht that night."

Ken Jackson mentioned the kayak left on the beach. I'd seen a photo of Stellene and Tinsley in a kayak. Stellene had kayaked over to the yacht, got the gun, and shot Patrick Yardley.

Henry smiled at me. "You've figured it out, too. The best part is that I can just see how Stellene's mind works. She's not a business mogul for nothing. She turned adversity into opportunity and grabbed it."

"When you came on the boat with Eden and Stellene from Montauk, you all handled the gun," I said slowly. "All your prints were on it. That's why the gun was left in the boat with Patrick's body instead of tossed overboard."

Henry's eyes were shining. "That was an opportunity Stellene just couldn't let pass. She had no idea that Lorel's were on there, too. Bonus. Though I don't know why she didn't just cancel her rendezvous with Patrick when Eden told her she wanted to stay on the yacht."

"Patrick's phone didn't work," I said. *Because Lorel knocked it into the water.* "Patrick was going to keep his appointment on the yacht. With me and Lorel going with you and Eden, there would be four suspects on the yacht, two of them with their fingerprints on the gun. Stellene nowhere near. When Stellene couldn't reach Patrick, she saw that it was actually a perfect setup to get rid of him. All she had to do was make sure we couldn't interfere. So she drugged us with the champagne."

Tinsley struggled upright, her sobs choking her

words. "Patrick was supposed to give all the money to Hayley. But he didn't! Hayley wanted her fair share!"

Henry laughed. "See? Wouldn't look too good for Stellene's foundation if people knew that difficult donors end up on the bottom of the ocean."

Keep him talking, Tinsley. I tensed my hands on the arms of the chair. Maybe I could run and grab a knife.

"Don't think about it, Allie." He raised the gun.

I froze, but not because of the gun. Above me in the gallery, Verity stood, her mouth an *O*. She was holding her cell, and I hoped she'd dialed 911. I kept my eyes on Henry, afraid to betray her presence with a glance.

"When Stellene and Patrick were done with her, what happened to Hayley, huh? They discarded her like trash." The muscles in Henry's forearm tightened. "Like I discarded her all those years ago. So I owe her. A life for a life. Justice for Hayley."

The vacuum still ran. Verity waved her phone. The police will be too late, I thought. Henry's mouth was set, hard. He pushed his hair back, slick against his skull.

My breath came in short gasps. We'll all end up like Hayley, under the water. *Cool it, Allie. Focus.* "My friends are upstairs. You won't get away with this."

The vacuum cut. In the sudden silence, the only sound was Tinsley's sobs.

Henry gestured out the window. "No loss if your boat goes up in flames tonight. With you all aboard. Then I'll head over to Montauk. I've got a friend with a private plane. I'll fly off into the sunset before anyone knows you're missing."

"It won't work." *Oh, God, it could work.*

"I'm sorry, Allie. Maybe I'll write a song about you one day." Henry raised the gun. Every nerve in my body hummed, every muscle went taut. The black circle of the muzzle leveled with my heart.

I centered my weight. Which way to leap when his finger moved to pull the trigger? Right or left?

Verity wrenched the fishing net off the wall and threw it. It whirled through the air onto Henry. He shouted. I lunged left. The gun went off.

Glass exploded from the mirror at my back. Needle pricks like winter sleet stung my arms. Someone screamed.

Henry thudded to his knees, thrashing in the net. Bertha shouted from the gallery. I looked up. With a roar she hefted the vacuum cleaner and hurled it over the rail. It thudded onto Henry's torso.

I'd flung myself onto an armchair, shoving it into the side table next to the couch. A lamp toppled onto Tinsley's legs.

Bertha and Verity ran down the stairs.

"The gun! Where's the gun?" I shouted.

Henry moaned but flailed against the net.

Tinsley pushed herself to her feet. She raised the lamp and brought it down on Henry over and over, then tumbled to her knees.

I scrabbled on the floor. *Where is the gun?*

Tinsley dropped the lamp and crawled back onto the couch.

Verity pushed aside the coffee table.

"There's the gun!" Bertha picked it up. "If he bats

an eyelash wrong, he's history." Bertha pointed the gun at Henry, her hand steady.

Henry whimpered and curled into the fetal position. What if he did try to get up? From the set of Bertha's mouth, she'd have no trouble shooting him. "Let's roll him in the rug," I said. "I don't want him to be able to move an inch."

Verity and I dragged Henry by his feet and laid him on the accent rug. He murmured but his eyes remained closed. Tinsley helped, but her breath came in ragged gasps by the time we finished. She sank back on the couch. Verity hurried to the kitchen and brought her a glass of water. Tinsley took a sip and nodded thanks. Henry's body was still, his handsome face peaceful above the edge of the rug.

Bertha high-fived me with her left hand while her right kept the gun trained on Henry. I sagged onto the couch next to Tinsley and put my head in my trembling hands.

"Stay still." Tinsley's fingers moved through my hair. "Will you get a cloth, please?" she said to Verity. "Allie, you've got some cuts and there's some glass in your hair."

Verity went into the kitchen and returned carrying a tray with a wet towel, an open bottle of wine, and four glasses. She put it on the coffee table and poured.

"I can't have alcohol." Tinsley took the cloth and dabbed my arms. I winced.

"I can." Bertha accepted a glass of wine and sipped as she kept the gun leveled at Henry.

Verity sighed. "Broken mirror. Seven years' bad luck."

Bertha toasted toward Henry. "For that slimy scum-covered chum bucket. Not us."

Chapter 37

By the time my breathing returned to normal, the sound of engines and voices streamed into the living room.

Tinsley lay back against the creamy leather cushions, her face gray. "I don't feel good. I'm supposed to take my pills on a schedule. Henry took me out on the boat for too long."

"Did you think you were going on a date?" I said.

She nodded. "He asked to see the island. I was so happy when he asked me to come out. I thought he'd been avoiding me."

Verity beamed, from the wine or the stream of muscular first responders it was hard to say. Mystic Bay Police, Coast Guard, and Harbor Patrol had answered her call for help. Thank goodness Mr. Miami Vice was not among them.

A Coastguardsman tended to my cuts. "Not too serious," he said.

The face of his colleague tending Tinsley was grim.

They stepped aside to confer. I heard the words "transplant" and "airlift."

"Tinsley." I pulled a cashmere throw from a chair and tucked it around her. "Tell me. What happened with Hayley after the operation?"

Tinsley's eyelids fluttered. "We had it done in New York. Everything was fine. My mom sent Hayley to a private clinic to recuperate. When she was discharged, Patrick picked her up. I thought she was going home."

"Did she tell you this?"

Tinsley shook her head. "We talked up until the day she was discharged. Then her phone went out of service. She only called me once more." Her voice got small. "She was angry. She wanted to talk to my mom."

To demand her payment in full.

Tinsley sobbed. "Hayley was my friend."

"I know she was." I squeezed her hand. "You gave her one of your new bracelets, didn't you?"

She nodded.

"Excuse me, miss." The Coastguardsman gently took my elbow and helped me to my feet. "We're going to airlift your friend out of here."

"Tinsley!" Stellene rushed in the French doors followed by Zoe Parker.

"That's her mother," I told him.

Stellene fell to her knees at Tinsley's side. Zoe hung back, clutching her hands to her chest.

I stood next to Verity. "Did you hear everything Henry said?"

"The vacuum was on, so I missed part of it. And when I saw the gun I kind of blanked out." We watched the Coast Guard guys load Tinsley onto a special stretcher that looked like a long metal basket.

Detective Rosato and Detective Budwitz stepped into the living room.

"Great," I muttered.

The law enforcement contingent unrolled Henry. He curled into a ball, whimpering and gasping. "They broke my ribs! The big one threw a vacuum cleaner at me!"

The detectives scanned the room and their eyes lit on me. Detective Budwitz did a double take. Detective Rosato's look was level as she removed her sunglasses.

"Here she comes," I whispered.

"Are you all right, Miss Larkin?" Detective Rosato said.

"Yes, thank you."

"And you, Miss—" Detective Rosato regarded Verity with her unblinking eyes.

"Brooks," Verity said carefully.

"If you'll go into the kitchen, please. We'll have to take statements," Detective Rosato said. "It may take a while."

"How long?" Verity said. "Allie's got opening night at the Jake."

I'd completely forgotten. Right now, I could think of only one thing: Stellene. What had Bertha said? Stellene wanted all the stuff in the bedroom packed up. *All traces of Hayley gone.* "Detective Rosato, please come upstairs with me. I have to show you something."

Detective Rosato's eyes flicked from me to Verity, but she followed me upstairs. Below, Stellene followed Tinsley's stretcher through the French doors. Zoe

Parker hurried after her. Approaching helicopter blades thudded overhead.

We went into the blue bedroom. Detective Rosato looked out the window. "How convenient to have your own helipad."

We watched the Coast Guard helicopter land. The crew rushed Tinsley on board. Stellene and Zoe spoke, their heads close together, then Stellene also boarded the helicopter. Henry's tattoo came to mind: *Let justice be done though the heavens fall.*

"Why are we here?" Detective Rosato put her hands on her hips.

"Hayley Castle died of a drug overdose, right?"

I showed her the pill bottles in the bureau drawer, then we went into the bathroom and I showed her the rest of the bottles and the hair dye. I told her in a rush what Tinsley and Henry had said.

"And you think?" she said.

"I think Hayley Castle was a liability. Stellene's husband was this saint who selflessly let another person take the kidney meant for him, because he thought they needed it more. And here was his wife, the head of his foundation, arranging a donation through her drug connection Patrick Yardley. I think"—I took a deep breath—"Stellene discovered that Hayley had struggled with addiction. I think Stellene left Hayley here alone, in pain, with all this medication, hoping she'd overdose."

Not a flicker of emotion crossed Detective Rosato's face. We went into the gallery and looked down at the chaos below, the rumpled rugs, the net, the vacuum cleaner, the broken mirror.

Zoe entered through the French doors, picked her way through the living room, went into the kitchen and moments later emerged carrying a white canvas shopping bag. She headed toward the stairs.

"If I'm Zoe Parker, what do I do now?" I said. "Detective Rosato, come quick." I ducked into the master bedroom.

"Miss Larkin, I don't know what you're doing"—she sighed and followed me—"but you've helped me before."

I closed the door almost all the way. "That's Zoe Parker, Stellene Lupo's assistant. I think she's going to collect those pill bottles and get rid of them."

Through the crack in the door, we watched Zoe walk across the gallery. She looked over the railing, then stepped into the blue bedroom. Detective Rosato waited. I stood behind her, holding my breath.

A few minutes later, Zoe, bag slung over her shoulder, left the room and went downstairs.

I looked at Detective Rosato. "Aren't you going to—"

"Thank you, Miss Larkin." She dashed into the blue bedroom and looked into the drawer. From the hall I could see it was now empty of pill bottles. Detective Rosato hurried after Zoe, calling to me over her shoulder, "Wait in the kitchen."

Zoe hurried out the French doors. Detective Rosato followed her. I stuck my head in the kitchen where Verity and Bertha sat at the kitchen counter.

"Come here! Quick!" I said.

We fast-walked through the dozen law enforcement types in the living room. In the distance, Zoe jogged toward the southside dock, Detective Rosato behind her.

"She's letting her get away!" I said.

"Miss Parker. One moment please!" Detective Rosato called.

Zoe didn't stop. She stepped onto Stellene's speedboat, threw off the line, and fired the engine. She ignored Detective Rosato and pulled from the dock.

"Stop!" Detective Rosato shouted.

Zoe didn't even turn.

"Bertha! Quick! Get *Queenie*! Make sure she doesn't get away!" I shouted. Bertha and Verity spun toward *Queenie*. I thought for a millisecond, then darted after Detective Rosato.

At the dock, a Harbor Patrol boat bobbed in the wake from Stellene's sleek wooden powerboat. The pilot looked up as Detective Rosato stepped aboard and pointed at Zoe's boat. He fired the engine and pulled away from the dock.

I leaped on board, jarring my ankle, and tumbling to my knees.

"Go!" I scrambled to my feet. "Follow her!" The engine roared to life.

Stellene's magnificent boat was powerful, but the Harbor Patrol boat had dual engines. They kicked in. The boat leaped ahead and soon closed the gap with Zoe.

Zoe looked back and turned her boat hard to starboard. A flash of white fell from her hand to the water.

"She's coming around," the pilot said.

"No!" I shouted. "She used the turn to hide the bag

she threw overboard on the other side of the boat. The white bag!"

Detective Rosato's eyes flicked from me to Zoe's boat.

"Let the boat go," she directed. "Go to the spot where she turned."

"There!" I pointed.

He cut the engine.

We scanned the water. I surged with anger. Zoe was doing Stellene's dirty work, dumping evidence that tied Stellene to Hayley, proof that Stellene left Hayley, a recovering drug addict who was still recovering from surgery to donate a kidney, in a candyland of pills.

Something white glimmered just beneath the waves.

"There!" I dove into the water, keeping my eyes on the flash of white. *Please don't sink*. I swam to the point where I'd last seen it.

I plunged into the shadowy depths, salt water stinging my eyes. *There!* I swooped up the bag. *Yes!* I kicked back to the boat.

The pilot pulled me aboard. "Are you crazy?"

Detective Rosato took the bag from my hands. I shivered and yanked up my sodden shorts. My flip-flops were gone.

She opened the bag, looked up at me, and smiled.

Chapter 38

Opening night of *Ondine* was one of the most electric of my career, one of the most electric in the history of Broadway by the Bay. It was too bad it was to be the first and only performance of Eden in *Ondine*.

Many people have told me that great dancers are great actors. I didn't trust my acting that night, so when the police car skidded to the stage door twenty minutes before the curtain was to go up, I told Mac Macallen I was late because I'd been in a minor boating accident with Henry Small. That was the story Detective Rosato and I'd spun on the way to the theater, a way to hold off the truth about the Coast Guard helicopter and all those police boats at Cat Island.

Eden and I took a dozen curtain calls together, showered in flower petals. She radiated star power even as she left the stage, trailing a black and green seaweed train into the wings, into the arms of her partner, Lars.

Lars held her and whispered in her ear. Eden's body

stiffened. They left immediately. She didn't even change out of her costume.

Aunt Gully, Verity, Bronwyn, and Lorel met me at the stage door with a bouquet of my favorite flowers—incredibly expensive, out of season white and lavender lilacs. Lorel came! The card on the bouquet read, *To our lazy mermaid, Love, Dad and Esmeralda.*

I skipped the opening-night reception. Instead, I iced my throbbing ankle while the rest of me soaked in a hot bubble bath to ease the cuts on my arms. They'd left splotches of blood on the illusion fabric of my costume.

Chapter 39

On the way to work the next morning, Aunt Gully asked if we could stop by the Yardleys' house.

I'd rather have a root canal. "Sure, Aunt Gully," I said.

Hayden's sedan was in the driveway.

Aunt Gully carried a casserole. Mediterranean beef tagine. Trying something new."

Mrs. Yardley answered the door. "Gully, you're a dear."

We all went into the kitchen.

"Hey, Allie." Hayden came into the kitchen and gave me and Aunt Gully a hug. His pale blue button-down shirt was crisp against my cheek and he smelled like Irish Spring.

He led me out into the mudroom while Aunt Gully and his mother spoke.

"How's your dad?" I asked.

"Sleeping it off," Hayden said.

Spar was always a sore spot.

"Listen, I need to apologize," Hayden said. "I got a little heated at the wake. I didn't mean to upset you. I'm sorry."

"It's okay, Hayden. I did some stupid things. It's the last time I'll interfere in police stuff, I promise." We sat on a bench by the door. Rubber gardening boots lined the wall. Jackets, backpacks, and sweatshirts hung from hooks in a neat row.

"Mom says she's going to clean out Patrick's things," Hayden said. "I'll help her and then I'm heading back to Boston next week."

"Lorel's already gone back."

A shiny fake leather bucket bag, hanging on a hook next to the door caught my eye. My heart rate kicked up. What had Franque said Hayley carried? *A cheap pleather bucket bag.* Could Patrick have taken Hayley's bag? Was there still money in it? "Hayden—"

"Listen, Allie, those Harbor Patrol guys." He looked away. "The police have been watching them and Patrick, too, as part of a drug-smuggling ring. That's why I lost it a little. The cops have to be careful. We don't want to tip our—their—hand."

How would Hayden know this? "Are you working with—" Hayden's look begged me to say no more. *You just promised, Allie.* I sighed.

So Hayden was hiding things from me. Marine insurance, my aunt Fanny. Growing up, he'd always wanted to be a cop, but had done accounting in college. At least, that's what he said. But the way he'd acted at the wake, all this stuff he knew about Patrick's smuggling . . . Was Hayden Yardley an undercover cop? I took a deep breath, decided to let it go, to keep his secret.

I punched his shoulder. "No worries, Hayden." I stood. "Aunt Gully and I'd better get to the Mermaid."

Hayden stood. "I'll get your aunt. When my mom starts talking it's hard to make her stop."

"I know how that goes."

As soon as Hayden went inside, I rushed to the pleather bag and looked inside. Stacks of cash were crammed inside. Thousands of dollars.

I jumped back as Hayden and Aunt Gully left the kitchen.

Hayden walked us to the van. We got in and he shut the door behind me.

"Hayden, be sure to check everything before you decide to toss it. Especially that bucket bag in the mudroom." I squeezed his hand. "Seriously, promise you'll check it."

"That's true." Aunt Gully clicked on her safety belt. "That happened on *American Pickers* the other day. Some guy almost threw away a hundred dollars."

Hayden gave me a long look. "Okay."

Chapter 40

"Allie, I almost forgot." Bronwyn handed me a small white envelope. "Detective Rosato asked me to give this to you."

"As long as it's not a summons." I set it aside. "I'm going to enjoy my champagne first." A fan had sent me a bottle of incredibly expensive champagne on the last night of *Ondine*. Thank goodness it wasn't Stellene's brand.

Eden's understudy had had her chance. Eden and Lars had left town, sending word that she was too devastated by Henry's arrest to perform.

Aunt Gully had stayed open until eleven to accommodate the after-theater rush and had just closed the doors of the shack. Verity, Bronwyn, and I relaxed on the Adirondack chairs on the Mermaid's lawn. The red, white, and blue bunting still hung on the shack, but the patriotic lobster had deflated and sagged off the roof.

"I wish I could've been on Cat Island with you." Bronwyn shook her head. "I'm always stuck in the office. You're always where the action is."

"You can have the action." My arms still ached where the mirror shards had sliced into them.

"So Stellene drugged you guys with champagne," Bronwyn said. "How classy."

We clinked glasses.

"I hope there's enough evidence to nail Stellene," Verity said.

"A lot of it is circumstantial." Bronwyn frowned. "With all the drugs, for example."

"Stellene isolated Hayley, a former addict who was recovering from a very serious operation, on an island with alcohol and drugs." I shook my head. "And I bet there was something in the champagne there, too."

"But does that make her guilty?" Verity said. "She didn't force Hayley to overdose."

"Well, Zoe sure knew about the drugs," I said. "She trotted right up to Hayley's bedroom and knew exactly where to find them. I wonder if Zoe bought all the extra drugs, too."

I remembered the Fourth of July party at Harmony Harbor. Zoe's friends toasting her promotion. Certainly that was payment for all the dirty work she did for Stellene.

Bronwyn shook her head. "Kudos on that recovery, by the way."

"I didn't think. I just reacted and dove in. I couldn't stomach her getting away with it."

"What about Zoe?" Verity said. "That was her at the Plex in disguise, wasn't it? She called and said she'd identify Hayley, right? Probably was going to make up some lie so no one would know the truth about Hayley Castle."

"But then she ran out," Bronwyn said.

"Remember Verity said she got a text. That was right after we heard the news on the radio about someone going to identify Hayley, maybe a coworker from New Salt, or her friend from Broadway by the Bay. Stellene must have heard the same news report and called Zoe back at the last minute."

"That outfit was a crime." Verity and I clinked glasses.

"That's how criminals get in trouble. That was taking a crazy chance, walking right into the police station like that," Bronwyn said. "Zoe's going to make a very effective witness against Stellene."

"She's gonna sing like a canary," Verity said.

"Like Aunt Gully," Bronwyn said.

"Hey!" I laughed.

"So if Zoe put the drugs in the house with Hayley, is Zoe responsible? Even if Stellene told her to do it?" Verity said.

I thought of Henry's tattoo of the scales of justice. He'd been ready to be judge, jury, and executioner. How he could be, all at once, the fun-loving guy on *Model Sailor,* the sexy dream in the beer ad, a man who hit a woman so hard he left his handprint on her cheek?

I closed my eyes.

"I wonder what would have happened if Patrick

hadn't skimmed the money from Hayley?" Verity smacked a mosquito.

"If he hadn't gambled. If he hadn't picked backers that"—what was Lorel's term?—"put the screws to him." I remembered my promise to Hayden and didn't say any more.

"Police work's slow, but methodical," Bronwyn said. "Patrick's phone is open and there's stuff there—"

I sat up. "What stuff?"

"Pictures of Lorel?" Verity said.

"No pictures of Lorel," Bronwyn said. "Patrick recorded Stellene telling him to get rid of the body. There were lots of saved messages from Stellene about the money. And here's the smoking gun, there are several messages telling him not to come to *Model Sailor* at midnight because Eden was going to be there. She told him to return her call ASAP."

"So he never got the message and he went out to keep his appointment with her." Because Lorel threw his phone in the water. When Stellene realized she couldn't cancel their meeting, she put her murderous plan into action. "You guys. We can never, ever tell Lorel that."

"But won't it come out at Stellene's trial?" Verity said.

"Stellene can buy so many lawyers, I don't know if she'll ever come to trial," Bronwyn said. "How cold she was to kayak out there and wait with the gun for Patrick. And then kayak back."

I imagined Patrick, panicked, on the phone to Stellene after finding Hayley's dead body. Stellene instructing Patrick to dispose of the body. Patrick following her orders instead of doing the decent thing. Dragging Hayley's body onto his boat—or maybe *Miranda*. I shivered. It would be fine with me if Hayden sold *Miranda* now.

"Did the cops test the champagne bottles from *Model Sailor*?"

"Budwitz is on it. I checked. See, Allie, the cops can do their jobs. They just don't do them as dramatically as you do."

"What about Mac? Was it against the law not to come forward to identify Hayley?"

Bronwyn shrugged.

"What about Tinsley?" Verity said.

Bronwyn shruged again. "Who knows what she knew and when she knew it?"

"Tinsley thought she and Hayley were friends," I said.

"And the utter worst part." Verity poured champagne into her glass, shaking the last drops from the bottle. "Henry turns out to be an almost murderer. What a waste. I feel so cheated."

"Do you still have that top hat?" Bronwyn asked.

"Yes," Verity said.

"At least he paid for it," I said.

"Just from what you've told me he's guilty of assault, kidnapping, and attempted murder," Bronwyn said. "Not good boyfriend material."

Music thumped from the Mermaid. "Watch out, Aunt Gully's in a disco mood." I drained my glass.

"Let's go dance." Verity stood and shimmied toward the shack.

"Right behind you." Bronwyn gathered the bottle and glasses and followed her.

"I'll be there in a sec." I opened the envelope from Detective Rosato.

The card had one word. *"Brava."*

Aunt Gully's Lobster Love Sauce AKA Lobster Bisque

If you can't visit a real, waterside lobster shack you can cook up Aunt Gully's Lobster Love Sauce for a taste of the award-winning Lazy Mermaid Lobster Roll. Lobster Love Sauce is a rich bisque, which you can enjoy by the bowl or spoon on top of lobster meat in a buttered and toasted hot dog roll.

Aunt Gully always has plenty of lobster carcasses—the lobster body and shells left behind after all the meat has been picked for lobster rolls. Start by cooking 4 (1–1½ lb.) lobsters—there are lots of good tutorials online for this step. Then enjoy a lobster feast or use the meat to make lobster rolls.

4 cooked lobster carcasses, remove intestinal
    tract and sac behind head, break up shells
4 tablespoons butter
1 medium onion, chopped
2 cloves garlic, smashed
1 medium carrot, peeled and chopped
1 bay leaf
4 sprigs fresh thyme or ½ teaspoon dried thyme
1 cup sherry (or you can substitute a dry white
    wine)
1 cup diced tomatoes (canned is okay)
4 cups chicken stock
1 cup heavy cream
Salt and freshly ground black pepper to taste

Over medium heat, melt 2 tablespoons butter in a large saucepan or Dutch oven. Add onion, garlic, carrot, bay leaf, and thyme. Stir until the onion is soft, 5 to 10 minutes.

Add the lobster carcasses and any extra shells and cook, stirring, about 5 minutes.

Add the sherry and tomatoes. Turn the heat to medium-high and bring to a boil, then turn down the heat to low, cover and cook for 10 minutes.

Add stock, turn heat to high and bring to a boil. Turn heat to low, cover and cook 20 minutes. Remove the bay leaf, thyme sprigs and lobster shells.

Puree bisque in a heavy-duty blender or food processor. Strain well. Return the soup to the pot and bring to a boil. Turn down heat and add the remaining butter in small pieces, let melt fully. Stir in the cream and heat through. Season with salt and pepper. Serve as a soup with crusty bread and a green salad, or spoon over lobster meat layered in buttered, toasted rolls. Serves 4. Enjoy!

Coming soon . . .

Don't miss the next novel in the
Lobster Shack mystery series

DRAWN AND BUTTERED

Available in March 2019 from
St. Martin's Paperbacks